A
WESTERN
BEAUTY

Sherry!

East meets West!!

Ruth Trippy

Pp. 19:1

A
WESTERN
BEAUTY

COLORADO – 1879

BY RUTH TRIPPY

MILL CITY PRESS

Mill City Press, Inc.
2301 Lucien Way #415
Maitland, FL 32751
407.339.4217
www.millcitypress.net

Printed in the United States of America

1. Art—Fiction. 2. Colorado—Fiction. 3. Single women—Fiction. 4. Spirituality—Fiction. 5. Ute Indians—Fiction

Cover Design by Sean Allen
seanallencreative@gmail.com

ISBN: 9781545614464

C.S. Lewis

Beauty descends from God into nature; but there it would perish and does except when a Man appreciates it with worship and thus as it were *sends it back* to God: so that through his consciousness what descended ascends again and the perfect circle is made.

From a letter to Arthur Greeves, August 28, 1930

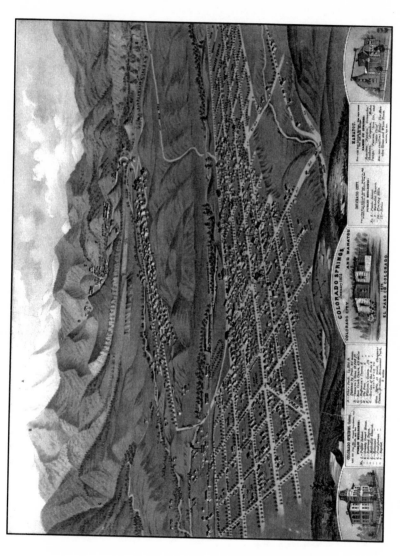

Lithograph drawn by F.S. Glover and Strobridge & Co. Lith. Cin. – Courtesy of Special Collections, Pikes Peak Library District, 001-4078

BOOKS BY RUTH TRIPPY

The Soul of the Rose

The Language of Music

A Western Beauty

ACKNOWLEDGMENTS

A research trip to Colorado was in order, as this story and its characters are based on what took place in 1879. Even though I had carefully researched this book for a number of years, when I visited the sites described in this novel and purchased books by local authors, I discovered additional facts, as well as corrections I needed to make. Also, a research trip can be like trying to find the needle in a haystack when the author isn't sure what needle requires finding.

Camping at 9,000 feet in the backcountry west of Pikes Peak, my husband called me one night to come out of our tent (where I was trying to stay warm), and sit in one of two camp chairs he'd set up. I reluctantly agreed. However, when I looked up at the black night sky and saw the myriad of stars revealed at that high elevation, absolute wonder took hold of me. Right overhead was a large black space and I imagined myself shooting up to Heaven itself. To the left spanned the grand Milky Way, and without the usual atmosphere to "cloud" the air, this massive galaxy looked like dust. As I gazed at this amazing sight, a thought came to me: If I, the Lord, can create all this and keep it in order, don't you think I can direct your research?

This proved to be true. The next evening while reading a local history book, I discovered the dinner party I'd so carefully constructed at General William Palmer's Glen Eyrie home (founder of Colorado Springs), couldn't have taken place because his wife, Queen Palmer, wasn't in the area at the time. Stunned, I looked to the Lord for a solution. Later that night, I discovered General Palmer's close business associate, Dr. William Bell and his wife Cara had lived nearby in Manitou Springs, and their home had been the center of Colorado Springs' social life. Briarhurst now existed as an upscale restaurant. So, the next day my husband and I went to visit it. I am grateful to Ken Healey, the present owner and operator, who gave us a private tour and shared interesting facts about the house and anecdotes about this unusual couple, the Bells.

I'd also like to thank the librarians in the Special Collections section of the Penrose Library in Colorado Springs for their timely and generous help: Bill Thomas, Toni Miller and Emily Anderson. I especially appreciated the lithograph of Colorado Springs and a copy of the 1879 map of Colorado. The Colorado Springs Pioneers Museum gave me valuable resources including *Legends, Labors & Loves of William Jackson Palmer*. And Dale McClure, archivist at First Presbyterian Church of Colorado Springs, shared pictures of the area in the 1870's and stories of the early settlers. I smiled when he quoted the local organist's description of their church's first organ as sounding like an asthmatic hurdy-gurdy.

And, of course, my heartfelt gratitude goes to my critique partners. Laurie Fuller, LeAnne Benfield Martin and Gloria Spencer read the earliest chapters, then those hardy souls who critiqued the entire book line by line: Donna Lott, Peggy Moore, Bette Noble and Hope Welborn. My beta reader, Jan Whitford, who understands my "voice," made welcome suggestions, as did my editor, Gloria Spenser. Also, I'm so thankful for the spiritual support of these writing partners, and particularly the faithful prayers of my aunt, Anita Van Wyk and my friend, Candy Menedis.

This trip to the West wouldn't have happened without the transportation (and help in pitching that tent) provided by my husband, Ernie. However, I told him the next research trip west will be conducted differently. The tent will stay behind as well as that air mattress with the slow leak which had to be re-inflated in the middle of the night in cold temperatures!

A last note: I am grateful to Celinda Reynolds Kaelin for taking my phone call in Florissant and for her excellent book, *Pikes Peak Backcountry, The Historic Saga of the Peak's West Slope*, as well as a thank you to the archives of the California Digital Library for preserving *The Ute war: a history of the White River Massacre*, that described the treatment of the women survivors, which I used for my story.

To all my readers who appreciated the first two novels, set primarily in the East, this book gives a taste of the West, and I hope you enjoy it as well.

Sincerely,

Ruth Trippy

CHAPTER 1

Sarah Whittington chanced a covert glance at the back of the church. Had the wedding party arrived? Yes, she saw the knot of groomsmen.

When would this wedding begin? How very unorganized these western affairs seemed to be. Just then a tall man joined the others, another groomsman? Why hadn't he arrived earlier? But maybe this event would get started now. Sarah turned to the front of the church, settling herself to wait.

Aunt Amelia had assured her this would be quite the occasion, the pump organ reputed to be one of the best for miles around. Sarah thought its sound rather uninspiring. Could one call it quaint? Like this small clapboard church with its simple, sparsely furnished interior. Maybe this was all one could expect out west.

Just then, a strident voice rose from the back. "Le' me through, I want tha' old preacher! I can sell whiskey—" The man's voice cut off. Sarah craned her neck again to look at the rear of the church. A gaunt man in soiled, worn clothing belligerently shook off a wedding guest who'd grabbed his arm. A scuffle began. The unkempt man flung away and accidentally knocked down a lady in formal wear. Sarah felt her eyes widen. Was that the bride's mother?

The tall groomsman who'd just arrived shot over and helped the woman from the floor. "I never!" she said. "Please, do something!" The man took a moment longer to soothe her, motioning the other man involved in the fray to lead her to a seat. He then seized the angry man by the arm and the back of the collar and forced him toward the door.

"I'm goin' to settle—"

"Not here, Hob." One of the other groomsmen hurried to open the door and offered help, but the man holding the ruffian shook his head, and out the two men went. The door closed decisively behind them.

Sarah felt herself mesmerized. What was that all about? Were western weddings always this rough?

She turned around and settled herself to wait for this most unusual occasion to begin, then glanced down the row to catch her aunt's eye. Aunt Amelia just shrugged.

Well, if her aunt could shrug it off— Sarah sat still a minute, then began envisioning her own wedding which would be quite different...in the august Church of the Holy Trinity in Philadelphia. The grand pipe organ would play "Trumpet Voluntary" as she walked with measured step down the long aisle. Her bridesmaids' dresses would suggest the ethereal, giving the town's prominent citizens a foretaste of her own gown, a vision in satin and iridescent pearls. The delicate veil would soften her golden hair.

How she wanted to be beautiful on her wedding day. For Prescott. She hadn't been able to tell him about—he was such a perfectionist—but if she didn't tell him beforehand, he would certainly discover it on their wedding night. What would he say then?

However, she wouldn't think of that now. Her wedding would be all such an occasion should be. She could picture it. Passing under the church's expansive arched ceiling, she'd gaze up at the glorious dome above the altar where she would meet her groom. Through the dome's lofty windows, the sun would smile on her wedding day. A great and glorious affair!

Sarah blinked, abruptly bringing herself back to the little church in which she sat. A corner of her mouth went up in a self-deprecatory smile. Here she was envisioning her wedding when its date hadn't even been set. Prescott had agreed to wait until she returned from this trip—which was fortunate, since Father had told him in no uncertain terms he must first prove himself as a lawyer before their engagement be made official.

That was fine with her. She was in no hurry to be married. Here in Colorado Springs, she could certainly amuse herself. Her cousin Jean was always up for a little fun. What was life for anyway, if not to live with zest and appreciate its beauty?

She changed her position on the hard church bench crossing her ankles and carefully straightening her filmy skirt. This morning her uncle had affectionately poked fun at the time she had taken with her toilette. "You're a peacock—" he chucked her under the chin, "—but a fetching young peacock for all that." She supposed he spoke a measure of truth, though no one else dared say such a thing. All the same, she loved him. She had sat on his knee as a tot when he and Aunt Amelia lived in Philadelphia, a mere mile from her home. And yesterday he had pronounced he was "dad gum" proud of her. A western expression, surely. Her uncle's sense of humor wouldn't allow for too much seriousness. Maybe that's where she got her own love of fun.

Sarah felt her drop earrings dance as her head turned quickly to observe the men in the wedding party finally start to walk down the aisle. She noticed their suits, their variety of styles. Yes, this was a most modest wedding.

The groomsman leading the way caught her attention. He was the one who had taken that ruffian in hand. The cut of his coat had more style than the others. The groom, then? If so, this bride was fortunate. He walked confidently, a tall, broad-shouldered fellow with brown hair tending dark. Her artist's eye took his measure. He had a rugged look. From his profile, his strong chin jutted a bit. Would that denote stubbornness or strength of character? His bride would certainly appreciate the difference. Reaching the front, the man turned to face those assembled, the other men keeping to his left.

So he wasn't the groom. The minister, then. He turned his head to say something to the man at his side.

What! A scar? She felt a slight tremor in her chest. From the temple it curved to his upper jaw. She considered it a moment. It gave him a tough, rakish appearance—a look one hardly associated with a man of God. On him, however, the scar wasn't unsightly.

It would be different on a girl. For a moment her heart sank. How could a scar be other than ugly on a girl?

The organ music changed key. With soft, measured tread the bridesmaids started down the aisle, followed by her own little cousin Hildie as flower girl. Sarah immediately assessed their dresses. The light blue, pink and green hues were pleasing, but cut in quite different styles. She supposed after this wedding they would do double duty as party dresses.

With the bridesmaids in place, the music changed again, this time to Mendelssohn's noble "Wedding March." Or rather, the organ tried to be noble. Instead, it wheezed like an asthmatic hurdy-gurdy. Confound her thoughts! Mother had said time and time again not to be so critical. Being judgmental did have a tendency to spoil one's enjoyment. But Sarah believed this same outlook, the artist in her, enabled her to enjoy a thing of beauty so intensely.

She rose with everyone else to see the bride begin her slow progress down the aisle. Her gown was quite lovely, simple and appropriate for this unpretentious ceremony. Sarah was glad she could approve the bride's choice. But her mind couldn't help envisioning her own wedding, which would certainly rank first on the society page.

———————— ∞◦⟨⟨◦∞ ————————

"Can I find you a chair, Miss Whittington?" A man with the bluest eyes Sarah had ever seen looked at her intently. The outdoor light intensified the blue. Taking her acquiescence for granted, her aunt and uncle's next door neighbor led her to two vacant seats at the edge of the crowd.

"May I bring you some lemonade?" Sidney Carlton gestured to the reception table on the side lawn of the church.

"I've had some already, thank you."

Carlton smiled, an engaging quirk to his mouth. "I feel fortunate to have discovered a moment when you weren't talking to someone else. But your cousin Jean warned me."

"I like people, that's all."

His infectious smile widened into a full-blown grin. "Colorado Springs has much to offer in desirable acquaintances. And places of interest an easterner such as yourself would be pleased to visit. I'll be glad to take you—and Jean—wherever you need an escort."

"Well—thank you, Mr. Carlton."

"Growing up as neighbors, Jean and I had all sorts of adventures. The fact that your cousin visited you in Philly—I know you're acquainted with her adventurous spirit."

"Oh, yes."

"Then you should be prepared for life in the Wild West."

Sarah lifted her handkerchief to cover a smile. Until this afternoon's incident at the beginning of the wedding, Colorado Springs seemed to her no more wild than one of their lovely, sedate towns back east. Except it had more space—wide-open stretches.

"You'll take the waters while you're here, Miss Whittington?"

"Yes. They're just west from us in Manitou Springs?" At his nod, she added, "Aunt Amelia wrote the springs have become quite famous, attracting people from across the country, even abroad." She considered him, wondering how he'd react to her

5

next statement. "However, one of the main reasons I came west was not only to see the mountains, but to paint them. I also plan to view art in Denver—what they have of it." She let her eyes light up with amusement. "And maybe conduct a little business while I'm there."

"A businesswoman? A lady as lovely as yourself? Is that allowed?"

"Oh, yes. I'm acquiring western art for the Pennsylvania Academy of the Fine Arts—where I studied two years. Also, I'm buying for a friend who runs a gallery in Philadelphia."

"The Pennsylvania Academy? You know Mr. Larkin, by any chance?"

"Yes. Do you know him?"

"A friend of the family." He smiled at her again. "So you studied at the Academy? Impressive."

"Under the famous Thomas Eakins, no less."

"That *is* impressive. So, he inspired you to paint the west?"

"Not exactly. It was another artist. Maybe you're familiar with Albert Bierstadt?"

"The name is familiar...I'm trying to remember."

"His grand paintings are the reason I looked forward to coming west. I should think anyone would admire his work."

"I'm sure! So, when are you leaving for Denver?"

With the quick change of subject, Sarah thought it obvious Mr. Carlton wasn't familiar with Bierstadt's work. How disappointing. She would have liked nothing better than to discuss the artist's paintings with someone. "In about three weeks."

"Sounds to me like you would benefit from my escort, as someone who knows Mr. Larkin—"

"How *very* kind of you. I'll mention your offer to Aunt Amelia." Sarah felt herself smile at the man's obvious ploy to ingratiate himself. "I'm not sure what her plans are, but we'll probably stay in Denver several days."

At that moment Hildie sidled up to Sarah, then leaned against her. Jean's younger sister had adopted Sarah the minute she'd stepped off the train. The youngster lifted her basket for inspection.

Sarah looked inside. "What's wrong? Didn't you throw all your petals when you walked down the aisle?"

"No!" The child's expression was as tragic as any accomplished actress.

"Well, let's see. You could throw them when the bride and groom leave the church—right after the reception."

Hildie asked if she could sit, so Sarah moved over and let her perch on the edge of her chair. Sarah didn't have a sister and found Hildie an endearing, rather precocious bundle of femininity.

Hildie cocked her head. "Sidney, do you like Sarah? I thought you liked Jean."

"I *do* like your sister." He reached over and tweaked her nose. "But have you ever heard of greener pastures?"

"Uh—" Hildie scrunched up her nose in reaction, "—no. What does that mean?"

"Miss Whittington here is a delightful newcomer. She could be termed 'greener pastures.'" His head tipped to the side. "You know, you're both very pretty."

Hildie looked up at Sarah.

"Oh, dear!" Sarah laughed.

Just then Jean joined them. "What's going on?"

Sarah batted her eyes at her cousin. "Jean, your neighbor is a shameless flirt. Philadelphia men don't talk such nonsense."

Sid Carlton's mouth had a decided smirk. "I told you this was the *Wild West*."

"Overall, Colorado Springs seems pretty tame to me." Putting this man in his place wouldn't hurt him.

"That might be, but wait until you visit our fair city's neighbor, Colorado City. If you take the waters in Manitou, it's right on the way." He looked at Jean. "Would you like my seat?"

"No, thank you. I've come to claim Sarah. I want her to meet someone *else*."

"I would think she's already met everyone else—with the number of people that have congregated around her all afternoon."

"Oh, Miss Socialite hasn't met *everyone*. Come on, Sarah." Jean grabbed her cousin's arm to lead her away. In a low voice she said, "Mother wondered if you and Aunt Martha have been introduced to the minister." She squeezed Sarah's arm. With a giggle, she added, "I'm glad you're already spoken for— so I don't have to worry about you taking a perfectly good prospect from under my nose."

For a rare moment, John Harding stood alone. Conversation buzzed around him at the outdoor reception.

What a happy occasion this had turned out to be. He was relieved—after that confrontation before the start of the ceremony. Hob had been a handful. He'd reeked of whiskey, and for a few moments John had seen red. But the import of the occasion had helped him quickly get himself in hand. Thankfully, Hob's brother had shown the good sense to stay outside. Once these brothers got started on drink, there was no telling what they'd do.

Besides that, before leaving for this wedding, he'd been notified of Jake's sudden death. He'd rushed over to his old mining friend's house. Thankfully, one of Jake's old cronies had taken over to determine if any relatives existed to be notified, so John could leave, making it just in time to conduct this ceremony.

He looked around at the assembled guests. He was sure many of them wouldn't have been able to see value in Jake. Most would think him just an old geezer, but John felt privileged to have known him. Jake had introduced him to the Ute Indians, invaluable to his mission here. Also, Jake had been a man of his word—with the proverbial heart of gold.

John's eyes skimmed the gathering, his height enabling him to see over most in the crowd. Whom had he not yet greeted? Jean Garland had just returned from an eastern school and brought along an older lady and a cousin. If he knew what was good for him—his social standing, that is—he'd say hello to Jean and welcome the other ladies to Colorado Springs. He was surprised Mrs. Garland hadn't already herded her little group to meet him. She usually took the lead in such things.

At that moment several people in the crowd stepped away and the Garland group came into view. John's eyes rested on the cousin next to Jean. He'd noticed her as soon as the ceremony had concluded. Her sunny blond hair stood out in the crowd, but it was her vivacity that continued to attract his attention. She laughed and talked as if she'd known everyone here for years. Of course, as outgoing as she was, she might be lacking the ability to discuss more serious subjects. And that mattered a great deal—to him, in any case. Well, he'd do his duty and greet the newcomers from the East.

As he walked toward the group, he caught Mrs. Garland's eye. She quickly apprised the family of his approach and drew in her flock. John smiled, recognizing the sheep-herder at work.

"Reverend Harding!" Mrs. Garland looked up archly. "How nice of you to come over. What a wonderful wedding ceremony you conducted this afternoon. The minister of our former church in Philadelphia couldn't have performed it with more dignity. And especially after you had to escort out that angry man. I know everyone was relieved you took care of him so quickly."

"Yes, ma'am. I'm just sorry it happened."

"It certainly gave my relatives from the East a memorable experience!" Mrs. Garland motioned to the older woman at her side. "Now, let me now introduce my sister, Martha Spaulding. She is here to take the waters in Manitou Springs."

Mrs. Garland's sister extended her hand. John thought the lady appeared delicate, but her handshake said differently. This woman had definite ideas, or he'd miss his bet.

"If she finds the waters beneficial and likes it here," Mrs. Garland continued, "she might stay the year. Our healthy, drier weather may be good for her." She turned to the younger woman next to her. "And I'd like you to meet my niece, Sarah Whittington. She's a favorite cousin of Jean's. The two are looking forward to some enjoyable times this summer."

John waited to see if the cousin would extend her hand. When he saw it lift, he quickly offered his to meet it. Her grasp was gentle, then firm. *Soft and feminine—then solid.* As her hand released his, he speculated pleasantly when he might have a repeat on that shake.

Warmth traveled from her mouth to a pair of deep blue-gray eyes. "Nice to meet you." Her smile welcomed him as if she were truly happy to make his acquaintance. He could see how people would respond to such warm-heartedness.

Jean held out her hand. Her energetic shake was like the kid he remembered. Being away at an eastern school hadn't changed her much. Still the same tomboy. He caught his thoughts up short. That wasn't too complimentary to the young lady she was obviously becoming.

He should let Jean be herself and hope she'd enjoy her visit home. With the influx of tourists from the East and the growing numbers from England, she and her cousin should have plenty of society to enjoy. General Palmer had succeeded only too well in advertising Colorado Springs as a resort town from which to make forays to Manitou.

John said his goodbyes and continued around the reception area, scanning it for anyone he hadn't yet greeted. Looking over the crowd, his mind wandered to next week's responsibilities. He would take a trip back into the mountains, scouting out any Ute band hunting the area. The young braves had been restless and didn't want to be confined to a reservation. They didn't remember Kit Carson accompanying their Ute leaders to Washington in '68 to hammer out a treaty. And they paid scant attention to the Brunot Treaty of '74 carving out more of their lands to mining interests. However, little by little a bridge was being built between himself and these Indians. Old Jake had helped him there.

He glanced at the buffet table. Still plenty of food. He'd had no time to get anything with the meeting and greeting that was part of his position. Maybe he'd eat after the bride and groom left. Right now he didn't see them. Were they inside? Maybe he should check.

Already the guests were heading to the front doors of the church to see them off. He noticed Sid Carlton approaching Miss Whittington, and then her aunt from the East turning toward them. He caught the look in the woman's eyes as they settled on Sid. If that man were to show any more marked interest in Miss Whittington, he would have to face the aunt's displeasure. John wondered why. The man certainly had enough money and social standing to satisfy most families.

Then his eyes rested on the lovely, straight back of the blond-haired cousin. And forced himself to look away.

———————⋘⋙———————

Sarah followed the other guests crowding to the church doors. The bridal couple would appear shortly.

Where was Hildie? Sarah had promised the little girl she'd let her know when the bride and groom exited the church. She saw Jean ahead in the crowd and excused herself as she wove her way through people to join her cousin.

"Jean, I don't see your sister. She desperately wanted to throw the remainder of her petals at the bride and groom."

"Oh dear." Jean gestured to the side of the building. "Quick, go around the church. The children were playing hide and seek. Hildie might be taking cover in the bushes. I'll look inside."

11

Sarah threaded her way back through the crowd and hurried past the reception tables and chairs. She glanced at the greenery at the side of the church. No pink dress.

As she rounded the corner at the back of the church a little boy ran past. "Have you seen Hildie?" she called. He stopped long enough to shrug his shoulders.

Several yards behind the church clustered a dense clump of bushes. The perfect place to hide. Sarah ran to the spot and parted the branches as best she could, leaning in. "Hildie! Are you here? The bride and groom are coming!" No answer. Well, she obviously wasn't here— Sarah's hair caught on something, and she pulled it free.

At the church's back door, the minister stepped out. Sarah rushed up to him. "Have you seen Hildie?" She tried to conceal her heavy breathing.

"No, I haven't, but I just left the bride and groom inside. They're about to walk out the front. I'm rounding up the strays."

"If you see Hildie, will you send her to the front of the church? I'm hoping Jean found her."

Just as she was about to hurry away, she caught an amused twinkle in his eye. Hadn't he ever seen a lady rush about before?

Reaching the wedding guests, Sarah noted how a path had been cleared through the crowd for the wedding couple. Just then, Jean opened the church door, exiting with Hildie in tow, and placed her little sister near the top step to throw her petals.

One of the doors swung open again and the best man appeared. Grinning, he announced, "Ladies and gentlemen! May I present Mr. and Mrs. Kirby!" The couple exited the building and stopped a moment while the crowd cheered. Hildie threw a fistful of petals. They landed at the couple's feet. Hildie frantically dug for more as the groom pulled his wife forward. This time the little girl threw the petals up so that the couple ran right into them.

The bride laughed and rewarded Hildie with a quick wave.

"Bravo, Hildie!" Sarah shouted. The crowd closed the path after the hurrying couple and followed them to the carriage.

After the bridal couple departed, Jean rushed toward Sarah. "I found Hildie hiding under a pew. Poor thing, she didn't know whether or not to stay hidden for the game. I told her to come out and make it quick in order to see the bride and groom." Jean grasped Sarah's arm. "Wait! You've got some dead leaves or something in your hair." She laughed. "And a twig is sticking out the side of your head. Oh dear—"

"What?" Sarah gingerly felt her hair.

"No, the other side." Jean was still laughing. "Let me help." She pulled the loose debris off Sarah's head, extracting the twig, but a section of hair became unpinned. "How in the world?" Jean's nose scrunched up. "Here, I'll get your hair back in place. Step over here so we're not so obvious."

Chagrin washed over Sarah. She remembered the minister at the back door and his amused smile. He had seen the debris, and that twig sticking out of her hair.

Well, she certainly wouldn't tell Jean. Her cousin would never let her hear the last of it.

CHAPTER 2

John Harding shaved the last of his stubborn dark whiskers, rinsed the sharp blade and wiped it dry.

"Breakfast in five minutes, John!"

"Thank you, Hannah." He doused his face in the bowl of warm water and toweled it dry with the rough, sunshine-dried length of cotton. He scrunched the towel in and out to soften it, then dried the cleft in his chin.

He had smelled frying bacon and known the eggs weren't far behind, and for that reason had hurried, but not so much as to miss any whiskers. This funeral would be far from fancy, but he wanted to honor the dead with a neat appearance. And do justice to the words he would share with those gathered.

Entering the kitchen in the small, wood-framed house, he caught Hannah plunking down with a flourish a plate loaded with eggs and bacon on the red and white checked tablecloth. Her mature, rotund figure was a comfort to him, as much as her kind but rather rough voice. Hannah was housekeeper, neighbor, and mother all rolled into one.

"You're lookin' a sight for these old eyes," she said, dishing out fried potatoes. "I hope the folks Colorado City way appreciate the fine preacher they've comin' to officiate. If you ask me, you're a sight too good for them."

John seated himself. "Now, Hannah, you know Jake was an old friend, someone who did a lot of good. And the Lord doesn't look at the outward appearance."

"I know. But I hope they had a decent suit to bury him in. Did he have two cents to rub between his fingers?"

"I don't know if he had much of anything, but he'll have a decent suit."

"Now, you didn't go and buy him one, did you? Because you can't afford it! Besides, *he'll* never know." Hannah poured a steaming cup of black coffee. "Your wife had a heart of gold, but she wouldn't have stood for that. She looked out for your money. Would have buried him in a nice shirt and tie and left it at that."

"I'm laying up treasure in heaven, my girl."

"Lands sakes, you give away your money like it was sand. What with medicine for the Indians and all. You need someone like Rosalind to look after the little money you got."

"What's money for, Hannah, but to help others? Like I help *you*—by hiring you." He smiled up at her.

"Don't get sweet with old Hannah. Hiring me helps us *both*, and you know it."

"Ah—" His housekeeper was quick on the draw.

"God's truth!" She shook out her dishtowel, straightening it. "Though I'd stay on if you needed me, money or no." Hannah looked at him pensively. "I did feel kinda bad when you first brought Rosalind here as a bride—after your visit to that Philly church board back East—you know, after she said she didn't need me. Me, after seeing to you all those years! Course I could see you didn't need us both in a place this small. Real soon I saw she was nice enough to keep me on once a week."

"Now, Hannah, after Rosalind began visiting the sick with me, you *were* needed."

"Like a hole in the head."

"There's nary a hole in my head, Hannah, and my wife didn't have one either. However, if I didn't keep you on for

15

any other reason, I would for your coffee." He bent over and breathed in its aroma. "Rosalind never did have the knack. What's your secret?"

"That's between me and the good Lord." Hannah grinned suddenly. "I've got to give you some reason to keep me on." She shook her finger at him. "But I do a lot more around here. You keep that busy you don't notice. Now, take the shirt you're wearing. No one, and I mean no one, would bleach it and starch it and iron it the way I do—just so you can look like one of them eastern gentlemen with their fancy shirts."

Hannah walked over to the counter and picked up the butter she'd put out to soften from the ice box, then went back and placed the dish beside his toast. She looked him over. "A mother couldn't be prouder of the way you look, your dark handsome face against that white shirt. My, if I was a few decades younger and a mite more educated, I'd go after you myself. I sure would."

John felt his face redden and laughed. "Hannah, don't worry. You're my girl no matter what. My next wife will just have to put up with you, can't do without your coffee."

"Pshaw!" Hannah shooed his words away with a wave of her hand as she shuffled to the pantry.

Pike's Peak soared in the distance. A neighboring mountain sloped down to a meadow dotted with white and yellow wild flowers, dark purple blooms scattered among them. In one corner of the cemetery, a hole had been dug for the wooden coffin. John stood waiting as a few people climbed the slight incline, their horses staked, left to crop grass a short distance away.

After the graveside service finished, the few friends of the deceased came up to shake John's hand, telling him how much they appreciated what he'd said. Well, the words were real to him. Had to be. "I am the Resurrection and the Life," Jesus said. "I go to prepare a place for you and will receive you unto Myself." What a comfort those promises were for those who knew the Lord and had lost loved ones.

John had expected only nine present, ten at most, but twice that number had come. While dirt was shoveled over the rough-hewn box, a man in a severe black suit stepped up to him.

"Jake had a will and I'm going to read it next Tuesday in my office. I'd like you to be present."

Who would have thought Jake had a will, or anything to will away? John nodded his acquiescence. His visit to the Utes would have to be postponed a few days.

He climbed into the saddle and leaned over to pat his horse's neck before he prodded her down the trail. Leaving the mountain meadow, he marveled at the burial site, surprisingly lovely for the poor folks of Colorado City. Peaceful, too. A contrast to the ruckus that often went on in that settlement.

Just as he was beginning to clear the last rise into town, he saw two riders coming off a trail below him. Something familiar about them made him stop his horse to keep from being skylined.

The taller, gaunt one he'd had to exit so forcefully from the wedding. These two brothers were a thorn in his flesh, way back when he'd caught them selling whiskey to the Utes. He felt the old ire rise in his chest. If there were two more good-for-nothings on the face of God's earth, he hadn't met them. He hated the thought of what drink was doing to the Indians. That, and the gambling and overeating. General Palmer's aide had told him Chief Colorow had ballooned to over 300 pounds, unusual for an Indian. What was the Department of Indian Affairs thinking—giving tribes allotments to live away from their traditional hunting grounds—confident they were somehow making it up to the Indians?

17

John kept to the back of the knoll as the two men ambled down into town. Months ago, after their big confrontation, he'd hoped they would keep traveling west. They drank enough whiskey themselves to provoke inevitable fights. Hang it, he didn't want to be officiating at any more funerals.

When they were lost to sight, he started the mustang down the trail. After the service he'd just conducted, he needed some time alone. Since Rosalind's death, a funeral triggered that in him. Thankfully, it was not as heart-wrenching as it used to be. Time was when he could hardly get through the words of a service. But folks understood when he paused, struggling to hold his features in place. Whoever said men didn't cry, or that they shouldn't? They'd never been married to Rosalind.

The sturdy gait of his horse comforted him.

He still missed Rosalind's quiet support of his work, the little curve of her lips that preceded her eyes lighting up. Yes, she could be stubborn about money. But that had all been for their good.

Reflecting on the morning at home, he realized again how grateful he was for his housekeeper. Not only for food and a clean house, but the way she let him talk about Rosalind. His wife was still valued, not forgotten. Hannah never claimed to be smart, book-learning smart. No, she was better than that.

CHAPTER 3

Sarah stepped off the porch steps of her aunt's house and gazed up at the glowing summit above Colorado Springs. Pikes Peak. Such a prosaic name for a beautiful mountain. It towered above the town. She was told the Indians called it Shining Mountain.

What a subject for a painter. But how could one capture the mountain's majesty? She had come west to paint, but now doubted her ability. She had tried a sketch last week when they made the outing to Manitou to taste the springs, but her attempt looked rather flat. How had Bierstadt done it, achieved such grandeur in his paintings?

Maybe her foreground was wrong. One would need to do it just right to do justice to that mountain.

"Sarah! Join me on the porch." Jean beckoned from her chair and threw a magazine on the one next to hers. "Here, this one's got all the latest fashions."

Sarah mounted the steps and adjusted a pillow in the fan-backed wicker chair before taking up *Lady's Godey's.* Her cousin had been difficult all morning. Sarah was tempted to say, a little sarcastically, "You're in a sweet mood," but she refrained, wanting to set a lady-like example. Seeing her cousin resting, perusing a periodical, seemed too good to be true. Sarah opened the proffered olive branch.

A striking white and black dress caught her attention. It would be perfect for paying afternoon calls as Prescott Bellamy's wife. Wearing that, she would certainly help drum up business for Philadelphia's up-and-coming lawyer. Then she sighed. By the time her father let her marry Prescott the dress would be out of style.

She might as well not dwell on that or try and wheedle her father into changing his mind—for Colorado Springs did have its compensations. She was finding society unexpectedly genteel. And on this late spring day, the Garland's deep front porch couldn't be more comfortable. Her eye rested on Jean scrunched up in a wicker chair near her own.

Her cousin looked up from her magazine. "You know what I'd like to do?"

"What?"

"This!" Jean suddenly rose up and threw a pillow with a vengeance. Sarah raised her magazine just in time to block it. When Sarah lowered her periodical, a second pillow caught her full in the face.

"Stop!" Sarah held up the offending pillow. "I won't throw this on your porch—in full view of everyone—"

"Oh, don't be such a wet blanket." Jean rolled her eyes.

"You could act a little more ladylike."

"*Dearest cousin*, I'm just letting off a little steam, celebrating the last of my girlhood this summer before becoming a *woman*."

Sarah closed the magazine. "At nineteen you're supposed to already be a woman. Better yet, a lady."

Jean stuck out her tongue. "You just like to lord it over me because you're a year older."

"I lord it, as you term it, because I do, in fact, act a bit more grownup."

"I was just expending a little energy *now*, so when we go out *later*, I won't *embarrass* you. And," Jean's eyes glinted, "so

I won't embarrass myself—in case we run into you-know-who. Remember his house near Limit Street, the one I pointed out on our way to Manitou?"

Sarah knew. Whom else had Jean talked about in bed last night? Sarah assessed her cousin in her yellow dress. Jean was certainly comely enough with her figure and glossy chestnut hair. But her hoydenish behavior!

Sarah shook her head. "If *he's* what you have in mind, you'd better reform. When you first described him, I thought he was your average, serious-minded, decent-looking man. But he's *quite* a bit more than that, my dear."

"That's why I primed you before the wedding. You're the best person to help me acquire a little more polish and sophistication—when you aren't acting crazed like me." Jean smirked. "I should know, the weekends I spent at your house this last year."

Jean settled herself more comfortably in her fan-backed chair. "In fact, I'm rather surprised Prescott is enamored with you. He is *so* serious." She flipped a page in her magazine. "As I mentioned before, it's a comfort you already have Prescott—the third. When you finally walk down the aisle, he'll keep you in the furs and jewels you're accustomed to—after he makes his mark as a lawyer, of course."

"Now you sound like my father."

"Do I? Then maybe I know your father pretty well. Surprising, since he doesn't talk much."

"But he's invariably at dinner. He makes a point to be home for that."

"I shouldn't wonder with a cook like yours. Though I don't think he'd dare stay at his club for fear of affronting your mother."

Sarah sat up straighter in her chair. "I'll admit Mother does run a tight ship. She is very much in charge at home. But then Father's bailiwick is his law office."

"Nice division of labor. Although I will have to say, between the cook and the different maids doing laundry and cleaning the house, your mother doesn't labor too hard."

"She *has* to have help if she's going to keep up with her society work."

"Certainly." Jean flipped a page in her magazine noisily. "And you, *of course*, will follow in her footsteps."

"Of course. But if you haven't noticed, art also interests me. That will take quite a bit of my energy. Next time we go to the waters in Manitou for Aunt Martha, I'm taking my sketchpad again. Another idea is forming for a painting."

Jean's eyes narrowed. Sarah could see the wheels working in her cousin's head.

"I just thought of something." Jean pushed herself upright. "Maybe I should have some such interest to catch the minister's eye."

"It wouldn't hurt. What did you study, anyway, during your time in Philly?"

"The usual. Literature. History. A little geography. I don't know."

"Oh!" Sarah laughed. "With all that you'll be just the wife for a finely educated minister. I hope you studied a little *religion* as well."

"Yes, last term something called, 'Religions of the World.'"

"That's a start, a topic to talk about until you get his interest up."

"Oh, Sarah, do you think I could do so?" Jean looked at her, admiration gleaming in her eyes. "Jiminy, I just know I would have a fighting chance with you on my side. Oh, I wish I could see him soon. If I can't—" she tapped her magazine with a fingertip.

From the look on her cousin's face Sarah knew something was coming.

"You know that town on the way to Manitou—Colorado City? I think we should visit it. The place will give you a taste of a typical western town, like the frontier you read about in the papers back east."

"It's not too wild, is it?"

"No. Besides, a mining town like Colorado City is part of our state's history." Jean jerked up in her chair. "And, the more I consider it, the more I think it's part of my job as hostess to show you around, to *educate* you in these matters."

"Why do I see that mischievous look in your eyes?"

"You're too suspicious." Jean settled back in her chair. "I will have to admit Colorado City is a bit more lively than our town. You know when General Palmer founded Colorado Springs, he forbade saloons and houses of ill repute. He wanted a nice peace-abiding place. As a result, we've enough upper crust people living here to satisfy the most persnickety persons, including yourself. Have you seen any more lovely homes in a western town? Especially one of this size?"

"With scant experience of the west, I wouldn't know."

"Well, you'll have to take my word for it. Having said that, I think you should acquaint yourself with the most historical town in our area."

"I'm perfectly willing to be exposed to a little history. But we can't go with just the two of us. What about your famous next-door neighbor accompanying us?"

"Sid? He's busy on Thursdays." Jean's index finger tapped her chin meditatively. "My brother might do. He'd be more than willing to take us to a place like Colorado City."

"Isn't Ben only fifteen?"

"Kids grow up fast in the west." Jean put down her magazine, "but I'll probably just tell Mama we're going for a ride." She glanced at Sarah. "Now don't look at me like that."

John stood gazing out the parlor window, then stepped back when he spotted the Garland carriage. Jean's young brother was handling the reins. Ben looked like he had the Garland way with horses. John stayed near the window a little longer, his eye caught by the very becoming hat on Miss Whittington's blond head.

He smiled at himself. He didn't usually spy behind curtains, but at least he wasn't making a fool of himself by being seen. The lace his wife had brought west was heavy enough to conceal him. She had liked pretty things, this parlor a testament to her efforts. Since her passing, its order and beauty had comforted him.

But here he was, looking out the window at another woman. Was that wrong? It'd been well over a year since his wife's death, almost two. He had wondered if that dead feeling inside him would ever lift. Rosalind had meant so much to him. This was the first time his interest had stirred in another woman.

A relief almost. Many a week he had tried to get up a sermon on sheer grit, grieving as he was. Finally, he would go to the Heavenly Father, pleading for help. God always came through. That pure dependence on the Lord was probably what had worked wonders in his sermons.

He leaned closer to the window. The carriage was traveling down the road that would take them to either Manitou Springs or Colorado City. Surely they wouldn't be going to the latter. No—more likely they were driving to Manitou Springs. But then, wouldn't the girls' aunt be accompanying them? That was the reason she'd come west— to take the waters.

So why wasn't she with them? He watched the carriage as far as he could before it disappeared from view. A buggy followed in its wake before John turned and crossed the parlor to enter the spare room he'd converted into a study. He passed his desk and looked out the back window. If this back yard hadn't been enclosed, surrounded by trees and bushes, the place would lack the peace he often craved. Its serenity settled him. Quiet and shade ruled most of the yard, but a small patch of continual sunshine nurtured Hannah's herbs and flowers.

His backyard was the perfect image of the serene Colorado Springs the General had envisioned for its residents.

John sat down at his desk and took out his notes for next Sunday's sermon. The topic would provide a good focus for his mind.

But after a minute his thoughts veered to that carriage. Jean came from a circumspect family. She wouldn't take her cousin to Colorado City without proper escort. Surely not.

John's pencil ground out a few words. Concentration on his topic was coming hard. A cunningly-wrought bonnet on top of blond hair kept intruding.

He looked up. Compromise was in order. After completing this next section on his sermon, he would go out for a while. Sunday after church he'd promised to visit the widow Cunningham. That should cure his restlessness.

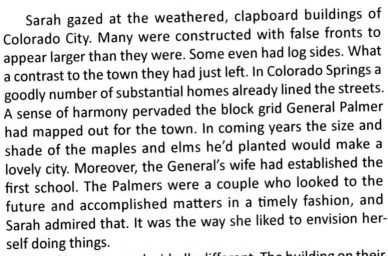

Sarah gazed at the weathered, clapboard buildings of Colorado City. Many were constructed with false fronts to appear larger than they were. Some even had log sides. What a contrast to the town they had just left. In Colorado Springs a goodly number of substantial homes already lined the streets. A sense of harmony pervaded the block grid General Palmer had mapped out for the town. In coming years the size and shade of the maples and elms he'd planted would make a lovely city. Moreover, the General's wife had established the first school. The Palmers were a couple who looked to the future and accomplished matters in a timely fashion, and Sarah admired that. It was the way she liked to envision herself doing things.

But this town was decidedly different. The building on their right was worn, weather-beaten. The horizontal slats of its boards stood out in the light. Interesting from an artist's viewpoint. A little seedy, though. Most of the wooden buildings on the outskirts of town had already seen hard years. A number of people walked the streets, mostly men it seemed. Some lounged in chairs out front.

As their party drove slowly through town, a man standing in front of a saloon on the left stared at their carriage. Without meaning to, Sarah caught his eye. His bold gaze brought embarrassed warmth to her face. Sarah glanced at her cousin. But surely Jean knew what she was doing.

"The business district is several blocks. We're going to drive to the end of it before parking," Jean said. "The south side on the left, we need to stay away from. You noticed that saloon? Well, that's typical. Respectable people don't walk that side. Ben, let's go to that general store at the end of the street." Jean pointed to a building coming up on their right. "I'd like to see what kind of goods they have inside."

Sarah clutched Jean's arm. "Don't you think we should just ride around a bit, then leave?"

"I declare, Sarah. Where is your sense of adventure? You've left all your fun at home."

Mentally, Sarah threw up her hands. "Okay, this is your outing."

Ben drove behind the store then jumped off his seat and tied their horse to the hitching post.

"Now you can help us down," Jean instructed him.

He came around and assisted Sarah first. When his sister held out her hand, he said under his breath, "You better treat me nice or I'll tell Mother where we've been this afternoon."

Jean's eyes flashed a warning. Sarah pretended not to see, but it confirmed her suspicions. Jean was skating on thin ice.

The door's jingling bell announced their entrance. Behind the counter, the proprietor looked up. Sarah's eyes scanned the full-to-bursting store, shelves stacked with rows of cans and bottles of every size and shape. On higher shelves sat clocks, lamps, a yellow and red ceramic rooster and cardboard and wooden boxes. From the walls hung rifles, tin pictures, and a bleached ram's skull with dark curling horns. Floor to ceiling, objects of every description filled the place, a hodgepodge of shape, texture and color.

Down the counter from the proprietor, two men eyed them.

Jean ignored them, ambled through the aisles, fingering the merchandise. Sarah followed her lead.

"Hey, look at these, will you?" Ben stopped in front of a jar filled with empty bullet cartridges.

"They don't throw anything away here, do they?" Sarah said quietly to Jean. She wondered what in the world those would be useful for. A nearby crock held pickles.

Jean approached the counter. "Do you have any ribbon we could see?"

The storekeeper nodded, then reached behind him for a box on a high shelf. "Here you are, miss."

Jean removed its cover and examined one colorful roll after another. "Look at this yellow striped one, Sarah. Wouldn't it be perfect for my straw, the hat I wear with that sunny-colored dress?"

"It would. Yellow brings out the color of your hair."

As Jean continued to look over the ribbons, Sarah noticed one of the men leaving the store, while the other, dressed in a black frock-coat and flowery vest, moved down the counter toward them to examine a box of loose cigars. He took one and held it out to the proprietor. "I'll take one of these." After pocketing the change, he edged nearer Jean. "That ribbon's certainly pretty. Was wondering what to buy my sister. Now you've given me an idea. Something for a hat, you say?"

Sarah thought he stood unnecessarily close.

Jean's lips twitched into a small smile. "After I finish I'll be glad to let you have the box to look for yourself."

The man's white hand rested on the counter near Jean's. It inched closer as he tapped the counter lightly with his long, slim fingers. "I'd take that right kindly, miss." Then he smiled and moved away.

Sarah stepped closer to Jean and whispered, "He wasn't even introduced to us!"

Jean whispered back, "People out west are friendly. You don't always need an introduction like you'd expect in Philly."

Sarah's eyebrows lifted and plainly said, *If you say so.*

Jean's brisk nod back said, *I do!*

Just then Ben walked up. "You ready to go?"

"Not yet." Jean's response was clipped.

"Well, I'm done looking. When you get whatever you want, why don't you buy me that candy over there—the gumdrops." Jean didn't answer so her brother pressed. "You know, for taking you out riding and all."

"Can't you get it yourself?"

"I don't have any money; besides, I'm going outside. I've seen enough here."

Jean gave him a hard look. "Well, I suppose I'll get you some. But don't wander far."

"Jean, would this color make me more feminine?" Sarah held pink ribbon near her face, batting her eyes.

Jean batted her eyes right back—fiercely. "If you get any more so, you'll have every man in the county after you and I won't have a chance."

Sarah laughed. "With your gorgeous hair? I don't think you have to worry. Just *act* a little more like a girl and you'll have the boys lining up. That yellow striped ribbon you were looking at earlier was pretty. Are you going to buy that?"

"Oh, I don't know." Jean straightened the last of the spools in the box. "Maybe some other time." The proprietor had moved to the end of the counter. "Here, Sarah," she snapped. "Give me the pink. I'll get it for you. I know *you* won't buy anything in a place like this."

Browsing a little longer, Jean finally bought the penny candy along with the ribbon. Sarah noticed the man who purchased the cigar at the far end of an aisle.

Stepping outside the store, Jean glanced around. "Now where is that boy? Don't tell me we have to track him down." She stood a minute longer scanning the street, then looked at Sarah. "Should we hunt for him along the boardwalk or wait in the carriage?"

At this juncture, the general store door opened. The man who'd asked about the ribbon paused beside them, putting on his wide-brimmed, flat-crowned hat. "You ladies lost your young escort?" He smiled. "I was all for adventure at that age myself. Browsing through a general store wouldn't have qualified."

"I'm not sure where he could have gone." Jean cast the man a doubtful look. "If you were a boy his age, where would you go?"

"Why, I'd continue on this side of the street and make my way through town. Of course we do have a number of saloons—the other side. Those might'a gotten his curiosity up."

"I hope not."

They stood a moment longer. The man then offered, "Why don't I accompany you ladies down the street while you glance inside some of the buildings. If you want, I can step inside any to see if the boy's there." Without waiting for an answer, he extended first one arm, then the other.

Jean took his arm. Sarah followed her cousin's lead, but felt most uncomfortable. She wasn't sure she liked this town's easy ways.

Just then a man called out, exiting the hotel from across the street. Dressed in a dapper suit with lapels outlined in darker material, he hurried up to the threesome. "Are you in the need of assistance, my friend? Three's a crowd, you know."

"Hello, Luke. We're doing just fine, but maybe one of the ladies would like her own escort. We're searching for this one's brother. Here," he handed over Jean. The gentleman took her gloved hand and placed it on his arm.

Sarah's escort patted her hand on his arm, "Now, little lady, isn't this more comfortable?"

The impertinence of the man. Sarah wanted to draw away, but didn't know how to do so without making a scene. Jean was going along with this nonsense. What was she doing, encouraging these strange men? Oh, she would get a talking to when they returned home.

Sarah steeled her back. What if her friends back east saw her now? Or Prescott? He'd think she had taken leave of her senses. He might even reconsider becoming engaged to her. She looked in despair at the length of street they were to travel. God spare her from meeting anyone they knew.

As they walked, Sarah's escort asked if she was enjoying her time out west, then bent close to hear the answer to his question. She could feel his breath against her cheek. When she backed away, he held her hand a little more firmly under his own.

At the end of the block, Sarah called out ahead, "Jean, don't you think it might be a good idea to go back to the carriage and wait there for your brother?"

Sarah's escort laughed. "Now, Miss! We've just started looking for the boy. Besides, you haven't seen much of Colorado City. We're only too glad to show you around. Isn't that right, Luke?"

Luke turned to answer. "Certainly! You ladies let us help you now. That boy will turn up. We'll keep an eye open for him and in the meantime we'll show you the town."

"Jean?" Sarah willed her cousin to look at her.

Jean turned and shrugged a shoulder. Sarah could see it was three against one. She renewed her commitment to give her cousin a piece of her mind when they returned home.

"Now, don't you fret," Sarah's escort advised. "Even if the boy appears in the next few minutes, why, I'll bet he'd like more time to explore. You stay right here with me," he smiled down at her, "and you'll do just fine."

CHAPTER 4

John put down his work. He'd made himself stick to it while restlessness nagged at him. However, he'd finished in record time.

Now he'd visit the Widow Cunningham.

He tightened the cinch on Flossie, then finally admitted the real reason for his uneasiness. He couldn't help thinking Jean's mother or the aunt should have been with the girls.

Climbing into the saddle, he wondered if the widow couldn't wait until later in the day. Out on the road, instead of heading in the direction to her house, he kneed his horse in the direction of Colorado City. He argued with himself. He wasn't even sure the girls had gone there. They could have driven instead to Manitou Springs. And even if they had gone to the former, they should be safe in broad daylight. He didn't really need to go.

On the other hand, with Colorado City one never knew. The rough element might be drinking early, and with pretty girls walking around town— But surely they could take care of themselves, coming from a big city like Philadelphia.

Despite his double-mindedness, he continued down the road to Colorado City. Was he a fool? Well, no one need know.

As far as anyone was concerned, he was making one of his usual visits.

When he came to the business district he looked down its main street, aware of the underground tunnels that connected the disreputable saloons and gaming houses of the south side with the reputable north side. The tunnels also provided a quick way to exit the illegal gambling houses should a raid occur.

Turning his horse to the right, he headed to the street that ran behind the north-side establishments. The women folk of the town had insisted no horses be tied to the boardwalk to taint the appearance of the street, so he directed his horse to the rear of the buildings, examining each carriage. At the end of the business district, he spied the Garland carriage behind the Tappan Building. Everything seemed peaceful, normal enough. Yet, he argued, it wasn't the better part of wisdom for these girls to visit this town in the first place, particularly with only young Ben as escort.

He tied his horse, stepped around the building and walked into the general store. The proprietor looked up. "Can I help you, sir?"

John's cursory glance around showed two old prospectors sitting by the potbellied stove, smoking pipes. He walked up to the counter. "I'm searching for two young ladies and a lad of about fifteen."

The proprietor rubbed his chin, took his time answering. "That group was here... awhile ago. Sort of wandered around, just looking. Finally bought a few things."

"How long ago did they leave?"

"Oh...not long."

John stepped out the door and looked down the street. Where would the girls and Ben have gone? Individuals or small groups of people were either on their way to do business or strolling the boardwalk.

He decided riding was the faster way to search the town so he went to the back of the building and once again climbed into the saddle. He patted Flossie's neck. "Well, girl, let's make the tour." Directing her back around the Tappan Building to the main street, he walked her slowly enough to glance in alleyways. Because he looked for two young women and a boy, he missed the two couples a block away.

The hat caught his eye. And then the woman's figure of the rear couple.

He quickly assessed the situation, taking in the men's dress. Dapper. Too dapper. And one man in a black frock coat. The girls shouldn't be walking with *those* men. Men, he'd bet his bottom dollar, they hadn't known an hour ago.

The foursome was walking in the same direction he was riding, so they hadn't seen him. He pulled in his horse and considered the situation. It was a mighty strange one. Where was Ben?

John didn't figure his job description included nursemaid, so he wasn't about to extract the ladies from those gentlemen if they didn't want it. On the other hand, he was sure the families of these two young women wouldn't approve of the association. The couples had only another half block before they'd reach the end of the boardwalk. Maybe he'd just follow slowly at a distance to determine what was going on.

John watched as the couples reached the last building that could be properly called the business district. Would they turn and come back the same way they'd gone? They had to. No gentlemen would take ladies to the opposite side of the street. Low-lifes and criminals frequented those unsavory establishments, drinking and gambling. Further south on Cucharras Street stood houses of prostitution. He kept his eyes particularly on the statuesque blond, wondering what she was thinking. Was she comfortable with what was going on?

He saw her motion her intention to return the way they'd come. The man held her arm, urging her to cross the street. She tried to step away from him.

John immediately kneed his horse into a canter. Halfway there, he heard a hail. Glancing to his left, Ben rushed out of an alleyway where horses were tethered. John motioned him to follow and urged on his horse.

Jean was the first to see him coming. "Pastor!" she called.

Coming up abruptly on the couples, he decided not to dismount. He would need all the authority he could muster in this situation. At closer range, these gentlemen appeared to be men of wide experience, more than these young ladies were accustomed to handling.

"Hello, Miss Garland, Miss Whittington." He tipped his hat. "Can I be of service?" Both girls were rosy faced. Embarrassed, he was sure.

"These ladies are with us, sir." The taller of the two men gave him a direct, steely look.

"We were just to suggest eating at the El Paso House back down the street," the other man volunteered. "As you might know, it has a spacious dining room. We've offered to show the ladies the town," he gestured with his free hand, "such as it is at this hour of the day."

John turned in his saddle. Ben was just coming up. "Weren't you ladies showing Ben the town?" he asked smoothly. "Too bad to leave him out of things."

"Yes, Ben!" Jean said. "We lost track of him. And oh, I promised Mother we'd be home early for dinner because Aunt Martha's visiting." She looked for confirmation from Sarah. "You remember?"

Sarah hesitated just long enough for John to suspect the promise had been invented on the spot. He decided to step in. "Well, if you ladies are ready to return, I'll escort you back to your carriage."

He didn't wait for a response. He climbed off his horse and handed the reins to Ben. "Follow us." He stepped onto the boardwalk, notching up the authority level in his voice. "I'll take you ladies now."

The taller man who was Miss Whittington's escort put his hand firmly over Sarah's resting on his sleeve.

John looked him in the eye. "Excuse me, sir. These ladies are particular friends of mine. I'm sure you understand."

"Yes," Jean quickly volunteered. "You see, he's our pastor." She jerked away from her companion and took John's proffered arm. Sarah followed suit. "Thank you, gentlemen," Jean said. "You've been most kind, but Reverend Harding will see to us now."

The tall gentleman had reluctantly released Sarah. "Downright convenient, you being a reverend and all." He snickered, looking sideways at his friend. "Wouldn't want to fight God almighty now, would we, Luke?"

The snicker was an insult, but John was accustomed to brushing off intended offenses. He merely said, "Good day, gentlemen. You ready, ladies? Ben?" Then he adroitly turned his little group back the way they had come. Each lady clutched his arm, confirming his instincts of how grateful they were to be rescued.

They walked the length of the block, then just as they began the second, John's eye caught two familiar figures exiting a saloon across the street. The men recognized him and one of them shouted. He kept the girls going, pretending not to notice, but the two men in buckskin stumbled into a run, one lagging behind the other. The laggard finally caught at the other's shoulder. "Now Hob! You leave that parson alone. He's mean poison!"

In just moments the leader of the two cut in front of the group. John stopped. The man swaggered, his breath exuding liquor and tobacco.

"Why-y Parson. Seems ta me like you've got one gir-r-l too many." The man's hand dropped suggestively on his six-shooter. "I'll ferget last time...if yule be friendly like...and do a little shar-r-in'."

John had purposely left his gun at home. "Hob, I'm clean and don't want to get into anything. I'm just escorting these two ladies home. They've had enough sightseeing for one day."

"Tha' so? I'm thinkin' we ought'a ask th' ladies." Taking a step to one side, his boot stepped on the hem of Sarah's dress. He clumsily removed it and offered his arm. "Sorry, Ma'am, but may I have...th' honor?"

John felt Miss Whittington's hand clutch him harder. "Thank you, Sir, but Reverend Harding is escorting us home. Both my cousin and myself."

Hob looked up at John, anger suddenly flaring in his eyes. "Aw now. Parson don't need *two* women."

Everyone stood very still.

John considered the situation, knowing if he made a sudden move, Hob and his brother would use it as an excuse to start a fight. If not now, later. He wasn't opposed to a good slugfest—his blood was up from the gamblers he'd just got rid of—but he had these two ladies to consider.

He disciplined his voice to be quiet, injecting just enough authority. "Men, if you'll let us by...these two ladies have had quite an afternoon and are ready to go home. Their carriage and brother are waiting."

Hob chomped on the plug in his mouth, glanced over at the boy leading the horse then back at John. "I might 'a known you'd hide behind somethin'." He sneered. "Next time... yule find yerself a fight, Brother Hardin'. With none of them skirts to hide behind neither." Holding up his hand to his hat, he gave a jaunty salute with his index finger. Pointing it like a gun, he lowered it and fired. Then took an unsteady step back and waved them on.

John carefully guided the ladies past.

That's what had made him uneasy back at the house, he now realized. Somewhere back in his mind, he'd taken into account these two whiskey-selling brothers in town. With two very naïve, unsuspecting young ladies.

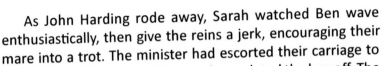

As John Harding rode away, Sarah watched Ben wave enthusiastically, then give the reins a jerk, encouraging their mare into a trot. The minister had escorted their carriage to the outskirts of Colorado Springs then saluted the boy off. The reverend had said very little, treating them respectfully—but distantly, she thought.

Afterward they sat quietly in the carriage, their own thoughts keeping them company. Sarah had never been so glad to see someone—or so embarrassed. Colorado City had been a situation where she'd been thrown off balance, hadn't known what to do. Those men! Jean said western people were friendly, more casual than back east. But the situation they found themselves in hadn't felt particularly friendly or casual. She had depended on Jean to lead them out of it, but Jean just kept going along. Even now, Sarah couldn't believe her cousin.

She had hoped no one from Colorado Springs would see them. Then to have the minister, of all people, help them out of their predicament. Jean had explained it to him as a lark that had gotten out of hand. Sarah felt the less said the better. Frankly, she hadn't known *what* to say. All she knew was that she'd never let herself get into such a situation again. If she did, she would take measures *herself* to get out of it.

When the minister handed her up into the carriage, his eyes had a *look*—was it questioning, judgmental? She hadn't been sure, but once again she felt a wave of embarrassment. Back home she was highly respected, at least her family was—

Ben gave another slap to the reins. "Boy, did you see how he handled those men?"

"Which men?" Jean asked.

"The men that jumped out in front on the boardwalk. They looked bad, real bad. Couldn't you tell they'd been drinking? And Mr. Harding was as cool as anything. Man, I wish the boys could've seen him."

"Ben! You're not to say anything. Not to anyone!" Jean scooted up from her seat to grab her brother's arm. "Do you hear me? That was part of the agreement for your going."

"Ah, you don't mean it."

"I do mean it. Mother and Father would—I don't know what they'd do, but I don't want to find out. All you need to say is that we were on a ride. That's *all*."

"Drat!" Ben flicked the reins again. He guided the horse down the street, his shoulders communicating a sulk. Then he suddenly burst out, "But did you see the way he sat his horse? Those other men, the first two I'm talking about now—they didn't want to tangle with *him*, not the way he looked on that horse. And they didn't look none too pleased—"

"I know, I know!" Jean all but shouted. "You don't have to tell me. I was terribly embarrassed he found us in that situation." Jean dropped back, very decidedly, in her seat then glanced at Sarah. "But he did look grand, didn't he? Imagine! He, of all people, rescuing us. Oh, Sarah, if you could have heard my heart pounding."

"What are you talking about?" Ben looked over his shoulder.

"Never mind. I was just saying how glad I was to be rescued."

As Ben turned back to his driving, Jean gave Sarah a warning look. "This *has* been quite an afternoon. When we get home, just act as if nothing happened." She glanced at her brother then again at Sarah, and put a warning finger to her lips. "And nothing did happen. Really!"

———∞◦⟨∞⟩◦∞———

Martha looked up from reading to Hildie. From her vantage point on the front porch, she noticed Ben driving the carriage down the road at a good-paced trot, approaching the corner into their drive much too fast. Why did these young people always have to be in such a spanking hurry? No wonder the girls looked—

Martha quickly patted Hildie's arm. "I'm going down to meet them." Hurrying down the steps, she waved them to stop. Hildie followed.

Ben brought the horse to a halt near the aunt.

Hildie stepped to the carriage. "I want to go for a ride. Can I get up with you?"

Sarah leaned over to help lift her.

Hildie plopped herself down on the seat. "Where'd you go?"

Jean reached over to tickle her. "Hildie! Little girls should be seen and not heard."

"So, girls, how was your afternoon?" Martha asked.

"Jean, stop!" Hildie, laughing, begged.

Jean answered, "Fine, Auntie, just fine."

Martha tried to catch either Jean or Sarah's eyes, but to no avail. She remembered at lunch the girls had been mighty general in talking about the outing. Sarah was her responsibility. Martha raised her voice. "Jean, stop tickling Hildie!" When Hildie quieted down, she asked again, "Now, did everything go all right?"

Jean's answer took longer this time. "Oh, pretty much the usual, I guess."

"Where'd you go?" Hildie chimed in again.

"Hildie!" Jean warned.

Martha noticed Sarah gazing off to the side. The lack of a direct look confirmed her suspicions. Something *had* happened, but the girls didn't want to say. She was weighing whether or not to cross examine when Sid hailed them, pushing his way through an opening in the hedge separating the two yards.

"Hey, everyone!" He waved a white envelope with an accompanying sheet of heavy paper. "This came this afternoon. Did you receive one?"

"That looks like the Bells' invitation," Martha said. "My sister showed it to me."

"It's to Briarhurst." Sid held out the invitation to Jean. "It'll be a big event. Inform your cousin the treat she's in for."

Jean grabbed the letter. "Sarah, an invitation to the Bells' home is about the biggest social affair in these parts—Dr. William Bell is General Palmer's business associate—General Palmer, remember who founded Colorado Springs?"

"The one who wanted an upstanding town," Sid interrupted, "not a place like Colorado City with its strong drink and wild living."

Martha saw the warning look Jean gave Sarah. "Where did you say you girls—"

"Not now, Auntie," Jean interrupted. "Come inside Sid, and let's tell Sarah more about the invitation to Briarhurst over a glass of lemonade. Anybody thirsty? I'm parched." She reached ahead to grasp Ben's arm. "You take the carriage round the back. Then come inside for something to drink. Sid, will you please help us down?"

Martha looked at the girls hurrying up the walk with Sid in their wake. Jean had nicely dispatched everyone. And she couldn't have looked guiltier if she tried. Martha had half a mind to talk with her sister Amelia right now. She picked up her skirt and followed everyone inside.

CHAPTER 5

John stepped out onto the stoop of the solicitor's office. When he had walked into the lawyer's place earlier this morning it had been sunny, weather Colorado Springs was known for. Now as he gazed up at Pikes Peak, the sunlight, the atmosphere seemed even lighter. Probably no different from when he'd entered the office, but his perception had certainly changed.

The solicitor's precise words came back to him. "Jake Mullins has appointed you benefactor of his estate. That includes the cabin and its contents. His mine. And a bank account in Denver. Here is a copy of the will, Mr. Harding. As well as authorization for you to obtain funds from the account."

For some moments, John had sat in the chair, stunned. Then he asked the first question that came to mind. "I wonder why he didn't bank here in the Springs."

The lawyer adjusted his spectacles. "My reading of Jake is that he didn't trust people overmuch, especially regarding his claim. So he did his business in a city where he was not known. Regarding his mine, I have no idea if it produced anything of real value. I only know he was a very careful man."

The lawyer stood to indicate their business was concluded. "And if you will take my advice, I'd ride up to his place as soon as possible. When word gets out he's gone, our less deserving friends will pay his claim a visit. There's always some slacker who wants something for nothing."

John climbed into the saddle. Jake and he had been good friends; still, he hadn't expected the results of the will. He hadn't been prepared to make a trip into the mountains today, but as Flossie trotted down the street, it dawned on him the lawyer's advice was well given.

He pulled out his pocket watch. Almost eleven. He'd ask Hannah for an early lunch and be in the saddle shortly after twelve. He'd travel up Ute Pass and in about three hours get to the trail that went north, then arrive at Jake's late afternoon. He'd have time to have a good look around before dark. Thankfully, he had a good start on his sermon and, at the moment, no parishioners needed visiting.

A little over an hour later, he slung saddle bags over his horse. They contained a few cans of food and coffee—enough to get by. He strapped on his six-shooter and shoved his rifle into the scabbard. Though he considered himself a peace-abiding man, he never went into the wilds unprepared.

He stepped into the stirrup. "I'll be back in a couple of days, Hannah. At least I plan to. I'm taking food and a blanket to spend the night at Jake's."

"Be careful, John."

"Yes, Ma." He gave his best imitation of a fifteen-year-old son appeasing a worried mother.

Flossie easily climbed the grade out of town. Her name was something of a joke, making her seem less of a horse than she actually was. Most horses of her breed stood only fourteen hands high. She was nearly sixteen. The gritty mustang was ready to take to the mountains. He could feel her eagerness to get going.

This time of year the noon sun was warm, the air invigorating. Looking back over the trail he had just scaled, he saw a pleasant, orderly town with trees lining the streets and avenues. Much had been built and planted in the few years since the town's inception. He recalled reminiscences by the early settlers and visitors—how in 1871 the site had been a level, elevated plateau of greenish brown sloping a quarter mile to the railroad track with not a single tree or plant higher than a two foot Spanish bayonet. A couple years later, Helen Hunt Jackson had written about her first look at Colorado Springs. On that grey day in November, she said she'd never forget her sudden sense of hopeless disappointment to see a town so straight, small and treeless. That very next year Colorado College had been established, and John well remembered when the General brought in thousands of trees to be planted. They had both agreed there was nothing like a tree to bring beauty and graciousness to a street—or a town.

John turned back in the saddle to look at the mountains and the majestic landscape before him. He felt the intense vibrancy of the day. Adventure, and its accompanying excitement, seeped into his bones. He and his horse were in agreement.

Jake's claim was his. For some moments he allowed his thoughts to expand. What would he do if there was actually gold in that mine? Jake had never said as much. However, the Denver bank account hinted at something. A little extra money—what couldn't he do with that? But he wouldn't let gold fever take hold. Besides, with his present commitment to his pastorate, when would he have time to do anything more? And what about the Ute Indians? Over this last decade they'd been moved farther west. In years past they had come to Manitou during the spring and fall for their religious festivals and to treat the buffalo meat and hides they'd acquired on the plains. But now, instead of their free roaming life, they'd been given specified lands to settle on, only allowed to come east into places like South Park to hunt. It had become more difficult to minister to them with the distances involved.

43

His congregation here in Colorado Springs was his primary responsibility. A good many congregants were from town, but their church always had visitors from back East. His thoughts veered suddenly to the Garlands and one guest in particular. Miss Whittington. He might as well admit it right out—she had caught his eye. She was a beautiful, striking woman. And it didn't take a perceptive observer to note she was accustomed to the best. The style and cut of her clothing, the way she carried herself spoke Philadelphia high society.

His thoughts reverted to Jake's claim. The cabin was absolute bare bones. He recalled one of its few pieces of furniture, the rough-hewn table. Miss Whittington had probably never eaten off a bare table like that in her life. He could imagine the fine napery and silver at dinner in the Philadelphia home—and some servant to wait on attendance, no doubt.

Of course, Hannah served him. But that was different. His life was unpretentious, had become even more so since Rosalind's death. Once a week, Rosalind would have a formal meal with a lace tablecloth and her wedding brass candlesticks. She insisted they eat off their few pieces of fine china, and Hannah had used them—reluctantly. "Land sakes, Mrs. Harding," he remembered Hannah saying, "I wouldn't use that china. Just put it on display. I'd be too afraid of breaking it."

Well, Hannah should be happy now. The china hadn't been used since Rosalind's death. And he hadn't wanted to either, it brought back too many memories.

But thinking now about that china, those candlesticks, and the lace tablecloth—he missed them. He suddenly wanted the refinement they represented and wondered how Hannah would react if he mentioned bringing them out.

Strange—this sudden desire to use those things. Was it because the pain of his wife's death was receding? Or because of this new woman who had crossed his path?

The elegant Sarah Whittington was as unsuited to his simple way of life as anyone he'd ever met. He couldn't see her having

44

anything to do with him. Yet, if she could exorcise this grief that had him by the throat, then she was an angel of mercy.

That business in Colorado City—he felt it had been more her cousin's doing than hers. Of that he was sure. He'd been worried about the girls—and if he was honest, more about Miss Whittington because she was unaccustomed to the West. Especially the kind of west the south part of Colorado City was known for. At first, when he'd seen her on the arm of that man, he'd felt a sudden stone in his stomach. He hadn't known what to think. To his understanding, she was finer than that. Then his instincts proved right when she drew away from that man's insistence to cross to the rough side of the street.

Yes, she was finer than that. Fine clothes, fine figure, fine lady. For a rash moment, he saw her sitting at his table eating off his fine china.

Enough of that. He kneed his horse to step up the pace. Both of them had slowed down, gotten sidetracked from the purpose of the day. Why his thoughts had strayed in Miss Whittington's direction and stayed there so long, he didn't know.

He was determined to enjoy this day as from the Lord. The beauty of the surrounding area was enough to set one's thinking on higher things.

When he came to the trail where he'd turn due north, he stopped and dismounted. This was one of his favorite views of Pikes Peak. Its north slope. Even now, snow remained in the ravines traveling vertically down the great mountain.

Turning north, an hour later his horse skirted the base of a good-sized knoll. Jake's claim lay a half mile away. Finally, rounding a mound of rock, John saw the cabin in the distance. Its site had been well chosen, built in the open so no one could sneak up unawares. The ground was rough with rock and small stones, dotted with patches of grass, but no sign of anything like a garden to make it more like a home. Not even a corral. Near the cabin, a lone, spindly tree doubled as a hitching post.

For stabling, there was a lean-to, high enough to shelter a horse with a corner bin to hold corn or oats.

Nearby ran a small stream. He rode Flossie to the water, and while she drank, a few yards upstream he cupped his hands for a long cold drink himself. Walking the mustang up to the lone tree, he almost wrapped the reins around a branch, then thought better of it, remembering the lawyer's caution about unwelcome visitors.

No use announcing his presence if anyone happened to drop by. He led the horse into the shed, took off the saddle and gave her a quick rub down with an empty grain sack. Then he checked the bin. Sure enough, there was corn. Flossie would have fine dining today.

He decided to take a quick look inside the cabin before walking to the mine. Opening the door, at a glance he took in the simple but comfortable room. Jake had left the cabin in order. His two concessions to comfort, a rocker by the fire and a mattress covered with a quilt, were as John remembered. The few times he'd visited over the years, mainly to make contact with the Indians Jake befriended, either one of them would take the bench by the table or the rocker. As a rule, Jake hadn't encouraged visitors.

John turned from the spare comfort of the cabin and closed the door. Later, he'd fix himself something to eat before turning in. The mine, visible from the cabin, opened a couple hundred feet away. To the left rose the high mound of a mine dump. Jake had been busy.

A few feet into the tunnel a kerosene lamp hung from a peg. John struck a match and lit it. A couple years back he'd been in the mine after he'd gained Jake's trust. But only that once. How much farther would the passage extend since his last visit? Holding the lantern high, he peered into the darkness. When he'd visited, the tunnel had gone back seventy-five feet or so. Leaving the natural daylight, he picked his way carefully. So far, he could stand upright—he remembered this part.

He reached what he gauged to be about the seventy-five foot mark, but now the tunnel went considerably farther. Jake had used a good bit of dynamite.

Loose rock crunched under his feet then the passage cut suddenly left. He held up the lamp into the cavity to see as best he could, but couldn't make out the end. The floor was uneven and he stopped every few feet to examine the walls. This cavity wasn't as high, so after a few yards he had to stoop. Finally, on reaching the end, he went down on one knee and shined the lantern on the walls. The sides were rough, but he couldn't see anything out of the ordinary. Clearly, he'd better bone up on mining.

The space was unpleasantly close, and except for the lantern, very dark. He didn't have a particular yen to stay longer. Besides, he couldn't do anything here at present. He'd give the cabin a thorough going-over for anything valuable, but couldn't imagine Jake leaving any gold or ore, unless it was well hidden. Whenever Jake would have left—on a trip to Denver or wherever—someone might easily have helped himself to the comforts of the cabin or any valuables left behind. Jake would have had to be careful. No wonder the solicitor had labeled him such.

John was within a few feet of the mine's opening when he stopped abruptly. Two horses stood near the cabin, their reins slung over the branches of the lone tree. The cabin door stood open.

He gazed at the horses. Where had he seen that roan and dun before?

The two whiskey-toting brothers.

He stepped back into the tunnel, far enough so he couldn't be detected if one of the brothers came outside. Putting out the lantern, he considered what to do.

Then he heard a crash. His military training rushed up in him and he drew out his six-shooter. He ran, keeping to grass clumps to muffle his approach. He couldn't imagine anything good occasioning that loud bang. He was a great one for praying, for gentle entreaty, but these brothers didn't understand those kinder methods. Before rounding the doorway, he halted and closed his eyes a couple seconds so they'd adjust quickly to the dark interior. The faint odor of body sweat escaped from the open door. Body sweat laced with whiskey.

Stepping into the opening, John saw the men's backs to him, the cabin's contents strewed around. Hob had thrown the quilt on the floor, and was now dragging off the mattress. The younger Jeb was examining each pot before hastily shoving it aside. Both men searched the place with a vengeance.

"Hold it right there men." John held the six-shooter steady.

They jerked around, hands hovering near their guns, but neither yanked them out their holsters.

"What are you boys doing here?"

A big pause followed and then Hob answered, "Just lookin' for something we left."

"Yeah, the last time we was here." Jeb's eyes gleamed a challenge.

John paused, long enough to let the brothers know he doubted what they said. "You sure are making a mess of things."

Hob shrugged his shoulders. "Aw, you know—we was never much at housekeeping."

At the moment, John didn't appreciate the humor. His eyes narrowed. "I suggest you put everything back, like you found it. All nice and neat."

Hob's chin jutted out pugnaciously. "You talk big with that gun."

Jeb chimed in. "Come to think of it—we got just as much right here as you. Jake ain't never comin' back. He don't care what this place looks like. Not from six feet under."

"But *I* care. I prefer neat living quarters. And I won't be getting my housekeeper up here anytime soon to put this place to rights."

Hob's eyes narrowed. "Whatcha mean by that?"

"I own this place now. Courtesy of Jake. The lawyer read the will this morning." John saw a flash—was it anger or envy—dart from Hob's eyes. John gestured with his gun, keeping his voice smooth. "So if you men will straighten up, I'd appreciate it."

They didn't stay around long after that. He'd offered them coffee as a sort of olive branch, but they'd refused. Frankly, he was relieved. He didn't trust turning his back on either of them. Each was mean as a snake, Garden of Eden variety. For a few moments there, he'd felt cold anger. It was amazing how a man could feel godly one moment, then downright hateful the next.

Now he was glad he'd kept his temper. It would have served no good purpose to let it go. And he supposed, as much as he disliked these men and thought of them as hopeless, God could do anything, even with them.

He looked around at the straightened cabin. He'd fix a bite to eat then sit awhile. It was good he was staying the night, just to make sure those brothers didn't come back. Still, he couldn't be guarding this place day and night. Of necessity it would stand empty most of the time.

Perhaps in the next week or so he could get someone to stay here, maybe an old prospector who'd given up on his own claim. It would give the place a presence. And if the tenant wanted to work the mine, so much the better. Maybe they could go into partnership.

Until then, he didn't need to be stupid. When he left, he'd take anything of value with him. Then if those brothers came back, they could have at it.

CHAPTER 6

Martha enjoyed the ride as the two open Garland carriages spun along to the outskirts of Colorado Springs. Amelia and her husband had taken the one conveyance, assigning her to the other carriage as chaperone to Sarah, Sid and Jean. As they passed Reverend Harding's home, Jean leaned out the side. Martha could guess her niece's thoughts. She'd overheard Jean talking with Sarah just before they left, wondering if the minister would be at tonight's social gathering.

Jean, back in the seat and glancing over at her, had the grace to blush. "Aunt Martha, aren't you excited to attend the Bells' party?"

"Oh, yes." The party would be nice, of course, but she was relieved to be invited—to keep an eye on one niece in particular, and it wasn't Jean.

She'd warned Sarah only yesterday, "I'm responsible for you this trip, young lady. You have a way of attracting people like honey attracts flies. And some people, like flies, should be swatted and kept at a distance."

"You know by now," Sarah had said, laughing, "I'm also *very* circumspect."

"Well, I'll grant you that, but your mother expects me to chaperone you properly, so I won't allow even the *suggestion* of shenanigans."

Maybe she'd made too much of it, but she had noted soon after their arrival in Colorado Springs how Sid had come over to the Garlands' almost every evening, paying Sarah every courtesy. Martha hoped he wasn't serious in his attentions, because there was Prescott to consider. But as a result, she had decided to keep a closer eye on Sid. Sarah's parents certainly wouldn't want anything started with a western man.

That same western man now leaned over to address her. "Aunt Martha, you might keep your eyes open to spot our hostess. She's quite something, you know. Mrs. Bell has the reputation of being a delightful scatterbrain. She's been known to wave gaily to approaching guests as she drives past them on a hurried trip to town, oblivious to the fact that they are coming for dinner. Her charming absent-mindedness is becoming something of a legend."

"Sid! That's too bad of you," Jean scolded. "Telling such a story about our hostess when Aunt Martha hasn't even met her yet. Give Auntie a chance to form her own opinion."

"Just whetting Auntie's appetite."

"I don't countenance gossip, young man."

"Oh, this isn't gossip. It's fact. Anyone will tell you so!"

"Sid!" Jean gave an upbraiding stare. "We don't want to shock Aunt Martha's sensibilities. The Bells are actually very proper; in fact, they are moneyed Britishers with homes on both continents. And dedicated Episcopalians."

"Yes, Ma'am," he said in a subdued voice.

For the remainder of the trip, whenever Martha looked at Sid, he tried to look sheepish and apologetic, but the twinkle in his eye gave him away. That young man was incorrigible!

Reaching Manitou, the two carriages drove across the little town to a box canyon. On its edge a charming house appeared through the trees—Briarhurst. Sarah had heard the Bells call their home a cottage. If so, it was a very large one, more than equal to the large parties they hosted.

Mr. Garland offered his hand to his wife, helping her to alight.

Sid handed down Aunt Martha, then made much ado about taking Sarah's hand. Finally, he helped Jean. As a guest of the family, Sarah knew she should be assisted before Jean, but did he have to make such a show of it? After all, Jean was his life-long friend. That should count for something.

Having stepped from the carriage, Sarah looked around the grounds. Larkspur, phlox and peonies filled the flowered beds.

Sid said over his shoulder, "Looks every bit like England. The Bells take tea religiously every afternoon. Can't get more British than that."

"The rose bushes!" Sarah looked around, delighted. "I'm impressed."

Aunt Martha took Sarah's arm. "Come, my dear. Let's go inside."

On entering the house with other guests, Sarah gazed around the foyer. The Hepplewhite chairs and hunting tapestries showed an unmistakable love of English furnishings. It looked as if Sid was right.

Just then a petite woman breezed into the room. "I'm so glad you could come! Make yourselves at home!" And she was out the door.

"That," said Sid with a flourish of his hand, "is our hostess!" He laughed. "Now do you see what I mean? There's no one quite like Mrs. Cara Bell."

"But I must say," said Mrs. Garland, "the Bells are known for their hospitality. They're the social center of the community."

"Oh, certainly!" Sid agreed. "You won't find a more hospitable couple anywhere. They're just a bit unusual, not at all your stodgy, formal Britishers. They fit right in with us Americans and our spirited ways. Here, follow me."

Sid guided them from the foyer with its wide oak stairway, to a beautiful room on the left. "You see, this drawing room is generous in size without being overwhelming. Just the right proportions for a *cottage*."

Sarah could see Sid was enjoying himself. The Bells must be great favorites of his.

"We'll sit here until dinner is announced," Mrs. Garland said. "But why don't the rest of you circulate."

"And I'll perform the introductions," Sid offered.

"Yes, but let's return to a place near the entrance," Jean said. "I love to see what people arrive."

Sarah had a good idea which particular person Jean would be keeping a lookout for.

Jean latched onto Sarah's arm and led the way back into the foyer, stopping near the staircase. Sarah could see her cousin's intention. From here she could keep an eye on the entrance door. Guests were arriving regularly, some stopping a moment in the entrance to gaze at the oak paneled walls and staircase before moving on.

Sid came up from behind with Aunt Martha. "Over there by the fireplace is Dr. Bell. It looks as if he's free for the moment. Sarah, I'll introduce you with your aunt. Jean, you can keep company with the stairwell newel post."

Jean glared at him. "Oh, no! I'm coming with you. And *I'll* introduce my aunt and cousin, thank you!"

Would these two never stop sparring? Sarah looked across the room to see a dapper gentleman not much taller than herself. Both Dr. Bell and his wife were diminutive, but Sarah could see they made a charming couple.

"Dr. Bell! Thank you so much for inviting us this evening." Jean drew Aunt Martha forward. "I'd like to introduce my aunt, Martha Sargeant from Philadelphia. She's living with us for the summer and taking the waters here." Then she turned to

Sarah. "And this is my cousin, Sarah Whittington, also from Philadelphia."

"I'm pleased to meet you, ladies." Dr. Bell nodded his head in a courtly greeting. "Jean has such a reputation of energy, we're glad to see her back in our Little London. My wife adores high-spirited young ladies. They add zest to her already zest-filled parties."

"Well, sir, you set the pace." Sid grinned. "To accomplish all you do, you must sleep only three to four hours a night." He turned to the ladies. "Dr. Bell is *vice-president* of everything our town's founder, General Palmer, is *president* of. And Dr. Bell has the reputation of getting *any* job done."

"I'm glad that's my reputation," Dr. Bell said, laughing. "But speaking of General Palmer, he's just arrived. Why don't I introduce you, ladies." He stepped over to intercept the General who was heading to the drawing room.

Sarah saw an immaculately dressed gentleman with wavy brown hair.

After Dr. Bell performed the introductions, Jean jumped in. "Like yourself, General, my aunt and cousin are from Philadelphia. Sarah attended the Pennsylvania Academy of Fine Arts and hopes to paint here."

"Philadelphia!" General Palmer shook the aunt's hand, then looked at Sarah. "So you're interested in art. What do you paint?'

"Landscape and still life."

"I would think our locale here would provide much inspiration—Pikes Peak, then going north from here, the striking limestone formations in the Garden of the Gods, and farther on, my home, Glen Eyrie. We have some beautiful rock configurations there. You should come to our glen to paint."

"Thank you. We've driven by the rock formations once. The pink and orange colors were striking. I would love to see your home in its setting. How did you arrive at its name?"

"As soon as we saw eagles swooping down from the mountain heights, my wife Queen—who has a gift for naming things—knew what our home should be called."

"The General loves this area, and we're indebted to him for developing it, but his particular interest is railroads. In fact," Sid added, "he built the railway you rode when you traveled east from Kansas City and also the one south from Denver to Colorado Springs. And more rails are on the way across Colorado."

Aunt Martha, standing at Sarah's elbow, asked, "General Palmer, won't that be pretty rugged construction—with your mountains?"

"Ordinarily yes, except while visiting Great Britain, I discovered their use of narrow gauge rails. They are just the thing for our Rockies. A narrower rail bed will save time and money. We used it on the railroad between Denver and Colorado Springs."

Dr. Bell interjected, "From a more personal standpoint, trains have had an important place in General Palmer's life. A number of years ago, he was taking a trip west when he met his future wife and father-in-law on a train. That trip marked the beginning of their courtship."

General Palmer smiled. "Queen and I were married less than a year later."

Sid chuckled. "It only goes to show the General doesn't let grass grow under his feet."

"You have his measure," Dr. Bell, said laughing.

The general placed his hand fondly on his friend's shoulder. "I think we're two of a kind."

At that moment Sarah saw Dr. Bell's eyes flicker to the front door. He nodded to the General and said quietly, "John Harding has arrived. You wanted to talk with him?"

Jean pulled on Sarah's arm. Stretching on tiptoes to locate the newcomer, Jean whispered, "Sarah, you promised to help me."

Sarah happened to glance at Sid who was studying Jean covertly. Something about his look puzzled Sarah. Was he disturbed about something?

As soon as the two men moved beyond their party, Sid claimed Sarah's arm and drew her away from Jean and Aunt Martha. "What did Jean whisper?"

"I didn't think you were so nosy. Can't we girls have a few secrets?"

Sid was silent a moment and gave her a rueful smile. "Oh, all right!" Glancing over at the General, Sid's apologetic smile turned into sunshine. "So, what did you think of our General?" His eyes glowed with admiration.

Sarah found General Palmer pleasant and distinguished and said so. "Of course, I haven't had much opportunity to know him—but underneath his calm exterior he seems to have a good bit of suppressed energy as well."

"The General's an absolute gentleman, but he's also tough. Did you hear of our Royal Gorge Railroad War?"

"Was that associated with the Civil War?"

"Oh, no! This started just last year in a gorge just south of here. Near Cañon City. Competing companies want to build a railroad through the gorge and follow the Arkansas River up the state to the silver mines at Leadville. You can imagine how profitable that would be. One railroad is the General's Denver and Rio Grande, the other the Atchison, Topeka, and Santa Fe."

"I hadn't heard."

"Well, this so-called war is being waged in a narrow canyon with steep granite sides. During the daytime, each company lays track only to see it dynamited at night by the other side."

"No! Has anyone been killed?"

"Not that I've heard, but it's a wonder no one has. In April, the Rio Grande rail workers rolled boulders off the top of the canyon straight down onto the work site of the Santa Fe. That drop is five hundred to a thousand feet down. Santa Fe workers below said it was a nightmare out of hell. Boulders thundered against ledges, caroming off the bare granite. Men who fought at Gettysburg claimed it was worse than the first day's cannonading."

Shocked, Sarah said, "Did the General order that?"

"Some said it was his head engineer De Remer; others insisted it was the workers just blowing off steam against Santa Fe's tactics. You see, the Santa Fe had brought in Bat Masterson and his toughs to cow the Rio Grande. No, there was no suggestion of the General's involvement, but I'll say this, he wasn't promoted to Brigadier General in the Civil War for conducting tea parties."

Just then, Jean and Aunt Martha joined them. "I overheard you talk about the Civil War. You know, don't you, Sarah, that our reverend was part of the General's outfit in the war?"

Sarah felt something of a jolt. "John Harding fought with the General?"

"They both hail from Philadelphia," Sid explained. "When the General organized the Pennsylvania 17th, John Harding was one of his first recruits. He said the General was a natural leader. One time they crept on the enemy and captured two hundred of them without losing a single one of their own soldiers. The General lost very few men. He's often said the war forged bonds between the men and himself that none of them will ever forget."

"I wonder if that's where our pastor got his scar." Jean whispered to Sarah. "Don't you think it looks dashing?"

"I heard that!" Sid took Jean's arm. "I'll show you what *dash* is. Ladies, I'm taking Jean to the dining room buffet and see what's to eat. You may follow at your leisure.

John had entered the Bells' home and stopped just inside, letting his eyes adjust to the interior. The General had signaled him, wanting to talk, but had been waylaid by a couple of other guests. John looked over the crowded foyer, and his eyes were immediately drawn to a green dress. The color of Miss Whittington's garb was like trees leafing out. She literally brought spring into the room.

He left the doorway and stood waiting for General Palmer to finish talking with these others, welcoming the opportunity to stand quietly after his unexpected reaction to Miss Whittington and her attire. He thought back to his wife. Rosalind had always dressed tastefully in delicate grays and browns with the serviceable black. A light color or two for summers—he could hardly remember now. But he had always been proud of her, in attractive, yet appropriate clothing for her role as the minister's wife.

Sarah Whittington was different. Her dress was also appropriate and modest enough, yet it—it had a novel effect on him.

Just then Sid drew Miss Whittington away so John could no longer see her. Momentary irritation pricked him.

Then he told himself it was just as well and deliberately looked around the room. Cara Bell had invited a good share of the crème of Colorado Springs society. He hoped Miss Whittington appreciated it.

Supper was being served and John was hungry. The Bells had laid out a bountiful buffet including sliced beef running in its juices and the peanut-fed Smithfield ham Queen Victoria favored.

"Mr. Harding, sir, would you like some of both?" Antonio, the chef in charge of the kitchen, was doing the honors with the meats.

"Yes, sir!" While Antonio served John, he noted the various vegetables and fruits arrayed on the table. A grand Battenburg Cake, already partially cut to show its checkerboard interior, sat in state at the end of the buffet. The cake's almond paste frosting was his favorite part.

Tables were set throughout the main rooms for guests to find their own places after filling their plates. John stepped into the conservatory, just off the dining room. The atmosphere buzzed with lively conversation. He had waited until most were served before entering. Being by himself, he would have no trouble finding a spare place at some table. Many here were already known to him, but if not, he wouldn't hesitate introducing himself. He always liked to meet new people and find out their backgrounds and interests.

While he stood gazing around for a place, Dr. Bell walked up to him. "John, join our table, won't you? My wife is holding court." John smiled at the subtle reference to his wife's energetic and affable management of their guests.

Following his host across the room, he saw Mrs. Bell. She *was* holding court. Several members of the Garland party were seated at the table, Sarah Whittington next to her hostess. He started toward the empty chair at the end of the table.

"No, John, take my place next to my wife." Dr. Bell stepped over to retrieve his plate. "I'm going to circulate a bit."

John motioned his disagreement, nodding his intention to sit at the foot of the table.

"John!" Cara Bell said, smiling, "Do what my husband says."

John saluted with his free hand as if to say, "Of course," and walked to his hostess.

Mrs. Bell turned to John. "Philadelphia is also Miss Whittington's home. You wouldn't have by any chance already met there?"

John leaned over slightly to address his hostess and nod a smile at Sarah. "No, I lived on a farm about twenty miles out and rarely traveled into the city—"

"Well, then you will have much to talk about. Miss Whittington attended the Pennsylvania Academy of Fine Arts.

You have an eye for beauty—that was evident when I heard you speak a couple weeks ago."

Jean leaned over the table to address her hostess. "This last year I also attended school in Philadelphia. I visited Sarah's family weekends. We had such fun together." She looked at John with a lively interest. "And, before you joined us, we were discussing a painting at the Centennial Exposition. You didn't happen to be in Philadelphia that year?"

"No, I was busy with my work here. I only heard about the Exposition from my family."

"Well, Sarah and I were telling everyone we had the oddest experience. We had gone to the fine arts exhibit looking for the Thomas Eakins painting—he taught at Sarah's school—but we couldn't for the life of us find it." Jean blew out an indignant huff. "And do you know where we finally found it? In the medical pavilion, in an obscure spot. The famous Thomas Eakins!"

Cara Bell looked puzzled. "A painting in the medical pavilion?"

"Yes! Sarah, remember how shocked you were?" Then Jean's eyes took on a knowing look. "But we think we know why. His painting was of a doctor performing surgery with students looking on. Called 'The Gross Clinic.' And I must say, it was well named, it being rather—oh!" Jean jerked.

John noticed a *look* pass from Sarah to Jean and a blush rise quickly on Jean's face. John smiled to himself, wondering if one cousin had administered a warning kick under the table.

CHAPTER 7

*G*ross. Sarah was glad Jean had left the word unsaid—with a little help from her foot forced down hard on Jean's. Her cousin's "oh!" hadn't given away too much, at least Jean had that much quickness of perception. But to have begun to say that word in mixed company certainly cast doubt on Jean's lady-likeness. Their hostess had quickly overlooked the misstep, and with her vivid personality led her guests down another conversational path. Sarah had whispered a reprimand, but her cousin had shrugged it off.

Sarah could sing Cara Bell's praises. Just before Cara left the supper table she pulled Sarah aside. "You mentioned your particular interest in Albert Bierstadt before Mr. Harding joined our table. I recall him saying that he met Mr. Bierstadt on one of the artist's trips west. Out in California, I believe. You might ask him." The quick upturn of her lips suggested a conspiratorial intent. But just then she looked past Sarah and said, "Excuse me, my husband is signaling me."

That John Harding had met Albert Bierstadt piqued Sarah's curiosity. She must find out more. For the remainder of the evening she kept a sense of where the minister was, looking for a time when they would naturally come together or he would seek her out. But either she was surrounded by guests, or he was.

She finally settled on a chair in the drawing room, watching him as he spoke to a well-to-do couple. As Sarah waited for him to finish, her gaze wandered around the room. She couldn't help noticing the ladies' dresses. Colorado Springs had nothing to be ashamed of when it came to fashion.

But as he kept talking with this latest couple, Sarah became exasperated. Her mother would not have approved, would feel it too forward in a lady, but Sarah was about to walk up to the minister and draw him aside. Certainly, the free-wheeling atmosphere of the Bell party encouraged a more relaxed atmosphere. In fact, Cara Bell was known to eschew even formal introductions. She'd said that "being under our roof is your introduction."

Sarah was debating what to do when this particular couple finished conversing with Mr. Harding. Standing alone, he took out his pocket watch and looked at Mrs. Bell. Was he about to leave? He then glanced Sarah's way, but instead of coming to her, started toward their hostess.

A strange little feeling welled up in Sarah. She was accustomed to being sought out—if not for her beauty, she thought wryly, then surely her wit.

What should she do now?

All of a sudden, she didn't care what he or anyone else thought of her; she wanted to hear about Albert Bierstadt. She quickly circled two guests, purposing to cross his path on his way to their hostess. Then she abruptly slowed her walk. She would approach him with a certain nonchalance so as not to appear overly eager or forward.

But he moved with such decision she almost failed to intercept him. He had already passed her when she called out, "Mr. Harding, may I have a word with you?"

He stopped and turned. "Of course."

She couldn't tell from his expression if he was pleased to talk with her or not. Now *this* was a new experience. Was he remembering the Colorado City fiasco? Maybe she should say something about that first.

"I'm glad to see you here," she began, "for I never had the opportunity—" she faltered, "—I want to thank you again for coming to Jean's and my rescue in Colorado City. I have no idea how we came to get ourselves into such a fix."

"Oh, the two dandies—or more likely, gamblers?"

"What?"

"Dress often gives away one's profession."

"I didn't realize—" How out of kilter she felt, she who was usually so conversant with society's conventions. And *he* wasn't helping. Feeling the need to say something, she added abruptly, "They were certainly marked in their attentions. I'm not accustomed to that."

"No?" A ghost of a smile played over his lips.

Sarah felt herself blush. "Not in *that* manner. You must know." She knew her eyes had acquired a dangerous sparkle. "It was the same with the two men who crossed the street from the saloon. I take it they were *not* friends of yours."

"*That's* an understatement."

She couldn't help but smile at the vehemence of his reply. And as she remembered the ease with which he had handled the two rowdies, she felt moved to say, "However, you dealt with them most effectively."

"I was glad to be there for you ladies." He paused, as if debating whether to say more, then continued, "The rough-necks who exited the saloon—of course you know it is men like that you want to avoid. But in a town like Colorado City, it's difficult not to be accosted if you're escorted only by a youngster like Ben."

That was direct. Irritation pricked at her, but she quickly masked it with what she hoped was a penitent face. She hadn't forgotten what she had come to talk about. "In hindsight, I can see you're right. I'm afraid Jean and I were terribly naïve. So... am I forgiven?"

His eyes as well as his mouth broke into a smile. "Of course."

Suddenly, Sarah felt more in charity with him. He *did* have a nice smile. And that rugged exterior was rather handsome. No, he *was* handsome. In a rough-hewn way. Which for the west, she supposed, stood him in good stead. She couldn't imagine Prescott being able to handle those two ruffians.

Mr. Harding was looking at her questioningly, apparently waiting for her to say more. And here she was gazing at him. She dropped her eyes—he must think her extremely foolish. She made herself look up casually. "I almost forgot what I came to talk with you about." She drew her delicate shawl closer around her shoulders.

"After dinner Mrs. Bell told me you had met Albert Bierstadt. I'm interested to hear more. His paintings were one of the reasons I was so bent on coming west."

"Ah, that was in Yosemite, when I visited back in '72. Later, I found out it was one of his favorite locations; in fact he'd been there in the winter making sketches when the place was empty of visitors. In May—when I met him—he was staying in the Yosemite Mountain House. Because of my mother, I've been interested in art and she put me onto his painting, so when I had an opportunity to have dinner with him, I jumped at the chance."

Mr. Harding reached out to take her elbow. "Here, let me find you a seat." He guided her to two chairs on the edge of the room.

Sarah found herself looking up into very dark, interested eyes. Any feminine feathers which had been ruffled settled nicely. "Did you find out anything about how he worked?"

"Well, yes. Bierstadt would sketch in pencil, then make studies to get the colors and shading correct. He told of earlier visits to the West where he camped with other artists and hunters. Evenings, when the artists returned from their work in different parts of the countryside, they'd spend a half an hour viewing each other's studies. After supper, the tea-kettle was emptied into a pan and brush-washing ensued, along with talk and pipes until bed-time.

"I enjoyed our time together. He's enthusiastic about his work. The West gets his blood going; he loves its bigness, its vastness. When he discovered I was from Colorado Springs, he told me he'd visited the area about ten years earlier, before it was a town. But when the inhabitants had shown him their pride and joy, the Garden of the Gods, they were disappointed when he hadn't felt inspired to paint it."

He smiled. "But tell me, how did you become acquainted with his work?"

"I was introduced to his painting at the art academy, when we studied the Hudson River school of painters. But it wasn't until I saw his actual work—in an exhibition—that I became really interested."

"So what were your impressions?" Mr. Harding leaned back in the chair, crossing his arms.

He had rather turned the tables, wanting to know what *she* thought. Taken off guard, she fingered the gossamer threads of her shawl before answering, wanting to choose just the right words to make him understand how Bierstadt's painting had affected her.

She began slowly. "I first saw his work on exhibit when our new building opened for The Pennsylvania Academy of the Fine Arts. He contributed a painting to the new gallery, a huge picture *Mount Adams in the Rocky Mountains*. At the building's opening, quite a number of works by different artists had been hung. Bierstadt's large painting dwarfed most of them. But it was his treatment that interested me. Such grandeur. I wondered, could a scene be that majestic, that beautiful?"

For some moments her mind's eye left the Bells' party and she felt herself back in the exhibition hall, gazing at the huge painting. "It looked almost other-worldly. Luminous." Her eyes focused back on Mr. Harding. "Tell me, do you know if the places he painted actually look like that?"

"Hmm..." His eyes narrowed. "I'm thinking of a particular work, *Looking Down Yosemite Valley* that he painted in the 60's. The time I camped in Yosemite, I stood at its south entrance. The valley itself is about a mile in width and a good number of miles in length, but it was the sheer, vertical granite walls that amazed me. A half dome and other rock cliffs reached seven, some even nine thousand feet. Bierstadt caught the scene's magnificence, but he added something more, I think."

"And that was—" Sarah asked eagerly.

"When you're actually standing in the valley, it's not only grand, so grand it's hard to take in, but it's also *real*. The green of trees and grasses, the gray of hard granite walls, it's very much of this world. It seems familiar—something you can touch. With Bierstadt's painting—I think you put your finger on something when you mentioned an otherworldly look. Maybe it was the way he introduced light into the composition. The atmosphere is bigger, lighter somehow. The air seems rarefied."

"He's a bit of a romantic then?"

"I hadn't thought in those terms. In personality, Bierstadt is outgoing, very friendly. Big, like the outdoors he portrays." Mr. Harding looked over her shoulder, no longer focusing on her, but rather on the painting he was remembering. It seemed as though he was trying to find just the right words to express his thoughts, just as she had moments earlier. "I think his paintings depict the spirit of those who venture west. They're out for adventure, bravely taking chances for themselves and their families. They want a better life. I believe Bierstadt painted the ideals of those who see the West as their place of hope."

How eloquently spoken. She found herself smiling widely. "You sound a bit of a romantic yourself. You can empathize with an artist's mind, discover what he's trying to express. You know—" she leaned nearer—"we're planning an excursion to Denver next week to see an art exhibit. Would something like that interest you?" *Where had that come from?* Thankfully, she had stopped just short of inviting him. After all, this was her Aunt Garland's party.

But she'd felt so right telling him about the Denver exhibit. He seemed so sympathetic to artists and their views. Her interest in him deepened. How unusual for a rugged man to have such sensibility.

"I would be interested," he said. "Maybe I'll even attend."

Suddenly, his mouth curved upward. "But when *you* go, make sure you have a suitable escort. If you're arriving by train, the area around the Denver station is a bit disreputable."

A statement like that, following so closely on her recent apology for Colorado City, ordinarily would have nettled her. But his smile softened the directive. She cocked an eyebrow at his teasing.

At that moment someone came from her blind side and stooped to take her elbow. When she turned, blue eyes looked merrily into hers. "Sid! You startled me." *Couldn't you see I'm having a serious conversation? How rude to interrupt—*

"Sorry to break off your tête-à-tête, but the Garland party is ready to depart. The carriages are already at the door. My apologies, Reverend." Sid straightened and gave him a salute from the tip of an imaginary hat.

"I think we were finished." John rose and nodded with a slight bow. "It's been my pleasure, Miss Whittington."

Sarah looked at his departing figure—a departure that felt unexpectedly unwelcome.

"Did I hear you mention Denver?" Sid asked her. "What were you two talking about?"

"Oh—" Sarah toyed with the idea of not answering him. His question felt intrusive. But that would give more weight to her reaction than she wanted. "We were just talking about art, Bierstadt's paintings in particular. I happened to mention the art exhibit we'll be attending in Denver."

Sid looked at her a long moment. "Just as long as he doesn't tag along. A minister would put such a damper on our little party, you know."

He then extended his arm with a flourish. "Now, mademoiselle, let me escort you to yon waiting carriage with prancing white horses. But before doing so—" he nodded toward their hostess— "I will assist you in taking leave of your betters."

Sarah took Sid's arm and rose. "Betters?" She caught at his bid for repartee and decided to enter into his mood, ignoring the twinge of resentment his warning about the Reverend provoked. She could match Sid point for point when he joked. "My betters? Says who?"

Out of the corner of her eye, Sarah saw Jean intercept Mr. Harding and was talking animatedly. She suddenly wondered if Jean would be a fit mate for him. He had talked so knowledgeably, so sensitively about art. But she had promised to help her cousin pass muster.

He *was* a fine man. Finer than she had thought possible for a westerner. She caught herself up short. She had enough to think about with Prescott. He was trying to build up his law practice to satisfy Father, so they could be married. After which, she would take her place in Philadelphia society.

Casting a final glance at the two in conversation, she curtseyed playfully to Sid and followed his lead to depart.

CHAPTER 8

Sarah took her mother's letter to read privately in her bedroom. How she delighted in hearing news from home; yet, she was in no way homesick. She was excited to be out west, experiencing new things and meeting new people. Of course, staying with family made it all so much easier.

She opened the envelope and extracted the letter.

Dear Sarah,

Father and I wonder how you are doing. Aunt Martha has been our main correspondent on all your doings, but we need not tell you, we'd like to hear from you as well. You have such an engaging way of telling a story, of relating your experiences, and we miss that. Life here has been much the same since you've left....

Her mother went on to relate the latest society gossip, especially the engagement of her best friend's daughter. Then...

Regarding Prescott and yourself—he is working hard to acquire more clients. I think your father

*is softening about announcing your engage-
ment. Yet, he remains a little skeptical. You must
realize, dear, that your father wants the best for
you. He's worked hard to give us the lifestyle
we enjoy and he wants you to be able to continue in it. He also sees what a gracious, sunny
personality you have, and what a fine hostess
you'd make. He can see the mark you will make
in society. With your interest in art, you will
probably work to further the arts as several of
our friends do. And with your education at the
Academy, you have an automatic entrée there.*

*Your father and I are both proud of you. And if
Prescott can muster up, he would be a natural
choice as a husband. Our families have known
each other for years, and this is advantageous
for all concerned.*

*I'm sure you've noticed that Prescott is also a
man who looks after the details. This is something I particularly admire. Life is so much
smoother when a husband concerns himself
with them. And your father and I want you to
have a smooth running life, a fine life.*

Sarah stood with the letter in hand and walked to her bedroom window. The trees had just leafed out with the bushes
and grass a verdant green. Spring was one of her favorite times
of the year with everything so fresh.

What her mother had said about Prescott—that he looked
after details—made her think. In fact, it seemed almost an
obsession. Sarah felt it in his fastidiousness, even in his compli-
ments about her appearance—which was nice, of course, but
there was that critical spirit she'd noticed on occasion—the

way he apprised, judged another's house, buggy, appearance. These seemed to matter a great deal to him. As they did to her, of course, because she appreciated order and beauty. It was just that Prescott...well, she thought of her own hidden imperfection. But his last letter had been all that could be desired. He loved her, she knew, and was working hard to claim her as his own in marriage.

Yes, she could picture herself as a society matron, championing the arts. She'd been told here in Colorado Springs Queen Palmer fervently espoused the arts, especially music, having a fine contralto voice. Sarah wondered when Mrs. Palmer might be back in town. She was eager to meet her.

Just then, something caught her attention. Her second story window faced Sidney Carlton's house, and she saw little Hildie run across the lawn toward the hedge which had a pass-through between the two properties. Hot on her heels, Sid pretended to try to catch her, yet he never quite captured her.

A warm spot sprang up in Sarah's heart. He could have caught her easily, but he was letting her have the fun of the chase. How nice of him. On the spot, she forgave him for interrupting her conversation with Mr. Harding last night.

Hildie laughed with glee. She and Sid had apparently been on the Garlands' front porch and Hildie was leading him a merry chase.

"Hildie! Sid! Come back!" Jean appeared, crossing the Garland lawn. "Hildie! Stop being such a tease," Jean shouted. "We were having a nice board game. Come back to the porch, you two! Just because I was winning...." Jean passed through the hedge, and lifting her skirt, ran after them. The three chased each other around the Carlton yard.

Sarah shook her head. She could see Hildie and Sid tearing around like that. But Jean? Nice minister's wife *she'd* make.

Just then Sid turned from chasing Hildie and started after Jean. She gave a little scream and changed direction. But to no avail. Catching up with her, Sid tagged her shoulder. "I got you! Now, you're *it!*" He was running so hard he ran past her.

Jean stopped and yelled, "We weren't playing tag. I'm not *it!*"

Sid turned and approached her, out of breath. "You are, if I say so."

"No! You made it up on the spot."

Sid grabbed her by the shoulders. "What if I did? I can do anything around here!" He laughed good-naturedly. "You're on my property."

Sid now talked more softly, still holding Jean's shoulders.

Sarah stared down at the twosome. There was something oddly intimate in Sid's stance.

At that moment, Hildie came up and hugged the two of them. They now looked more like a brother and sisters having fun. Which was good, because Jean had her heart set on John Harding. Poor Sid.

Of course, Mr. Harding didn't have Sid's wealth. But the minister was a man of standing in the community. In fact, he was such a *man* it would be difficult for another male to compete with him in the marriage mart.

Jean was allowing Sid's intimate gesture to go on and on. Sarah would need to talk with her. One didn't allow intimacies with a man—no matter how long she'd known him—when she had her hat set for someone else. Sarah sighed. Ordinarily, it wouldn't be any of her business—but Jean had asked her help in attracting the minister. She was beginning to find her promise to Jean a bit distasteful. Her cousin needed such a lot of reforming.

Sarah turned from the window to finish her letter. Mother would be sure to close with some interesting tidbits.

John guided Flossie past the Garden of the Gods on his way to the General's house. Limestone jutted out of the ground, huge orange slabs isolated from each other. Green pines grew in their crevices. The scene was beautiful, almost otherworldly.

He wondered if Miss Whittington had seen the Garden at sunset. At that time of day the rocks turned a brilliant red orange. The light green oak leaves showing against the limestone made spring one of his favorite seasons.

During autumn, these same oaks would sport red and orange leaves, making the air seem almost warm with heated color against the orange rock formations. What a brilliant painting all this would make. No wonder the Utes loved the area. Queen Palmer had told him that until a few years ago, they'd camped right outside her home while the General was absent, even walking uninvited into the house. The General had finally appealed to the State to inform the Indians this area was now private property.

But he could understand the Utes affinity for this place. People who hadn't seen it personally would think the scene fashioned from an artist's imagination.

Suddenly, he wondered if he could take Miss Whittington riding here. He'd like to see how the artist in her would react. He smiled. Of course, Aunt Martha might have something to say about that. He'd caught her watching Sid with something like suspicion. He himself had been careful how he engaged her niece in conversation.

And what hope was there of a relationship, the kind that was beginning to nudge at his thought life? Miss Whittington was from the East, from high social standing, with money. Of course, money might not be such a difference between them now. He smiled again.

He kneed Flossie into a faster trot. General Palmer must not be kept waiting; he was a busy man. John left the Garden of the Gods and traveled north through a wide, treed canyon to the General's large, beautiful home. Glen Eyrie.

"Sit down, John." General Palmer motioned to an armchair on the other side of his desk. John noted how the General's study was much like his lavishly furnished railroad business car, its richly paneled walls hung with gilt-framed paintings. Heavy velvet draped the windows.

The General took a seat behind his desk. "Thank you for coming so quickly after the social last night. I'm gratified you granted my request with such dispatch."

John settled into the capacious leather chair opposite the General. "Your wish is my command, sir!" Of course, he wouldn't have done anything else. "It was a fine party last night. We missed your wife. Her graciousness would have added much to the occasion. I know our new acquaintances, especially Miss Whittington, who paints, would have appreciated getting to know her."

"Yes, Queen loves the arts. Unfortunately, she hasn't been feeling well. Is finding it hard to sleep at night. Her doctor thinks it's the altitude, so Queen is taking a respite at a lower elevation. You know, I'd do anything for Queen. Couldn't ask for a better wife." The General cleared his throat, signaling he was getting set for business. "I asked you to come today because I want to discuss railroads."

John was surprised. Railroads were far from his specialty.

General Palmer leaned back in his deep leather chair. "You're familiar with the unfortunate situation between my Denver Rio Grande and the Topeka and Santa Fe. The fight's grown ugly, both of us wanting to build that rail to Leadville to transport its silver. Presently, however, I'm thinking beyond Leadville—am considering other areas in western Colorado. One is to build a line near Animas City."

"Somewhere south of Silverton?"

"Yes. Back in '60 all sorts of miners, farmers and families flocked to the area after gold was discovered, but nearly twenty years later, there's still no rail."

"Sir, I know you're all for progress, but have you thought of what the introduction of railroads will do to the Ute homeland?"

"Well, the area around Silverton was opened to miners in '74, following the Brunot Treaty. So, legally, I believe we're covered. With your interest in the Utes, I know where you're coming from, but my concern is for this great nation of ours and its need for rails. Railroads are my business, have been so all my adult life. And as you know, rails have rarely been built to accommodate an existing population. They're built ahead of time with the intention of colonizing the area."

"Sir, that's exactly my concern. When settlers come in, they take Indian lands without so much as a by-your-leave or thank you. This is a particular problem with the Utes who are migratory. When the Utes leave one area in Colorado for another, settlers take the land, thinking it's uninhabited, only to find the Indians returning the following year. The result has been settlers and Indians at odds with each other. We need to respect the Utes and their life here in Colorado, not run roughshod over them."

"Roughshod?"

"What else do you call unfortunate situations like that affair at Steamboat Springs? U.S. soldiers roping off the springs, warning the Indians not to trespass—springs used by the Indians for generations."

"I agree, that was unfortunate."

"I'm sure you also know that the U.S. Government is considering taking the Utes out of the mountains and relocating them to the plains of Indian Territory, forcing our Indians to settle on that stark, wind-swept reservation where other displaced Indians are compelled to live." John felt his blood rise. "The government is barking up the wrong tree on this one."

"I know you're concerned. But I'm seeing a bigger picture." General Palmer rose from his chair and paced the area behind his desk. "Consider the impact rails have had on other states and territories.

"Take California, for instance. To reach it years ago, men from the East sailed around Cape Horn. California was considered dry and agriculturally so unreliable, it imported everything, even meat. Few deemed it valuable, except for washing gold. Men went to California with the intention of making a fortune, and then returning home to enjoy it."

The General stopped and looked directly at John. "Enter the railroad. In '69, it connected the east and west shores of our country. Do you know what happened in five short years?"

John felt the thrust of the argument coming. The General's usually mild eye now regarded him with a sharp look, like the eagle that claimed Glen Eyrie home.

"I'll tell you what happened. American ingenuity showed itself. By '74, California was exporting twenty million dollars' worth of wheat—yearly—and another ten million of wool. Fruit was being supplied to Eastern cities by rail, to say nothing of transporting visitors from America and Europe in search of a good climate for their health. They could cross the 3,300 miles of the American continent in just days instead of weeks."

John could see the General was building his case, but he was ready to argue the other side of the question. "You mentioned gold." He sat forward in his chair. "One of the problems with its discovery was the tremendous influx of settlers, and with that, skirmishes worsened between Indians and settlers."

General Palmer rounded his desk to stand nearer to John. "That's why I'm asking you to investigate what's happening with the Utes. Take a trip through western Colorado. It's not only the Silverton line I'm thinking about, but I want to build rails in other areas of western Colorado as well."

"I've got the church here to think of."

"Get someone to take your place. This is important. The Rocky Mountains contain rich deposits of silver and gold as well as every other known mineral. When Grant was President, he called the Rockies the 'strong-box' of the United States—from which we could pay the national debt."

The General grasped John's shoulder. "We have an obligation, John, a high calling to help our country."

John looked up into the General's eyes. "I still don't like the way we've treated the Indians."

"But Chief Ouray has been our ally. There's a good possibility a rail could be built south of Silverton, maybe up to Montrose, without disturbing the Utes. Think about it." The General removed his hand from John's shoulder and walked around his desk and reseated himself.

John moved restlessly in his chair. "I hear there's been trouble north of Montrose in White River country. That agent the government sent last year is trying to teach the Indians to farm." John shook his head. "General, you know as well as I do the Utes are nomadic. Farming's not part of their heritage, certainly not in their blood."

"Agent Meeker is a friend of mine. My understanding is that he has been successful in teaching the Indians to farm out Harmony way. The government wants to do the same in western Colorado."

"But Harmony is out on the plains. Western Colorado is mountainous, and the Utes are accustomed to migrating. Meeker has a tall order, taming the Utes to stay in one place."

"He's a strong personality, with equally strong convictions."

"But, sir, I wouldn't want to be in his shoes, convincing a tribe to do something they're dead set against."

"Well, I'm hoping he'll make a success of it. My job is to build railroads. And in this particular instance, to get a rail to Silverton and then add others." He paused. "Can we agree to disagree? I'm asking you to do this for both me and the country. Investigate what's happening with the Indians, especially around Silverton. You know some of the Ute language, have relations with a couple of the bands. I'm asking this as a favor because of our past association in the regiment."

John sat quietly, considering the request. "I appreciate your confidence in me, General. However, I don't know if I could be away from the pulpit that long."

"I've heard there's a minister from back East, taking the waters at Manitou. Or, I should say, his wife is. He could fill in for you."

John smiled. "You've got it all figured out, don't you, sir?"

The General smiled back.

"Well, let me think it over and pray about it."

"Good." General Palmer rose from his chair and held out his hand to shake John's. "That's all I can ask. Now let's see what refreshments we can drum up without Queen."

CHAPTER 9

Sarah looked at Aunt Martha sitting on the other side of the carriage. She hoped the waters at Manitou Springs were helping her. It certainly took enough time and trouble getting there.

Suddenly Hildie leaned over and whispered in Sarah's ear.

"Oh, Hildie, can't you wait?" The little girl shook her head. Sarah voiced Hildie's request to Aunt Martha. "Hildie has to stop."

"Hildie!" Aunt Martha looked exasperated. "We're too far from home, and we're too far from Manitou."

Sarah's glance rested a moment longer on her aunt. Sometimes Auntie had no patience with the eight-year-old.

Hildie craned her neck, looking around. "Reverend Harding lives near here, doesn't he? I think I can hold it until then." She leaned close to Sarah. "Remember the place?"

Yes, Sarah remembered the house, the one Jean kept pointing out whenever they drove by. But she hesitated to stop there. Invariably, she found herself in embarrassing situations with the minister. Oh, why hadn't Hildie seen to this before they left the house?

"Please! I can't hold it much longer."

Suddenly, the urgency in Hildie's voice swept aside Sarah's other concern. "Of course, Hildie." She leaned forward to address the driver Aunt Amelia had engaged for them. "You know where Pastor Harding lives? On this street, where Limit Street intersects with it." At least, she'd worn her delicate blue sprigged cotton. It was so much easier to *be* charming when one *looked* charming.

A few minutes later the driver looked back at his passengers. "That little white house?"

"Yes." Sarah caught her aunt's eye. "Aunt Martha, why don't you wait in the carriage. I'll take Hildie inside."

At the front door a short, plump woman greeted them. Sarah remembered seeing her in church. "I'm Miss Whittington, niece to the Garlands. Aren't you Miss Lee, Reverend Harding's housekeeper?

"What can I do for you?"

Sarah looked down at Hildie. "We have a problem."

The housekeeper's mouth quirked a smile. "Come right this way. I'll help you, Hildie. Miss, why don't you be seated in the parlor."

The warm fragrance of baked goods permeated the house, an aroma laced with sweetness. Sarah wondered if it was cookies.

Instead of taking a seat, Sarah stood, looking around the parlor. The room was certainly small. Could a person actually live and entertain here, someone with duties like a pastor? What would one do with out-of-town visitors? Did the place even have enough bedrooms?

But one thing she approved. The room wasn't overly fussy with knickknacks. No little chairs to sit primly on. Everything seemed well-proportioned and comfortable. One armchair was larger than the rest and well-worn. Was that where Mr. Harding sat? So many parlors were for show and seldom used, but this looked as if the minister spent time here. A pleasant thought.

Sarah glanced at the window. Lace curtains. She walked over to better examine and couldn't help fingering them. The quality was what one found in expensive shops in Philadelphia, imported from abroad. She looked at the room with new eyes. Obviously, a woman's touch showed here. Had it been his wife's? Surely not the housekeeper's. She looked capable, but hardly the artistic type.

Sarah walked to the fireplace over which a simply-framed watercolor caught her eye. It depicted a farmhouse and nearby field, with rolling hills in the background. Pennsylvania?

Was this, by any chance, the pastor's boyhood home? At the Palmer dinner, he'd said he had grown up on a farm twenty miles outside of Philly. She could imagine him working that field and sitting on the front porch at night. The painting's quiet scene calmed something within her.

She turned from the fireplace. The room—the entire house—was still, except for Hildie's chatter. Surely, if the minister were present, he would have heard and come to greet them. Minutes before in the carriage, she had been embarrassed he might be here. Now she was conscious of feeling disappointed he wasn't. She smiled at herself. Was there no pleasing her?

She heard Hildie laugh. And a chair scrape the floor. Where was she?

Just then the housekeeper appeared. "Miss Whittington, I have Hildie in the kitchen. She was hungry so I'm giving her a mite to eat, just a cookie with milk. Do you mind?"

Sarah thought it wouldn't do much good if she did. That Hildie! Obviously, the smell of cookies had gotten the better of her. "Of course not, though I do have my aunt outside in the carriage."

"We won't keep her waiting long. But your time will go better this morning if the child isn't hungry. That's sure."

Sarah smiled her acquiescence.

"Why don't you come into the kitchen?" The housekeeper was already turning.

It doesn't look as if I have much choice. Following the older woman, Sarah felt almost a little girl once more and wondered if she might be given a cookie and milk as well. She grinned at herself again. This house was affecting her in a strange way.

"Here, sit at the kitchen table. You'll have the place of honor, where the pastor sits."

"Well..." Sarah sat and eyed the plate of cookies, and when she glanced up, she saw the housekeeper had seen her hopeful look.

"Of course, you must have a cookie. This oatmeal recipe is a specialty of mine."

Sarah felt herself blushing. "Did I make that too obvious? The next thing you'll be asking me if I'd like a glass of milk."

"I never!" the housekeeper slapped her side. "That's the cleverest way of getting a glass of milk—I'd heard you could charm a cat out of its cream. Now I believe it." She laughed. "Of course, you can have milk with your cookie. Unless you'd like something hot. The minister swears by my coffee."

"Milk will be fine." Sarah found herself smiling. "I'm sure your coffee is wonderful, but I'm still thinking of my aunt."

"Maybe I should invite her inside," the housekeeper suggested.

"That's very kind of you, but I wouldn't dream of putting you out. And she wouldn't either. I do know, however, she's eager to be on her way to Manitou."

"Taking the waters?" At Sarah's nod, the housekeeper offered, "I'll send some cookies with you. Maybe your aunt would like one on the way."

"Thank you."

"So, are you here for the springs as well?"

"No, I came to paint and acquire western art. As a matter of fact, next week I'm attending an art exhibit in Denver. I'm hoping to purchase some paintings there." She took a sip of milk. "By the way, I noticed a watercolor over your parlor fire-place. Is it of a Pennsylvania farmstead?"

"Yes. That's the minister's home place, where his parents still farm."

"The work is exceptional. Do you know who painted it?"

"His mother. I've never been to the house, but I understand her paintings are all over the place. We have another one of hers in the pastor's study."

Sarah couldn't help herself. "You will think me absolutely shameless...but could I—?"

The housekeeper's eyes twinkled. "Yes, you absolutely could. Finish your cookie and I'll take you back to the study."

Just then a knock sounded at the kitchen door.

"Now who?" the housekeeper asked no one in particular. She glanced at Sarah. "I'm sorry. I should be used to people dropping in, this being a minister's house and all—"

She crossed the room and opened the door. "Well! Miss Tippet. And a pie, too. Won't you come in?"

Sarah saw a youngish, diminutive woman poke her head inside, then enter. She was neatly dressed in a brown, dun-colored dress. A wren immediately came to Sarah's mind.

"I hope I'm not interrupting. I did see the fancy carriage outside." The woman's eyes were all curiosity.

"You already know Hildie. And this is Miss Whittington. They stopped by with a little emergency."

The little woman gave a quick nod to Sarah, "Nice to meet you," then turned to the housekeeper. "I baked this pie only this morning. I know apple is one of the minister's favorites. Is he home? I wanted to give it to him." She peered at the door leading from the kitchen to the rest of the house. "You know, I still have a basket of apples down in our root cellar from last fall. I keep some just for him."

"I'm sure you do."

Did Sarah hear a slight weariness in the housekeeper's voice? One thing was sure, the little dark eyes of the visitor sparkled. It was as obvious as the nose on Sarah's face that this woman liked the minister, liked him very much indeed. So Jean wasn't the only one after him. It didn't surprise her, seeing what kind of a man he was, so rugged and hand— So devoted to God. A church-going woman like this would obviously be drawn to that. That sermon he had given Sunday—Sarah could still hear the fervency of his voice. Maybe the wren would be a better wife than Jean. Her cousin wasn't overly religious—

The housekeeper held out her hand for the pie. "He's not here right now. Won't be home for some time."

"Oh!" Such a well of disappointment rose in the wren's voice, but she reluctantly handed over the pie anyway.

"I'll be sure to tell him it's from you." The housekeeper put the pie on the side counter, then moved purposely to the doorway. In a matter of moments, she'd seen her guest out.

Sarah looked at the housekeeper appreciatively. Her mother should consider hiring her as housekeeper, with duties as "butler" thrown in. This woman knew how to show people the door.

"Now, where were we," Hannah said, turning from the entrance.

Sarah gave the housekeeper her most winning smile. "The watercolor you mentioned...but I wouldn't want to trespass into any place that's private—"

"Well, *you* appreciate art, so I'm saying it's all right. Besides, what Mr. Harding doesn't know won't hurt him."

Sarah whispered to Hildie, "Sit quietly, I'll only be a minute." On the instant she decided to disregard any negative ramifications from keeping Auntie waiting. She couldn't resist this opportunity. Stepping into the room, the first thing she noticed was its quietness and goodly number of books. For a parson of a small church, she was surprised, imagining how difficult it was to acquire books out west. The room was simply, but tastefully furnished. A large chair with a footstool—

"Here's the other picture." The housekeeper walked to the wall opposite the easy chair. "I imagine the pastor likes to look at this while sitting and meditating on life or his sermon."

Sarah joined her beside the painting.

"This is the back porch of his parents' home in Pennsylvania. He said his mother sits there mornings after his father has gone to the fields, reading her Bible and drinking a second cup of coffee. You can see her vegetable garden in the background, between the house and the barn—all neat and orderly.

What caught Sarah's eye were the zinnias and cosmos arranged artfully in a simple glass jar on the porch table, pin-points of delicate color in a wash of otherwise neutral shades of nature and farm property. She liked the picture. Very much. It was both restful and evocative. The woman certainly had talent.

The housekeeper folded her arms across her chest. "I don't know when she has time to do it all. A farm wife puts in long days. The minister said she's one of the women he most admires. I think he got his love of nature and beauty from her. He insists I plant those same flowers in this backyard. They remind him of home." She sighed contentedly. "But he loves it here. Says there's nothing like the west for wide open spaces and beautiful scenery. He says—but here I go talking—you can tell I set a great deal of store by him."

The housekeeper grinned sheepishly. "I don't know what's got into me. It's you just standing there so quiet, expecting me to say something, I guess."

Sarah was surprised at her own quietness. With someone new, she usually took charge of a conversation, but here she had so felt the peace of the place, letting it soak into her....

"Well, we don't want to keep your aunt waiting any longer. Now, I *sure* better send some cookies with you." She winked. "Nicer yet, I'll come out and tell her I kept you."

Sarah smiled in response. "I'll let you do just that. I love my aunt, but sometimes even *I* am at a loss how to—" she cleared her throat in amusement "—surmount certain difficulties."

"Now, that I don't believe! Not the way you got me to offer you a cookie, then see this painting." The housekeeper's jolly laugh rolled through her like jelly as she led Sarah out of the study.

CHAPTER 10

John surveyed the mountains from the church steps. The Rockies inspired him on any given day, but this morning in the clear bright air, they seemed especially striking.

Beauty.

He had always been aware of it, appreciated it. Yet the West particularly inspired him with its grand mountains and clouds billowing in blue skies. Its masses of wild flowers in high country meadows and its wide-open plains.

Drinking in the grand mountain scene another minute, he finally turned and entered his church. Mrs. Carey had sent word she was sick, unable to come and do her weekly service, so he'd decided to gather up the stray papers and such. What was the minister's job, but to encourage the flock to serve, then come along side and aid when it was unable. And he was glad to do so today.

Walking by the pews looking for litter, he visualized where each person sat. A renewed love for his people filled him, even those with peculiar ways. This morning he felt more tolerant—would he say, tender toward them?

Mrs. Rutland with her gravelly voice, but rough kindness came to mind. Another parishioner, Mr. Kendal, didn't have the perfectly pressed suits of the banker Mr. Greeley or stand quite so tall, but the slight droop to his shoulders hinted of a man who worked hard, maybe too hard, to support his family. Yes, Mr. Kendal was a man to be admired as well.

He smiled suddenly. Jane Tippet. Despite her hardships, the woman always had a cheerful smile for him, her eyes bright. And the pies and cakes she brought! If he ate them all, he'd be as big as a barn. Hannah saw to it that others shared in the bounty. Jane, always so neat looking, displayed the same trimness as his wife. Her dresses, while somber, displayed her skills as an excellent seamstress.

Just last Sunday he'd seen Sarah Whittington bend over Jane Tippet in the pew, then seat herself beside her, touching the long sleeve of Miss Tippet's Sunday dress, fetching forth a responding smile. Had Miss Whittington asked her who made it, only to find out that Miss Tippet had done so herself? He could imagine Sarah Whittington doing that. She had a way of reaching out to others, lighting up his or her day.

Sarah...she was high on Philadelphia's social ladder. Yet reaching down to engage someone like Jane Tippet, showed she felt secure in her own social standing. Besides that, she was above pettiness. He saw that in her.

He knew that whomever she married would be from the same social strata. Both she and her family would require it. But John could admire her nonetheless. Her beauty, her lithe movements, her springing step. She outshone the lot in his acquaintance. His eyes could single her out even when she was sitting quietly.

What was there about her? Was it her hair, a woman's crowning beauty? The cut and color of her clothing? Her figure? All these brought his thoughts to her again and again. Certainly, if a man were a connoisseur of beauty, she would fill the eye and the soul.

No, it was more than that.

Suddenly he felt on dangerous ground. He shouldn't let himself dwell on a woman like her. She was out of his social—and possibly financial—league.

The front door of the church closed with a decided thump.

He hadn't noticed it opening, so absorbed he'd been—

"Reverend!"

"Mrs. Garland."

"I didn't know you worked as janitor, too." The woman approached him with a decided step. "By the way, that was a fine sermon you delivered yesterday."

"Thank you, Mrs. Garland. As to being janitor, I'm just looking over the church; Mrs. Carey couldn't come today because of illness."

"Well, I'm sure that's very nice of you. If I'd known, I'd have taken Hildie along. Children that age think helping this way great fun. By the way, your housekeeper was so kind to Hildie the other day. Cookies and all! Will you thank her for me?"

"Certainly." He'd had quite an earful from Hannah about that visit. He wondered what Miss Whittington thought about his mother's paintings—

"—as it is, I've come to pick up the flowers from yesterday's service."

His mind refocused on Mrs. Garland's conversation. *They were on to flowers?* "Yes...they were exceptionally beautiful."

"Well, thank you! I can tell you, many a time I've been grateful for the little conservatory Mr. Garland built for my birthday. This time of year not much is showing in the garden, so I'm glad I can supplement what would ordinarily be a meager bouquet." As she spoke she was making her way to the front of the sanctuary.

Just before lifting the vase of flowers, she looked over her shoulder. "I wanted to tell you that we might not be in service next Sunday. We're traveling to Denver—for that art exhibit Sarah wants to attend. We're not sure how long her business will take."

"She mentioned the exhibit at the Bells' party. When...is it?"

"I believe it starts Friday, although we're leaving here Thursday to get settled into the hotel and all. Sarah wants to be at the Exhibition Hall bright and early to see what might be available for purchase." She gave John a little grin— "My niece, the businesswoman!"—and turned to pick up the vase.

John walked into his house whistling. "Hello, Hannah!"

His housekeeper looked up from her big crockery bowl and gazed at him. "Something's making you mighty happy. I could use a little cheering up. Care to share what's on your mind?"

For once he shied away from telling his housekeeper what he was thinking. "Oh, nothing much." He started out the kitchen to avoid any more questions but not before he heard her say under her breath, "Something's on that man's mind— or my name's not Hannah Lee!"

That Hannah didn't miss much. He'd better watch himself. *What of* his talk with Mrs. Garland? It was only by accident he'd found out they were leaving for Denver this week. But as soon as she'd said it, his mind had jumped to the possibility that he still hadn't taken care of Jake's bank business in Denver.

He retraced his steps back to the kitchen. "Hannah, in a couple days I'll be leaving for Denver. On business. Right now I'll be working on Wednesday night's meditation for prayer service and then my Sunday sermon." He saw the speculative look in her eyes. That woman. Did she have to know everything? Well, he would give her something else to mull over.

"Josh Barker mentioned taking a trip into the mountains for some hunting. If he drops by, let me know. I want to advise him not to go alone. Of course, it depends on where he's traveling. The Utes are a little high-strung right now. They've been pushed around a good bit, and we don't need our friend running into any young braves unaware. They don't always observe the treaties.

"And with the drought we had last year, the *Denver Tribune* blamed the fires on the Utes, starting its 'Ute Must Go' campaign. What is really at stake is too much gold and silver in those mountains for the like of the Utes," John added wryly, "even though the U.S. government has documented every one of those fires was caused by lightning—striking all that dry grass and brittle trees."

She nodded. "It didn't help the Ute reputation with that Chief Colorow—him and his braves giving those Bear Dances for the visitors up Denver way."

"Yes, but I'm not worried about Colorow, though he's had the reputation of being hostile with settlers moving onto Ute lands."

Hannah gave him a pointed look. "After that dance those Utes gave in Denver—pulling out fresh Cheyenne scalps right in front of those visitors? I declare, you know how it shocked the city fathers. That was the end of the city's *Indian entertainment!*"

"I know. But Colorow wouldn't make trouble now. It's the young braves that concern me. If a group of them are riding around and meet up with a lone man, there's no accounting what mischief will happen. So let me know if Josh stops by."

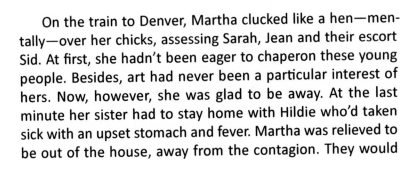

On the train to Denver, Martha clucked like a hen—mentally—over her chicks, assessing Sarah, Jean and their escort Sid. At first, she hadn't been eager to chaperon these young people. Besides, art had never been a particular interest of hers. Now, however, she was glad to be away. At the last minute her sister had to stay home with Hildie who'd taken sick with an upset stomach and fever. Martha was relieved to be out of the house, away from the contagion. They would stay a couple nights in Denver or longer, enough to let Hildie's sickness pass.

Martha looked out the window to her left. Mountains. Then to her right over the passengers' heads to the plains. Funny how this country went from mountains to plains just like that.

She was glad Colorado Springs was level, even though it was up some in elevation—what the townsfolk called high plains. She'd take flat land anytime. That climb to Manitou Springs, especially Pikes Peak looming nearby, was enough mountains for her.

Thinking of Manitou, she thought back on the conversation she'd had with her sister. "Why don't you stay in one of their hotels for a week?" Amelia had asked. "Then you can take advantage of the waters on a more regular basis."

"I don't know if I should be gone that long." Martha was thinking of Sarah. Why, what would her parents think, leaving her like that? They knew only too well their daughter's excessive warmth and sociability, how she could lead on a fellow to hope more than he should.

Mulling over the dilemma, Martha caught only the tail end of what her sister was saying. "...you know Manitou is quite the social scene these days. It was different in the old days. Why, the Ute Indians went there for years. And in the spring they had their Bear Dance nearby."

"Bear Dance?"

"Yes, the dance represented a bear coming out of his cave to greet the warmer weather. You know, that particular animal is very important to them."

"Gracious, all that happened near Manitou? Just imagine those Indians going to the springs and sloshing that water all over them. I'm glad I wasn't around. How could a person ever feel safe?"

"Well, you know, our minister attended their bear dances."

"What? Now, why would he do a thing like that? I should think he had enough to keep him busy at church."

"I heard even his wife attended. It was just too bad she died. A man needs a wife, especially a minister." Amelia took hold of her arm. "You don't know the way some mamas maneuver their daughters his way. And it's not only those in our church do it, either."

"Well!" Martha felt a smirk pulling at her lips. "I can understand that!"

She came back to the present and glanced at her two nieces sitting across from her. Jean, she noticed, nabbed the minister at every social function. It suddenly occurred to her Jean might be setting her cap for him. There was no way *that* was going to happen as she was certain Jean's parents wouldn't countenance such an alliance. Not enough future in him, meaning money.

She looked at Jean critically. And anyway, why would the minister be attracted to a nineteen-year-old tomboy? Anyone could see he was unusual. It would take more of a lady to get his attention. This minister was smart, though. Around the females of his congregation, she noticed he was reserved. Didn't give one more consideration than the others. She guessed he was what some would call godly. Now *that* she could respect.

Martha glanced at Sarah. She certainly had more social grace than Jean. Actually, she'd be a likelier candidate as a wife for the minister. But gracious, he must be as poor as a church mouse—she smiled at her churchy simile. No, he certainly wouldn't tempt her niece. Sarah had her standards. And besides, she had Prescott—*Prescott the Third*. Now, that had a ring to it.

Martha looked off to the mountains. Her mind jumped back to the Bells' party, seeing the Reverend and Sarah standing together. She didn't know if she'd ever seen them alone before, talking like that. Both had a *presence*, the way they moved and

93

carried themselves. They made a striking pair. Even though he stood almost a head taller than her, they seemed equally matched. If times were different and Sarah not her niece, she could see the possibility of them together. But as it was, there was no way in God's creation she would permit such a thing. That was one reason, besides taking the waters, she was here. Yes, she was here to see no such foolishness developed.

Martha settled back in her seat. One thing could be said for General Palmer's railroad. The tracks were as smooth as any she'd traveled on. And the seats were comfortable. She wondered if she had time to close her eyes and rest a bit before they arrived in Denver. She thought so. The young people were keeping entertained, talking quietly among themselves. And she must see to herself, too—with all her responsibility of the next few days.

CHAPTER 11

A buggy led by a prancing horse passed John as he stepped out of the Denver bank. Occasionally, he hankered for big city life with the advantages and hustle and bustle of Philadelphia. Colorado Springs had grown enormously in the eight years of its existence, and had surprised everyone with its orderliness and beauty, but *Denver* was a city. He knew he would enjoy it for a while, then he'd yearn to get back to the peaceful, quieter life of the Springs.

He thought back to his interview with the banker just minutes ago. Who would have thought Jake had squirreled away such a nice, tidy sum? And now thanks to Jake, it was his. Not enough to make him wealthy, but enough—to do what?

For starters, he'd give a portion to the church, make some provision for the poor, and buy medicine for his Indian friends. He rubbed his chin. Then what? He could take trips back east to see his parents—without worrying where the funds would come from. Next, he could make a few improvements on the house to make things nicer for Hannah and himself. And for a wife someday.

For the first time, he thought seriously what it would be like to live in that house with another woman. Other than

Rosalind. She had been happy there. Would someone else feel the same?

Did it need another room or two—to make it a place of comfort and, might he say, a home where they could entertain guests? Rosalind and he had done little of that, but now....

And then he thought of making his house a place of beauty. Already it was comfortable and pleasant enough, but now beauty came to mind. Why was he thinking in this particular term?

He would not name a woman, but a warm sensation entered the place where his heart resided. This woman, he was sure, would be accustomed to finer things. And he would want to please her, honor her.

He thought of the money again. Yes, before he left Denver, he would take out a portion for the church and charity. The remainder he would keep in the bank until such time as it was needed for other plans.

John stepped to the entrance of the Exhibition Hall. He'd just been to the hotel and asked for the Garland party only to be told they had already left for the hall.

Before leaving the Springs, he'd stopped by the Garland's. He was taking no chances of missing them in Denver. They had already departed, but Mrs. Garland had been home and told him which hotel they were staying in, even giving him a message for Aunt Martha. He hoped this was enough of an entrée so he could remain with their party, for he had a yen to see one of them—on a different footing than his usual ministerial role. After all, he was more than a preacher. When he thought of all he'd done in life—working on the farm, fighting and doctoring in the War, and finally going for further schooling—his position at the church represented just a part of him. Why, God Himself was as big as *all* of life. God wasn't confined to a church building.

The hall's sizeable entrance lobby displayed several large paintings, but a mere glance satisfied him. Ordinarily, he would have given time to examining them, but not now. He stepped into one of the large rooms, scanned the people, then exited as quickly as he'd entered. When he looked into the next room, he saw groups of two or three studying the pictures, but one lady stood by herself. Her back was to him. From her stance, John could feel her concentration, her intense interest in the large painting.

For the moment, he was unwilling to disturb her. The deep blue of the dress, her golden hair pleased something deep within him.

But there was something else—he searched for the right word.

Was it the cut of her clothing, the shape of her figure? Conscience brought his thoughts back to his wife. His *deceased* wife, reason reminded him. He had always been drawn to Rosalind's neat figure. But with Miss Whittington there was something more.

Allure.

He was suddenly taken aback. A minister of the gospel contemplating a woman in such a way—he'd better tamp that down. He hurried into the room.

Her peripheral vision must have caught him because she turned, her eyes alight with welcome.

"Mr. Harding!" She held out her hands. "What a surprise!"

"I had business in the city." He took her hands in his. Again, he felt that amazing softness, then a firm clasp. Did her hands linger in his? He gently let her go.

What was he thinking, catching at these straws of her favor? He was only a friend. And maybe not even that, for how long would she stay in the west? Well, he'd be a companion then. That might be possible for this short time in Denver. After this, they would probably see little of each other, for in all probability he would be spending an appreciable amount of time in western Colorado at General Palmer's request.

But here, for this short period, they could meet as equals. Not as parishioner and minister. Not as Easterner and Westerner. Nor as well-to-do and poor. His smile widened. He was poor no longer.

"It's good to see you smile," she said. "Has something particularly good happened?"

If only she knew. But he wouldn't tell of his good fortune, his windfall of money to anyone. He would leave it there in the bank, to be used only for emergencies or special items. "Just a thought crossed my mind, that's all."

"Then it must have been a very pleasant thought." She gestured with a hand that had just rested in his. "See this painting I've been studying? It's by one of our favorite painters."

He liked the way she said *our*. His eyes followed her gesture. Bierstadt, of course. "So he left one of his works here. Or was it sent from the East?"

"I'm not sure, but it's rather wonderful, isn't it?" She cocked her head a little and smiled. "He paints like an old-school European. Such attention to detail. I love the realism, the coloring, the smooth finishes. Do you see?"

"I hadn't thought in quite those terms."

"Well, look on this other wall, two paintings by George Catlin. You see the simplicity of his subject and execution. He's given us a record of the West and its Indians. That is valuable, and I view his works with interest, but they haven't elicited in me the same response as Bierstadt's. And that's why you find me by myself. The others in my party went on ahead. I just wanted to *be* with this artist's work. Letting its light fill me, brighten my afternoon, so to speak."

She glanced up at him, and for a moment the sparkle in her eyes held him. "When I studied at the Academy, I felt I could appreciate all centuries of art. In fact, I considered myself quite broad in my tastes, finding merit in everything, even the more modern pictures. But I have come to realize that, for me, I prefer this school of painting above all others. Realism, grace, beauty—obvious beauty, I guess. Not the kind one has to piece together or imagine. But right here, in plain view."

She talked with so much fervor, for some moments he forgot it was she he had sought, and concentrated on what she was saying about the artist.

"Maybe Bierstadt's art is an interpretation of the West, but it inspires something deep within me. For these few minutes I am transported to another place—a beautiful place that's grand. A place that is beyond one's present life, and maybe disappointing circumstances. A painting like this is a refreshment to the soul." Her smile widened. "Now, I've said my piece. You must look and draw your own conclusions." She turned back to the picture.

He stood and looked at the painting. For the moment he would try to put her observations aside. To do her justice as a painter and student of art, he would attempt to give an honest answer.

What impression did the painting make on him? Grand mountains enclosed a valley. Tiny figures of deer stood at a stream, one drinking. The animals brought a sense of life into the picture. Luminous clouds, shot through with light, hung over the scene. It made him want to be a bird, to soar up into those clouds and into that blue, blue sky.

He said as much to her.

"How delightful you and I share such similar feelings for Bierstadt's art." Pleasure was written on Sarah's face. "The others in my party said they liked it, but moved on rather quickly."

It seemed the proper time to suggest locating the remainder of her party, although he did so reluctantly. "Maybe we should join the others?"

He offered his arm as they left the room. When she put her hand so naturally on his forearm, he was tempted to place his other hand over hers, holding it securely. Yet, there was no reason to do so. She didn't need guiding over ruts in a road, or help over rough ground. But something in him wanted to steady, to protect her. Could he wrangle a dinner invitation with her party? He was able to remain in Denver this evening, could even stay until the following morning. Suddenly, hope sprang up in him. Was there a possibility of anything more between them?

But as they walked on, he realized he would probably make a fifth wheel to her group. Yet—he hadn't given Aunt Martha the message from her sister. That could be his bid to join them, and out of courtesy the aunt could offer him an invitation to dinner.

Sarah stood next to Jean, waiting, while the waiter deftly added a fifth dinner placing. The round table would work nicely, she thought. As their guest, Mr. Harding would be seated at Aunt Martha's right. Sarah wanted the place next to his, to talk more about art, of course—but Jean would want to sit by him as well. And she had promised Jean—why did she feel so honor-bound to help Jean attract the minister? Anyone could see how poorly they suited each other.

Aunt Martha insisted the two men sit on either side of her, and Sarah ended up between Jean and Sid.

"Why did you take so long in front of that big painting?" Jean's eyes held hers. "My gracious, you took enough time in that room."

"It was the grandness of the scene. The beauty—it was so expansive." Sarah turned from her cousin to the minister. "And Mr. Harding felt the same."

He smiled across the table at her. She saw understanding flash from his eyes. No, there was more, a spark of excitement. The same spark had been there this afternoon when she'd felt that quick perception in him. But now he was speaking. "For me, it was not only the painting's grand beauty, but the more personal element of deer in the scene. I have a partiality for animals. And, besides that, their smallness emphasized the scene's grandeur."

"So, you're an animal lover," Sid observed.

"I am. But I want to convey more than that. In the context of the almost impersonal quality of the scene—because of its grandness—the deer brought a particular kind of life into the painting, the kind of life the Indian and our first white settlers depended on for food, for survival. That simple addition to the painting brought in a human element for me."

"I know you help Indians," Sid interjected, "but the Utes in Colorado have been known to be tough—at times, bloody."

"It's true the Utes can be ferocious fighters, but that was mainly against their sworn enemies, the Cheyenne and Arapahoe Indians who wanted to infringe on Ute hunting grounds. The Utes were largely accommodating to white settlers, that is, until too many encroached on their lands as well."

"Well, for me, I think Indians are better on a reservation. And if not a reservation, you know what Sheridan said, "'The only good Indian is a dead Indian.'"

"Sid, you can't mean that," Jean scolded.

"Can't you see I'm joking—or half joking?" His face flashed a smirk.

"Well, here's another quote for you," John said, "by the same man. 'We took away their country and their means of support, broke up their mode of living, their habits of life, introduced disease and decay among them, and it was for this and against this that they made war. Could anyone expect less?'

"Now, Sheridan was no lover of Indians, but he understood why they behaved as they did. At the beginning of his career, he was a great cavalry commander under Grant, but after spending years out west, he had more experience of the United States' unfair dealings with the Indians. That's when he made this second statement."

Sarah felt the minister's eyes singling her out, though his next words addressed the whole group. "After the party at the Bell's last week, General Palmer asked me to take a trip to western Colorado to gauge how the Utes might react to railroad lines built in their territory, to investigate if another railroad could be built without too much trouble from them."

"Why would we want railroads out there?" Aunt Martha asked. "Isn't that all rugged country?"

"Yes," John answered. "But there is silver and gold in the mountains, as well as other valuable minerals. The General sees a need to transport it out—"

"That'll certainly make money for him," Sid interrupted, "if Leadville is any example. No wonder the General is looking to go west with his Denver and Rio Grande."

"True, but he also has the welfare of the country in mind. We're still in debt from the War, and he's looking to help out."

"Very noble," Aunt Martha said.

"General Palmer is all of that. Anyone who's served under him loves and respects him. But I worry about the Indians. While I want to be a good citizen and help the country, I also know our federal government has treated them unfairly. Sometimes, grossly so. The Bureau of Indian Affairs is riddled with men out for their own aggrandizement. Too many shipments of food meant for the reservation Indians are sold to others—with the money ending up in the agents' own pockets."

"Why, that's terrible!" Sarah could hardly believe such a thing, but if the minister said so... "What's being done?"

"A few of us are trying to address the problem. But it's a big one, and knotty. Our country is large, and with the waves of settlers coming west since the War, it's like trying to stem the tide of an ocean with a bucket. Someone has said that what the army didn't or couldn't do to tame or conquer the Indian, the mass of settlers is doing. And the railroad is bringing in even more. As you know, traveling west by train now takes only a few days instead of the months required by Conestoga. Those wagons are becoming a thing of the past."

"Really?" Aunt Martha looked at him with interest.

"Yes, they're still used to get back into the mountains—no railroads there yet. But once the rails take over, they will be rare."

Silence fell over the group. Then Martha suddenly asked, "So, when are you leaving on your trip?"

"I'll be in the pulpit one more Sunday, then will be absent for several weeks."

"We'll miss hearing you. It's likely we'll stay in Denver this Sunday. Then in a few weeks I will have to make a decision whether or not to return east."

"Still taking the waters?" John asked.

"Yes. I need to determine how much they are helping me. And there are other considerations as well. One is that winters here might be milder, and that would be better for my health."

"But," Sarah said. "I want to travel farther into the mountains to paint. I need something to show for my time here, both for my study at the Academy and because I haven't been able to purchase much art yet. The paintings in this exhibit are more expensive than I bargained for. As things stand, I don't know how much I'll be able to buy for the Academy or for my gallery friend in Philly. I've got to come back with *something!*" She turned suddenly to the minister. "What would you advise? Is there an area you might recommend to paint? An area beyond Manitou?"

John was silent a moment. "Well, there's country the other side of Pikes Peak. If you travel the trail over Ute Pass, there's even a place you might stay, a trading post with places to sleep. Castello's place in Florissant. In fact, it was first established as a Ute trading post.

"Then if you really want a spectacular view of Pikes Peak, there's the area south of the trading post. About fifteen minutes before sunset the Peak turns a brilliant red.

His eyes squinted, apparently visualizing the area. "If you turn and look west, in the distance is another range of high mountains. But traveling south from Pikes Peak one runs into some pretty rugged country." He smiled at Sarah. "More than you'd want to tackle."

"Well, if you want to paint, you'd better make quick work of it," Jean said, "because whether or not Auntie stays, you know you can't. School is waiting and then there's Prescott. He'll be eager to see you."

Sarah saw Mr. Harding lift his head from his soup spoon and give Jean, then herself, a quick look. Had he been a bit startled? There was a pregnant silence.

Finally, Aunt Martha said, "Yes, even if I stay, you will need to return. Poor Prescott, working so hard to build up clientele so your father will approve your marriage."

"Yes!" Jean shook Sarah's arm. "I would think he needs a little attention."

Sarah somehow wanted to turn the conversation away from Prescott. "I'd like to know what paintings impressed everyone most in this exhibit. And what type of work do you think my friend in Philly would most likely want for his customers?"

Everyone had an opinion, after which conversation drifted into other avenues. Sarah noticed the minister didn't engage her directly again. In fact, he gave Aunt Martha most of his attention. Something had changed between them. Before that, she had caught his eyes seeking hers again and again. When they rose to leave the table and make their way to the hotel salon for coffee, he excused himself. "I should be getting back to my hotel. I need to recheck the train schedule for the first one back to the Springs."

As their group left the dining room, Sarah watched his tall form walk to the big double doors leading to the street. Surely, he could have remained with them longer. Earlier in the meal, she had the feeling he was settling in for the evening. Now, it seemed he couldn't leave soon enough.

And he had been abrupt about his departure. In some way, she felt rather abandoned.

CHAPTER 12

Sarah extended her hand to Sid as he helped her descend the stagecoach. Aunt Martha and Jean had preceded her, and both looked as tired and dusty as she felt. Taking in the rough-hewn building that was to be their lodging, she looked forward to both a good meal and sleeping accommodations. John Harding had assured them the Castellos were renowned for their genial hospitality. She was glad he'd taken the trouble to help them before his trip to western Colorado. She didn't feel quite so *abandoned*.

Sid looked around. "Well, Florissant is quite the little settlement. And we've a crowd meeting the stage."

"For the mail and such, I suppose," Jean said. "I wonder if there are any Indians around."

"John Harding said this place had been friendly to the Utes. In fact, a few years back, Chief Ouray's camp was situated next to the trading post. The Utes taught the Castellos how to send smoke signals if any of their sworn enemies, Cheyenne or Arapahoe, were seen in the area."

Sarah stepped onto the open veranda of the hostelry. It looked like a veritable museum with its antelope and deer horns and those of Rocky Mountain sheep. Specimens of minerals and petrified wood were also on display.

Aunt Martha reached out to a post, steadying herself. "I'm glad to see we'll have some comfort. I feel all in after traveling. Coming down that last grade, I was afraid for my life, not knowing if the stage would keep upright or not!"

"When I saw all those boulders we had to steer through, I wondered myself," Jean said. "But that made the ride all the more exciting."

Sid laughed. "I bet those miles down that winding slope burned the brake. That *was* a bit of a spicy ride."

"Of course, packed in as we were," Jean added, "we couldn't bounce around much."

"That's something we could be thankful for," Sarah said. "Now let's go inside and see about rooms. We all need to wash up and rest a bit before dinner."

"Yes! You ladies go ahead. I'll bring in the luggage. Let's get settled so we can eat."

Sarah assisted Aunt Martha into the hostelry. Behind her, she heard Jean's intake of breath. "This looks like an old western outpost. Look at that large open fireplace!"

Sarah was glad for Aunt Martha's sake that the outpost showed a degree of comfort. The room evidenced a woman's touch, someone with an artistic eye. Indian blankets in orange, brown and red draped several chairs near the large fireplace and a few colorful pictures decorated the walls. This was a good place from which to make forays into the back country to paint.

A genial-looking woman stepped forward to greet them. "Welcome! I'm Mrs. Castello. I imagine you wish a meal? And to stay overnight?"

Sid set down the first of their things. "We'd like rooms for several nights."

"How many do you need?"

"Three. One for the two young ladies. One for their aunt, and one myself."

Their hostess said she had only two left for the night, but after that there would be plenty.

"For tonight, I could sleep near the fire on some blankets," Sid offered.

"Yes, we could arrange that—near the fire."

Sarah saw the question in Jean's eyes. Sid's lips twitched. "Unless you'd like me sleeping in front of your door to protect you. The fire, however, would be warmer."

"Leave it to you to look after your comfort," Jean retorted.

"Comfort? And me offering to sleep on a hard floor!"

"Please! Stop sparring, you two," Aunt Martha said. "I'm tired."

"It's good we have Aunt Martha along as peacemaker and... chaperone." Sid made Auntie an elaborate bow. "We are most appreciative of your presence."

"Well, I'm glad you've all come," Sarah said. "I've been itching to get out in these mountains to paint ever since we arrived. And the only reason Jean's mother finally approved was because the two of you persuaded her—and Aunt Martha finally agreed." She made a quick little curtsey. "I thank you."

Sarah glanced at Mrs. Castello. She probably thought them an odd lot, and she might not be far wrong. Sarah smiled to herself.

But it was a relief to find such accommodations this far out in the mountains and later, Sarah said as much to Sid as they stepped near the huge fireplace.

"Well, John Harding did recommend it," he said.

Sarah couldn't help ask. "He's been here...often?"

"A good number of times, I'm sure. You have to know he travels this region from time to time." He rubbed his chin. "Come to think of it, he would have traveled right through here, looking into that railroad business of General Palmer's. Who knows, if he's in the area, he might drop back in." He paused, and looked back at their hostess. "I wonder if she has any daughters?"

"You watch yourself, Sid Carlton," Jean said as she walked up with Aunt Martha. "You're supposed to be escorting *us*, not casting out lures for other women."

"Just wondering, dear neighbor. Actually, I was thinking more in terms for the pastor than myself. He needs a wife." Sid gave her a teasing grin.

Sarah frowned. "I hope this isn't a sample of what to expect from you two the rest of our trip. I need quiet to paint, not be distracted by squabbling."

"Don't worry, my sweet." Sid glanced at Sarah. "I'll take charge of Jean and make sure she doesn't disturb you."

"I believe I need to unpack." Jean flounced her skirt to the side with a kick. "I'll leave you two to decide on our itinerary tomorrow. You coming, Aunt Martha?"

"Yes." Aunt Martha looked pointedly at Jean, then Sid. "You're acting like an old married couple instead of nice, long-time neighbors."

Sid doffed an imaginary hat. "My most humble pardon. Fair ladies, au revoir!"

Sarah looked at Jean's indignant, retreating figure and Aunt Martha's lagging one, and chuckled. "Sid, can't you ever be serious?"

Sarah wet the heavy sheet of paper with large brush strokes. The bottom two thirds she'd wash in a light green. Her plan was to do a number of water color studies in *plein air*, then paint in oil at her aunt's house.

She looked around with satisfaction, taking a deep breath of air. A couple scenes here were readymade for her brush. Rolling treed hills swept up to an imposing Pikes Peak. It provided a restful, yet majestic vista. In the other direction, a grand plain dotted with forests led to distant majestic mountain ranges.

Jean and Sid had elected to take a walk, said they'd be back in an hour. "You'd better have something worthwhile to show us when we return, getting us up at the crack of dawn for this outing of yours," Sid admonished.

She would.

Setting to work with a purpose, she found herself enjoying the peace and quiet. Enjoying being alone. Aunt Martha had been true to her word when she said they couldn't get her on a horse. She had decided to rest at the post after their arduous journey yesterday. The three young people could go by themselves!

Sometime later, Sarah put down her brush. She'd just caught that particular cerulean blue of the Colorado sky with its wisps of bright white cloud when she heard a snort. In her peripheral vision, she saw several horses and turned to look. Indians. Sarah took a deep breath and sat up straighter.

Four muscular, young braves. Her eyes caught the leader's.

Her stomach tightened, then she remembered advice she'd heard Mr. Harding give. *Don't show fear. Not to an Indian. They respect courage as nothing else.* She nodded a greeting and continued with her painting.

Out of the corner of her eye she saw the Indians motion in her direction, bantering words back and forth. What did they intend to do?

Suddenly the lead Indian slung off his pony, jogged toward her and stopped by her side.

Liquor.

It was strong on his breath. Hardening her stomach, she disciplined herself to remain quiet. She *would not* appear weak.

He grasped her upper arm. When his fingers dug in, her first impulse was to jerk away, but she kept herself still. By sheer force, he forced her up. The pain let up slightly as she stood. Drawing up to her full height, she stared at him. As best she could, she would stay in control of this situation.

Sarah tried to disengage her arm, but found it held in a vise. The Indian drew out his knife, but one of the other braves shouted, motioning him to release her.

"Huh!" Her captor spit at the Indian who had just yelled. Then one of the other braves said something forceful in their native tongue, siding with the Indian who had shouted. At that the leader grunted approval and put his knife away, but with his free hand, he gestured emphatically toward the horses Sarah's party had staked nearby. He tried to force her toward them. Stiffening, she motioned toward her jacket and satchel on the ground. He jerked his head toward the articles, loosening his hold enough to let her scoop them up.

Approaching her mare, Sarah knew she couldn't mount without help. Certainly not without considerable loss of dignity, and dignity was something she felt she must maintain. Somehow, she had to keep a line of respect—something that would hold off these Indians from doing the unseemly. She reached up and looped her satchel over the pommel then lay her jacket in front. The Indian nudged her, indicating she should get up into the saddle, but made no move to assist. She wondered if this Indian had ever seen a sidesaddle. He pushed a second time, harder. Instead of complying, she cupped her hands, demonstrating how he should hold her foot to lift her up. Still, he made no move to help.

They seemed at an impasse. But when he muttered what seemed a threat, she grabbed the pommel with her right hand, forcing herself to lay her other hand on his shoulder. She pushed down and jumped, awkwardly thrusting herself up onto the saddle. Shifting herself and adjusting her skirt, she was finally able to curl her right leg around the pommel, awkwardly toeing her left foot into the stirrup.

The Indian grabbed the reins of her mare and leading it, vaulted onto his own horse. Sarah's heart sank when she saw the other braves gather the reins of Sid's and Jean's horses.

The lead Indian motioned the others to follow.

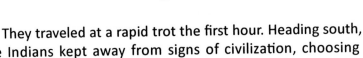

They traveled at a rapid trot the first hour. Heading south, the Indians kept away from signs of civilization, choosing country increasingly rugged: steep hills with stone outcroppings strewn with scrubby trees and brush. What would Jean and Sid think to find her gone? With their horses taken, they couldn't ride after her. Besides, what could they possibly do against four young, strong Indians? When they returned to the post they would surely send a rescue team. But would anyone be able to find and follow her trail?

The second hour the pace of the horses slowed. The Utes took out bottles of whiskey and took swigs at short intervals. They laughed, becoming increasingly ribald. The leader began to sing a pretty melody in slow tempo. But the way he looked at Sarah and then gestured, the song seemed obscene. When he finished he asked how she liked it. She kept her eyes cold and impersonal. She would not let him see she understood in any way.

The Indians talked louder, becoming progressively drunk, shouting occasional words in English. Mr. Harding had said a number of Utes knew some English and this proved to be true. A Ute who hadn't said much now drew his horse alongside Sarah and slapped her on the shoulder. "You squaw," he said. Then pointed to himself. She glanced at him. His leer suggested the worst. She looked away, willing herself to ignore him and ride with dignity. All the while, he talked indecently and made shameful gestures, and finally, laughing, he kneed his horse to trot ahead.

Sarah was relieved to see him move away from her. The uncertainty of what he might do had begun to wear on her. She tried to keep from slumping in the saddle, her back and limbs now aching.

She looked at the timepiece pinned to her dress. Did these Indians never stop to rest or eat? Breakfast seemed a long time

111

ago. At least Jean and Sid had food. The lunch basket had been hidden from view so thankfully hadn't been touched. They would need it, walking back to the post.

Finally, the Indians approached a stream where they watered their horses. Sarah was motioned to dismount. She drew her leg over the pommel and holding on, gingerly half slid, half jumped down. Her legs almost gave way when they hit the ground.

Her captor led her horse to water. She followed but walked a few steps upstream from where the horses drank. Once the horses had been watered, three of the braves sat down or stretched out. But the leader approached her, addressing her as "white squaw." He grunted at her, then with wild gestures and a few English words, recited wrongs carried out against him by soldiers. Greatly excited, he represented what had been done and what he thought and felt, as much by action as by word.

When he finished and walked away, Sarah warily stepped over to a tree and sat down. Propping herself against it, she tried to rest, but her stomach had tightened into a knot. Suddenly the leader grunted and approached her again.

She looked up.

Standing close, he drew up his gun and pointed its muzzle directly at her face. Involuntarily she cried out.

He lowered his gun, raised it again and took aim. His eyes glared with hatred. She held her breath. But then he lowered the gun and walked away. She looked at his departing back, fear gripping her. Would she be killed, even butchered?

For the first time in a long while, she prayed, a heartfelt, desperate prayer. *Oh God, help me*, she kept saying silently over and over. *Help me!*

One of the band made a sharp gesture toward the south. It seemed the signal to start once again.

Sarah held onto the tree as she gingerly rose, then approached her horse. The Indian brave who had earlier come to her defense walked up and jerked his head toward their leader. "He no hurt you. Only play soldier." He then cupped his hands as she had demonstrated earlier. Gratefully, she placed her foot in them and he hoisted her up. She thanked him and he grunted a response.

It was not many minutes down the trail before the Indians drank from their bottles again. They called out to each other, laughing, and kept looking at her, pointing. "You ours!"

What were they going to do with her? Sarah was glad her hair had been pulled back and hidden underneath her hat. She could only imagine what ribald comments or treatment such blond hair would incite.

The Indians chose terrain away from the stream. Sarah wondered if settlers would be situated near water and this band wanted to avoid being seen, especially with a captive white woman. They passed an abandoned mine, but other than that, they rode in rugged, lonely country. The prominent Pikes Peak had been left behind long ago. Even so, the craggy hills and trees would have obscured it from view.

Her situation seemed hopeless. She had heard of women being captured and then taken into the tribe, forced to work and perform. She shrank from what it meant to become some Indian's squaw.

But surely she would be rescued. Mr. Harding knew these Indians, or she hoped he did. Were these his Utes? But, then, she didn't know that either.

Again, she cried out a silent prayer.

Later, locating another stream, the Indians stopped, letting themselves and their horses drink. Then they led their mounts to a spot some distance away, out of sight from the water. Staking their ponies near clumps of grass and pulling off the riding blankets, they built a small fire where the smoke drifted up through the branches of a piñon tree. *How shrewd. No one would see the smoke.*

On hearing a sound, her head jerked around. The leader had suddenly appeared at her side and now unsheathing his knife, he raised it and pressed it against her throat. "No run away!" His eyes were cold.

"No run!" she said, holding her hands hard at her side to keep them from shaking. "I will not run away. And I am not afraid."

But she was afraid. And where would she go if she did run? She was at their mercy.

CHAPTER 13

John patted Flossie's neck and looked at Pikes Peak in the distance. It always felt like coming home whenever he saw that mountain. He was thankful for the mustang that had been bred into Flossie because they'd traveled some rough country these last weeks. This horse took to mountain trails as if she belonged there.

He directed Flossie around a hill to ground that leveled out, careful to steer her between rocks and scrub bushes, although by this time she instinctively knew where to step.

John's thoughts drifted to Jake's cabin. It was good he'd asked one of Jake's old friends to stay on site, because he'd reported those whiskey-toting brothers had paid another visit, only to be told the place was occupied. Otherwise, no telling what Hob and Jeb would have done. He'd heard via the grape vine they'd had enough of "that preacher." Another reason why he always carried a gun and rifle whenever he went into the wilderness.

He was still a good distance west of Pikes Peak, miles from Colorado Springs. Once he hit Ute Pass his horse would carry him home without much leading. However, first he might stop at the Castello trading post. A hot meal and an overnight stay would be welcome.

Traveling over a rise, in the distance he spotted two people. On foot. Something about them looked familiar. Jean? Sid? Looking closer, he was sure. Where they were, Miss Whittington was sure to be in the vicinity. He kneed his horse faster.

As soon as the two saw him, they started running, waving their arms frantically. He urged Flossie into a gallop.

"Mr. Harding! Mr. Harding, I'm so glad you're here," Jean cried.

Sid caught his breath. "Sarah's disappeared and the horses with her. Jean and I had just now started back to the post. Come and see what you can make of the tracks." Sid turned and sprinted, John following on horseback. As soon as they reached the place, John sprang off and scouted the area on foot.

"Several horses—unshod Indian ponies." He widened his circle. "They took off south, toward the canyons. Pretty rough country." He looked at both Jean and Sid.

"Indians!" Sid exclaimed. "But they weren't supposed to be in this area."

"I can't believe this!" Jean cried out.

"What happened?" John asked. "Was Sarah left alone?"

"She didn't mind," Jean said quickly. "She wanted to paint, so Sid and I went for a walk." She glanced at Sid and blushed.

"We said we'd be gone only an hour." Sid expelled his breath in frustration. "In fact, she wanted to be alone. Said she could concentrate better."

John strode back to his horse. "I'm going after her. There's nothing you can do. So go back to the post."

"I'll send for help," Sid said. "If we can get a tracker, I'll come. As it is—" He threw up his hands in vexation.

"There's no telling who will be at the post. I think I better figure on doing this alone. I know some of the Utes, have had dealings with one or two of the bands. I hope it's them. They've hunted this territory for years, are very familiar with it."

"Why did they take Sarah?" Jean's voice shook. "What will they do to her?"

John grimaced. "A white woman left alone like that—with blond hair—they probably couldn't resist taking her. The Utes have been friendly to whites around here, particularly the Castellos, but lately they've been unpredictable. Too many whites encroaching on their lands. There's no telling what's in their minds."

"I knew it—those dang Indians!" Sid's mouth set in a hard line.

Jean's eyes began to tear up.

John quickly added, "But there's hope. I've made friends with some of them, can speak a little of their language." He took hold of his saddle horn. "What kind of a lead do they have?"

"We left Sarah about ten o'clock," Sid said. "And it's now eleven-thirty. Surely, they couldn't be gone much more than an hour."

"You have water?" John asked.

"One canteen." Sid held it up.

"Fill it at a spring. There's one on the way to the post if you keep due north. With a few hours of walking, you'll make it okay."

Jean took out a couple of sandwiches and an apple from the basket she carried. "Here, for your lunch."

"Thanks." John shoved the food into his saddlebag, put his foot in the stirrup and swung up. "You can pray—for Sarah and me."

He traveled over rolling land, saw a few cattle grazing in the distance. But the Indians had kept shy of any possible settlements.

Riding over a pass, he came to a creek an hour and a half later. They'd stopped here; he found a soft foot print near the water—a moccasin. He watered his horse, took out a sandwich Jean had given him, and refilled his canteen.

He was somewhere southwest of Pikes Peak and entering a canyon. Why were these Indians heading into such rough country? To avoid the rolling plain to the west, where they might run into other travelers? His chest tightened at the thought.

He mounted Flossie once again. Even though the ground was rocky and dry, he could follow their tracks. It was plain enough to see they were heading through this winding canyon. He'd covered this ground once before. The elevation remained high. Rugged mountains rose to his left, largely unexplored. Miles ahead he remembered a large creek that ran into the canyon. Were they headed toward that?

These Indians taking a lone white woman—maybe he'd been too optimistic in giving Jean hope. Sarah's beauty and blond hair could work either way for her. If these were some renegades out roaming the countryside...once again his chest tightened.

Some time later he stepped off his horse, deciding to walk to give his mount a rest. In this terrain he'd progress almost as quickly as riding, anyway. Pushing on as fast as possible, a half hour later he climbed back on his horse. Time was getting on.

Lord, keep Sarah calm and strong. Help me to find her and get her back safely. He found himself praying the same simple words again and again—couldn't—wouldn't think much beyond that. Too much was uncertain.

Another hour passed. He stopped, both to give Flossie a rest, and to...then he heard a sound ahead, something that didn't belong to the wilderness. He listened closely. Had it been a whinny? Distant, but in this canyon sound carried.

That creek he'd been thinking of was ahead. Maybe they'd stopped nearby. He listened, almost certain now of camp sounds. He dismounted and led his horse to a piñon tree and looped the reins loosely over a branch, ready for a quick getaway.

John opened his saddle bag and took out the moccasins he used for stealing up on game. He slipped them on. Next, he unsheathed his rifle and advanced carefully through the rock outcroppings and scruffy brush.

What would he find when he reached his objective? He stopped again and listened. A voice. Too far away for words to be distinct, but its tone and cadence were different from a white man's. Yes, Indian.

Had they harmed Sarah? The fact they'd taken her at all suggested a group of renegades. They were far off their reservation.

What had she been thinking to be by herself? Or her companions to leave her? Suddenly he was angry.

He heard movement up ahead. Every muscle and nerve in his body became alert, his military experience rising up in him. For some yards he stepped carefully, silently. Then stopped again to assess the situation. With an act of will, he stilled his anger. He would need every bit of judgment and energy to deal with the unknown.

"Ahh—woo!" The sudden cry split the air. Another shout followed. Running feet thumped the ground. Cry after cry pierced the air.

John stole quickly forward, crouching to be less visible. He wanted to determine what he was up against before being seen.

He hadn't heard Sarah cry out, yet fear tightened his stomach. He reached a large rock outcropping and knew he was near. Slipping off his hat, he slowly inched his head around a large boulder.

Sarah stood in the middle of a clearing. Indians swooped past her, hitting her at each pass. One hit her shoulder. Another pulled at her hair that was falling down. One after another, their jabs became more and more forceful.

Four braves having some rough fun. Each wanting to prove his manhood to the others, their blood up. John shuddered to think where it might end.

He knew they wouldn't give her up. Would he have to shoot them down to get her?

119

If there were only two of them, he could disable them. He was a good shot and surprise would give him the advantage. Three? He'd have to have all the breaks in the world—once shots rang out, the Indians would move fast, either disappear in the rocks or charge him.

But four against one, an impossible situation.

He chanced another glance around the rock. Wait! Didn't he know one of them?

John had given that brave's sister medicine and she had recovered. Surely, that would weigh heavily in his favor. Maybe he could parley. The Indian girl's life he'd saved—for Sarah.

He quickly stepped from behind the boulder, his hand held up in peace, but keeping his rifle ready. "Stop!" he shouted in Ute.

The Indians halted, staring.

He made the sign for peace. Then pointed to the Indian he knew and signed to see if he remembered him. "Sister," he said. "Medicine."

The Indian's head jerked in recognition.

John looked directly at the Indian. "Your sister." He pointed at Sarah. "For her. She's my woman!"

"No!" Another Indian shouted and clenched his hand high. "Woman, ours!" The Indian's glance flashed to the others to gain their assent, then hit his hand against the brave's chest John had addressed. "No! Woman ours!"

It was plain who was the leader, and equally plain he wouldn't parley.

All this ran through John's mind in seconds. He still held his gun on the Indians. The odds were not in his favor, even with one possible ally. He'd still lose against their superior numbers if he tried to shoot it out. If he continued to hold the gun on them, and took Sarah by force, this band would take out after them, and he doubted if Sarah and he would make it more than a mile. Then no telling what revenge the Indians would extract. No, this needed to be decided here and now.

"Fight *me*!" John struck his chest, jerking his head at the leader, then pointed to Sarah, meaning she was the prize. He must prove his superiority in combat, otherwise he didn't stand a chance of taking her out of here.

The Indian John had challenged hit his own chest. "Fight!" John gave a quick nod. "If I win—girl goes free—with me." He gestured forcefully, underscoring each phrase. "No more trouble." He paused. "Agreed?"

The brave looked at him a moment, then a hard, savage smile crossed his face. The Indian had no doubt who would win.

John's fighting spirit rose. He would fight to win. Wouldn't consider anything else. He'd seen Utes fight in their camp games. Had paid attention in case he'd ever need the knowledge; the Utes were known as fierce warriors against their enemies.

Every trick he learned growing up wrestling, everything he gained in the War, he'd use. He'd give this Indian no quarter.

He glanced at Sarah. He could see resolve in her posture but also saw fear in her eyes.

His opponent drew out a knife, indicating his weapon of choice. John nodded and motioned Sarah back against the rocks and set his rifle and six-shooter at her feet. He looked up at her. She held herself proud, like any queen or Indian princess.

"Pray," he said quietly. "Protect yourself if you have to." His eyes held hers a moment, then purposely glanced down at the weapons.

He turned to find the Indian crouched with feet planted wide, knife grasped in front. John took his bowie from its sheath and stepped forward. Just as he took the same stance, the brave jumped in and jabbed. In that split second John instinctively sucked in his stomach and his fist came down hard on his opponent's wrist. The Indian's arm dropped, but the weapon remained firm in his hand. In that brief second John assessed the strength of the Indian's arm and wrist—that blow would have dislodged the knife in an ordinary man.

Before the Indian jumped back, his hot breath hit John's face. Then thrusting away, the Ute kicked up dust. For a moment John flinched but was vaguely aware of noise near the Indian ponies, a man's deep voice.

But both he and the brave quickly crouched, ready to spring again. The Indian's dark arm cut in with the intent to gouge. Once again John jumped away, but this time the knife caught his shirt. For the fraction of a second the knife held in the cloth, and John grabbed the Indian's wrist, slicing out with his own knife, catching the Indian across the cheek.

Blood unleashed the Indian's fury. He twisted his wrist out of John's grasp, quickly thrusting to the right then left. John jerked one way, then another, the last slash ripping through his shirt drawing blood. But before the Indian had time to jump away, John thrust his knife down hard into his opponent's shoulder, sinking it deep.

"Halt!" a deep voice shouted in Ute.

The renegade continued to swipe savagely, one stab after another. The deep voice shouted again. Two Indians grabbed the brave and John at mid-section and dragged them apart. John felt a shock of disbelief. The Indian code of honor dictated no interference in a fair fight.

A tall Indian had stepped into the clearing. John looked and saw an elder from the tribe he had brought medicine to. This man designated as chief stood not three yards away. He motioned the Indians to release John.

Drawing himself up, John greeted the elder in Ute.

The older Indian looked around at the others, then swept out his arm to indicate John. "Friend! Strong medicine man!"

John glanced at his opponent and the other Indians. Did he see a measure of respect in their eyes? He stretched his shoulders back to relieve their tightness.

The chief questioned him, what had happened? John answered in halting Ute. The elder Indian glanced around for confirmation. Reluctantly, the braves nodded. The chief then motioned one of the Indians with him to dress John's wound and that of his adversary. The brave quickly moved to his horse and extracted herbs from a pouch.

John looked over at Sarah. She looked pale but stood quietly. He walked over to her and grasping her elbow, helped her sit. "You've been brave." He pressed her arm. "No one could have handled herself better."

He gestured to the chief that Sarah needed water, and one of the Indians brought Sarah a worn canteen. "It's all right," John said. "Just drink." He was grateful she did as she was told.

"Rest as best you can," he said softly. "The chief's instructed one of his braves to see to my injury—just a surface wound—but afterwards we'll leave. So rest now for the ride home."

While John and the chief sat on the ground and talked, another Indian threw herbs into a tin cup with water and placed it on a stone in the fire. After steeping the concoction for a while, he signaled the potion was ready.

The chief pointed to John to be cared for first. The Indian took a piece of cloth, dipped it in the herb water and held it to John's wound. "Only a scratch," John tried to say in Ute. "Not serious." But the Indian dipped it again and again at the chief's insistence.

Then while the Indian took care of the brave's injury, John wiped his knife clean and heated it in the fire.

Afterward the chief indicated they should eat. A brave who had been with the chief, had already taken strips of freshly-cut meat—deer from their hunt—and had roasted them.

Sarah was sitting sideways against the rock, resting her head. John approached with a portion of the roasted meat. "Just a little longer, Miss Whittington." She was silent, but her eyes communicated gratitude. "Take this for strength," he said. He could see fatigue in her shoulders. "I need to eat with the Indians. Stay here, and rest as best you can."

He sat with the chief, but after they finished eating, he stood, indicating the need to leave. He motioned that Sarah would go with him. The chief nodded.

The Indians watched John as he helped Sarah up from her sitting position. He held her arm as she walked to retrieve her hat. She placed it on her head, quickly tucking her hair underneath.

John turned to the chief. "Her horse?"

One of the Indians left and returned with the mare, side saddle in place. Giving the chief and the others a respectful gesture in parting, he led Sarah and her horse out of the clearing, past the boulders and scruffy bush, and returned to the place he'd tethered his mount. Flossie had eaten the grass where she stood, and John now led her and Sarah's horse down to the stream.

"Why don't you wash your face and hands," he said.

Sarah removed her hat, and after refreshing herself with the water, took down hair that hadn't already fallen and combed it with her fingers, pinning it up as best she could. She did everything quietly and with precision. John couldn't help admiring her. Then she sighed, deeply.

John checked the cinch, then assisted her up. She barely made it into the saddle. He could see she was very tired. He took her horse's reins and mounted his own. "Just hang onto the pommel. I'll lead you." He thought of the country ahead, speculating where they might spend the night.

For the next half hour they skirted large rocks and trees, riding along the winding stream bed. With rocky cliffs rearing up on either side, the country had a rough beauty, but as John glanced back, he doubted Sarah was alert enough to appreciate it. He could see she was hard pressed to sit erect in the saddle. He decided the next likely place they'd dismount and rest. What she needed was to lie down.

He spied some trees with grass nearby, a sheltered spot. He could also see up and down the trail. No one could come up on them unawares. "We'll stop there awhile."

"Thank you." Her voice was so quiet, he almost missed what she said.

When they reached the place, he turned in the saddle. "I'll help you dismount." He slid off his horse and walked back to hers. With difficulty, she lifted her right leg over the pommel.

"Here, put your hands on my shoulders, and I'll lift you down." He raised his hands to her waist. How tiny it felt under his grasp. When her feet hit the ground, her legs folded beneath her and he instinctively held onto her, steadying her as a shepherd does a lamb he's just rescued from harm. She sank against him, her head resting against his neck. Then her shoulders started to heave with silent sobs.

He put his arms around her. "Just cry it out. You've been through a lot." She shook harder, and he held her a bit tighter. "There...let it all come out. No need to hold back." Rosalind had been this way. A soldier in the middle of a crisis, but when it passed, her guard would drop and the tears would come. He was glad Sarah was like his wife, for he knew what to do. He'd learned a lot from Rosalind.

After a minute, Sarah quieted, but he continued to hold her. Sure enough, the sobs started again. He had to smile above the blond head. *Just like Rosalind.* It might take another time or two before she got it all out of her system. He'd wait.

In fact, if he was perfectly truthful with himself, he'd wait a long while. He felt he could stand like this forever, holding her. Rosalind had been slight of build and he'd always wanted to protect her. Sarah was a bit taller and—quite a woman.

However, he wouldn't let his thoughts wander there. She was all but spoken for, and he was her pastor, of sorts. No, he would guard her and guide her like one of the sheep of his congregation. And that was that.

When she quieted, really quieted, he held her off a bit. "You feel better now?" That sounded like an inane question, but it would do for the present. As much normal talk as he could manage would be all to the good after her unnerving experience. And for himself, too, if he were honest.

"I'm putting my blanket on this grass, and we'll see if we can't make you comfortable enough for a short nap. Then we can travel another hour before making camp. Here, before you lie down, drink some water." He offered her own canteen.

"I don't know how I can thank you."

"Your saying it, is enough. However, I want to thank the Lord for helping me find you and for sending that chief." He went to her horse for the other blanket. "You sleep now, and I'll have coffee ready before we leave."

After Sarah lay down, John loosened the horses' cinches and staked them. Then he found a large tree and leaned against it with his rifle across his knees. He didn't anticipate any more trouble, but he'd be ready, and the horses would warn him if anyone was coming.

He thought back to fighting that Indian. Whiskey was on his breath. Not surprising then that they'd started in on the girl. But where did they get the whiskey?

His thoughts drifted back to Jake's cabin. And those whisky-toting brothers. Was there any connection? Too bad the cabin wasn't nearby. Sarah and he could stay there tonight.

Where were Jean's and Sid's horses? They had probably been tethered with the Indians' mounts. But he hadn't been up to bargaining for them, or leading them when he had Sarah to care for. His jaw tightened. Sid and Jean should pay for their foolishness. If worse came to worst, he'd pay the Castellos for the horses. He didn't want his friends out anything.

He looked around at the lengthening shadows in the canyon. Dusk would be coming soon. He wanted to put on a few more miles, and choose their camp with care. They would rest awhile longer, then be on their way.

CHAPTER 14

John had been on the lookout for a place to camp the last mile. Coolness now reigned and cold would descend soon enough at this elevation.

He glanced back at Sarah, for that's what he called her now, at least in his mind. Her shoulders slumped slightly forward; that straight back he so admired now told the tale of weariness.

Riding a little farther, John spotted a stream where several large rocks formed a pool. He pointed. "We'll stop there for water."

He filled their canteens. Handing Sarah hers, he directed, "Drink all you can, then I'll refill it. After that, we'll let the horses drink."

"Should I get down?"

"Only if you'd like to walk some. We won't camp here."

"No?"

"It's better to find a site away from the water. Animals or even people might use this. If they don't happen to be friendly, we're better out of sight."

They rode a short distance and spotted a wall of rock. Trees near the rock provided partial shelter.

John assessed the light coat Sarah was wearing. It would never give enough warmth against tonight's cold. A makeshift shelter against those rocks would help.

"Miss Whittington, would you like to get down off that horse now?"

Sarah nodded and he stepped over to her mount. She lifted one leg over the pommel of her sidesaddle, then trustingly leaned into his outstretched hands which grasped her at the waist.

To feel this bit of womanliness beneath his hands once again brought heat to his face.

Her knees buckled when she hit the ground, and he steadied her.

"You can tell I'm not accustomed to that much time in the saddle, I'm afraid."

"You did fine today. More than fine. Just stand by the horse a bit and get your legs back. I'll steady you." He transferred his hands to her shoulders. Somehow that felt less—intimate. Something he needed right now.

After a minute, he suggested, "Why don't you walk some. Here, I'll help." He held her elbow firmly, leading her a few steps. He had to admit he was glad for her weakness so he could lend his strength. But as soon as she seemed to regain steadiness, he suggested she continue to walk while he tethered the horses near grass. He took off their saddles and rubbed them down. Afterward, he gathered sticks and larger dead wood for their fire. As soon as Sarah saw what he was doing, she scouted around and did the same.

Working together, he felt their companionship. He could tell she felt much the same because when he glanced at her, she smiled. Since Rosalind's death, he'd been alone on the trail. Having Sarah here brought back memories of how much he and his wife had shared.

Finally, they had enough wood. "Now, you sit while I build a fire."

She readily acquiesced and, once again, he could tell her stamina had worn thin. Once again, he was glad to show his strength.

After the fire took nicely, he unsheathed his knife and walking to some nearby pines, cut the lower branches that fanned out. Thankfully they were pines with soft needles running in a similar direction. He layered some for a bed, then cut and shaped larger branches, leaning them out from the rock wall so that a small lean-to was formed. With the fire in front, they'd have some heat in the shelter the first part of the night.

He took out food from his saddlebag. A can of beans. Biscuits. Coffee and dried jerky. Not exactly gourmet eating, but it would keep them from starving.

"I wonder about Sid's and Jean's horses," she said. "I know the Indians took them with them. But I didn't think to mention them to you."

"Oh, I thought of them." He smiled. "However, I didn't think it worth troubling the waters to get them back. Indians aren't dumb; they were thinking of them, too, when I asked for your horse." He shifted his folded legs. "But I considered you the priority." He smiled again. "Thought you worth two horses."

"*Two* horses?"

"You should be flattered. Indians set great store by theirs. If I know anything, my friends at the trading post wouldn't have given Jean and Sid inferior mounts. But Sid and Jean should never have left you alone. At least, not for the length of time they did. They should have remained within earshot."

"It seemed safe enough."

"One can never be too careful. The Utes aren't in this area as a rule. They live on reservations—or are supposed to. But they still have hunting rights here, in fact, used to camp and roam all over this territory. With the trouble the agent has been having with the White River Utes, one can never tell. But if it isn't the Utes, it's bears and mountain lions to watch out for." He looked at her pointedly. "So, I'm not in charity with

Sid and Jean for leaving you alone. Sid, at least, should have known better."

It was nearly dark after they had eaten their spare but welcome supper. When the sun set, the temperature dropped noticeably. John suggested, "Shall we turn in?"

"I'm very tired, so I'll probably fall asleep right away. Thank you for the food."

In the light of the fire, he could see her wan smile convey gratitude. "You might not smile so gratefully when you hear my suggestion." He tried to soften his next words with a crooked smile. "It's going to get cold tonight, you can feel it already. We're at a good elevation here, about nine thousand feet. I suggest we both sleep in the lean-to—back to back to help generate heat for each other. I've slept alone out in the open many times with just the gear I've got with me, but you have only your thin jacket. That's not nearly enough to keep you warm. If we sleep fully clothed, covered by my blanket and slicker...."

He said carefully, "I know the conventions of society, what my matrons at church—or ladies, anywhere—would think. They would be shocked. But it's much warmer when another human being is near you. I discovered that camping with my wife." He looked at her, trying to gauge her reaction. "So that's my suggestion. We'll keep things purely businesslike. What do you think?"

She looked at him a long moment. "Whatever you say," she said quietly.

"All right." I'll put my ground cover on top of the pine branches. Over us will be my blanket and slicker. That'll make as good a bed as we can get in these parts." He paused. She was so quiet, he looked at her again. "We don't need to mention this arrangement to anyone. I wouldn't compromise your reputation for the world. It's just the necessity of the situation. It *is* all right with you, isn't it?" His eyebrows lifted in question. "You trust me?"

"Oh, yes!"

Some time in the middle of the night, Sarah awoke. Gradually, she became aware of where she was. Her exposed nose and face were absolutely freezing, but the rest of her felt reasonably warm. And protected.

A big shoulder shielded hers and an arm encircled her. She almost started up in confusion. What was this? At the beginning of their sleep, they had positioned themselves back to back, under the blanket and slicker. Just as she had started to drift off, she had felt warmth begin to permeate her. Grateful, she had drifted off into what must have been a deep sleep.

In fact, when she first awakened, she thought she was in her own bed in Colorado Springs, only to discover her nose so cold. Then she felt the shoulder shielding hers, an arm clasped around her middle, a warm body pressing close to her. And her head nestled against John Harding's neck.

What should she do?

She could feel him breathing softly, regularly. He was sound asleep. No doubt he was completely unconscious of his change in position. He was too much a man of honor. In his sleep, he had thought her his wife. This had been their accustomed position sleeping in the wild. And in all probability, in their bed at home.

Feeling his arm around her, holding her close, wonder filled her. She hadn't considered what it would be like to be in bed with a man. Her thoughts had never gone in that direction with Prescott. Theirs was quite a formal relationship.

Her father and mother seldom showed each other outward affection. Sarah had supposed that was just the way couples treated each other in upper crust society.

But now, she wondered what it would be like to be in bed with a man. Together. Sleeping. Almost she could breathe in rhythm with him. Two souls, acting as one. Was that how marriage was?

Would she have this with Prescott? *Could* she?

If this was a foretaste of what she would have with him, she didn't want to wait another year or two to marry. She should be there to help and encourage him when he came home from a hard day in the law office. And at night, be in bed to comfort and love him.

Doubt surfaced. But would she have this with Prescott? She didn't know...she honestly didn't know.

She stared into the dark at the sheltering pines. At the opening by their feet a dim light shined—probably the moon glowing somewhere in the sky.

What should she do? Should she wake Mr. Harding and ask him to turn over so they would be once again back to back?

Somehow she felt that would be small of her. He was oblivious—and they were both warmer—his shoulder shielding hers, his arm around her, his legs bent to cup hers.

After all, she was the only one awake who might be bothered. Well, if it was only she...in the end she decided to wait. Maybe he would change position on his own while he slept. Meanwhile, she wouldn't let it affect her. She would go back to sleep as if nothing was unusual.

For a few moments, she gave herself up to enjoying the closeness, the warmth, the feeling of protection. She felt herself relax and was drifting off to sleep when suddenly, she felt him jerk. Startle. Long moments passed. She waited for any little movement he might make. His breathing had changed. It was no longer slow and even.

Then she felt his muscles tense. His arm carefully lifted off her. Next, his shoulder backed away. Slowly, slowly, she felt his legs distance themselves from hers. And then in small increments he backed his body away.

When there was enough room, he gingerly turned over. Through this—this ordeal—she had been lying as still as possible, breathing regularly, not letting him suspect she was awake.

She wouldn't embarrass him for the world. He had meant nothing by it; she instinctively knew it was his wife he was holding. If she let him realize she was awake, it would embarrass them both. By pretending sleep, she would avoid all that.

Once again they were back to back, except now he had put space between them. Cold was creeping in. Hadn't she heard somewhere that just before dawn the air was its coldest? She was getting *cold*.

He had gone too far. Besides, as far as he knew, she had been asleep this whole time, unaware of what had happened.

She started to feel upset and was afraid she'd never get back to sleep. She felt her comfort gone.

It came to her then—she would remain perfectly still for another minute, yawn and then settle herself back against him. All while supposedly *sleeping*.

In the next minute she gently settled against him, and in large measure, her comfort returned.

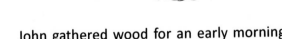

John gathered wood for an early morning fire. He'd left Sarah sleeping with only a small part of her face exposed. She had been cold during the night. He'd been cold, too. Was that why he'd found himself embracing her, just the way he'd done with Rosalind? That must be it. While sleeping he must have instinctively sought to protect and give warmth, just like he always did with his wife. He felt his face flush. It was good Sarah hadn't awoken, that only he knew about this. That way, there was no compromise to herself or to their relationship as pastor and parishioner.

Now, he would build a fire and make coffee. He could do with some of Hannah's brew. That woman. She still wouldn't tell her secret of making it.

He looked up at the sky; it would warm later this morning.

This day! He glanced at the makeshift shelter. He felt like a boy again. He stretched his arms with the wonder, with the glory of this sparkling morning. He wondered if Sarah would feel the same way—once she got moving and warmed up.

But he would move quietly, get a good fire going. He wanted to make things nice for her, so that after the horror of yesterday she would have the pleasant memory of this day. Looking over at her form beneath the slicker, he could hardly realize she was here or admit his own particular gladness to have her near.

Yes, he would do something beautiful for her, for she appreciated beauty. That he had discovered early on. He would not get in the way of her relationship with Prescott. No. He would merely show her something beautiful. And help her to see God in it. Surely, Prescott would not object to that.

Sarah smelled coffee. The air was still cold, and she supposed she should get moving. Could she take the blanket with her to the fire?

Then self-respect kicked in. She was a lady, not a child. Even if it was cold, she could still look presentable at the campfire before setting out on the trail.

She heard singing. A bass voice. Mr. Harding! She sat up.

To hear a man sing—it felt both comforting and inspiring in these wilds. How protected she felt with such a man, and how beautiful to hear music.

When she poked her head outside the lean-to and saw him, she asked, "What song was that?"

"A hymn." He smiled and obliged her with the opening words, "*When morning gilds the skies, my heart awakening cries. May Jesus Christ be praised.*"

"I like that part about morning gilding the skies." She got to her knees and slowly rose. "I'm glad someone else feels that way about mornings. It's the best part of the day. Often I'll rise before anyone else in the Garland household and look to the mountains. From our front porch, I can see Pikes Peak in the early morning sun. It's glorious."

"Often, I sing in the morning," John said. "That fragment I just sang—well, this is one of my favorite verses:

Let earth's wide circle round
In joyful notes resound:
May Jesus Christ be praised.

Let air and sea and sky,
From depth to height, reply:
May Jesus Christ be praised."

"That's beautiful."

"It's an old German poem, adopted for a hymn."

He added a few sticks to the fire. "Just to see the beauty of a new day—it reminds me of a verse in the book of Revelation where Jesus said, 'I am the root and the offspring of David, and the bright and morning star.'"

She stepped away from the bed of pine boughs. "I love to see the early morning sky, especially with its tint of orange or pink just as the sun breaks the horizon. Of course," she smiled, "sometimes in the summer the sunrise is too early even for me." She looked up at him brightly. "Then as winter is turning to spring, I like to see the rising sun move north through the tree trunks. I like to mark its progress day by day."

She stretched at the entrance to the shelter, then bent over to straighten and brush her skirt. "My uncle laughs at me. He

135

calls me his peacock and doesn't understand how I can get up so early. He thinks a preening bird like myself would loll in bed till later in the morning." She smiled. "Well, I've fooled him. My uncle thinks he knows me so well because he bounced me on his knee when I was young. But I usually have a few surprises up my sleeve."

"I'm sure you do." He stood before her, looking at her with a glad light in his eyes. Something warmed in her and then she looked down. Obviously, she had pleased him. And she felt pleased. He was such an *unusual* man. Things around him often reminded him of God.

Yet she had also seen him very human, very much so when fighting that Indian yesterday. He wasn't turning the other cheek then. Had fought in earnest. What would have happened if that chief hadn't stopped them?

But he had. What high regard John stood in that Indian's mind.

She glanced up again at the man who stood before her. Would John have killed that brave? What kind of a man was he really? He puzzled her.

Later as John saddled the horses, he looked over his mount and said, "I thought we'd veer off from this canyon trail a little. Go part way up a mountain, just a short distance—to a bench on its far side."

"A bench? A place to sit out here?" Her eyes showed disbelief.

He laughed. "That's a geographical term. A bench is a shelf-like area with steep slopes above and below. It can be very narrow on the side of a hill or mountain, or it can be large enough for a good sized dwelling with enough land for outbuildings and horses."

"Oh! Is there something special about this one?"

"The view. I'd like to show it to you."

"I see." She felt a blush start up from her throat. She hardly knew why.

CHAPTER 15

John looked at the elevation ahead, then back at Sarah. "This will be steep going for a ways. This ghost of a trail leads up to that bench I talked about. Just follow closely behind. Half way there, we'll rest." This seemed farther than he remembered; he didn't want Sarah to become overly tired.

He'd calculated the extra time this side trip would take; there should be enough for them to arrive at the post before dark. From the vantage point of the bench, a person could see far to the west, a vast valley with mountain ranges rising from it. He wanted her to see it.

Beauty. He thought about the two women uppermost in his mind. Sarah had an innate appreciation and love of beauty. And Rosalind. She had been more practical at heart, and beauty was something he'd had to teach her to look for. But Rosalind had certainly worked at his side, helping him with the ministry. She had been just the right companion, the wife he loved and needed for the early work in this developing country. And he loved the Lord for bringing her to him.

Then she'd died. For what reason? Her death had been incomprehensible. She had been such a help to him.

But even through his grief, John believed God was somehow working this all out.

Now he saw something else. Sarah, this other woman uppermost in his mind—she'd brought him back into Society. To the Palmers and the Bells. He had drifted away from them, busy with his church.

Sarah had a way of relating to people like the Palmers and Bells that was second nature. A question fleetingly presented itself: could she ever make a place for herself in Colorado Springs—this western town unlike any other? With the Palmers' vision and with the Bells' help, it was already a place for Society to visit, some to stay and make a home. Could Sarah be comfortable in a place like this?

He turned in the saddle to see how she was faring. She looked to be doing well, but he must be careful not to overdo on this trip. She'd had a hard day yesterday.

His mind went back to his question—could she ever be comfortable here in the west?

But why was he asking such a thing? She would be returning to Philadelphia. Back to a man who was building a legal practice so that when she married him, she could take her place in the society for which she had been reared.

Marriage to that Prescott fellow...he turned his mind away from what was becoming an increasingly unpalatable thought.

Well, he would enjoy this day with her. Accept it as a gift from God—and leave it there.

Nearing the mountain bench, John pulled in the reins. His horse had pricked up his ears. Immediately, John was on his guard. He looked back at Sarah, held a finger to his lips and dismounted. As he came alongside her horse, he reached into an inner pocket of his coat and held out a derringer. He said in an undertone, "There's something I need to investigate up ahead. Can you use this?"

"Why, yes." Her voice was almost a whisper. "My uncle took us shooting."

"Keep this gun ready. And stay here while I go ahead."

Quietly, he stepped back into the saddle and started up the trail. A rock let loose on the path and bounced noisily down the incline. Inwardly, he cringed.

Coming to the last corner before the bench, he edged his way around it.

A camp. In that moment he saw a fire still smoldering, but no one nearby. The better part of caution, he quickly guided his horse behind some bushes.

No one seemed to be around, but he couldn't be sure with all the boulders. The messy campsite and its silence made him uneasy. He moved forward, keeping to cover as much as possible. Whoever camped here either knew he was coming and hid, or else they were away. Hunting? But to leave a campsite like that—a fire still burning and dirty clothes and pots scattered about. He saw a whiskey bottle and a few Indian knives piled up. Suddenly, he wondered if he'd stumbled on—

A shot whizzed past his ear. He sprang off his horse, keeping the animal between him and the direction of the shot. Another bullet spit the ground near him, and he lunged behind a boulder to his left. Then a shot ricocheted off the rock and hit his hat. His blood raced as he gripped his gun. Memories of the war came back with a rush.

This person was shooting to kill. But why, and who was it?

From behind the boulder, he surveyed the area as best he could. Another large rock was off to his left and up a ways. He could see part of the camp. Two saddles. It would stand to reason one of the men would try to circle around and pick him off while the other held him at this position.

He wouldn't stay to be pinned down. Lowering into a crouch, he got off a quick shot from the right side of the boulder, then darted to the one on the left. A shot rang out, but hit only the dust near his feet.

Scanning the area beyond the boulder, he saw the rumps of two horses. They were tethered on a plot of grass some distance from the edge of the bench. They looked familiar.

Ah, his two *old friends*. His jaw clenched. They were out to get him this time. Hob and Jeb usually liked to talk things up a bit to rile him. But this time they were quiet. This gave him pause. It looked like they were cold-bloodedly setting about their objective.

And he had Sarah to think about. If they got him, what would they do to Sarah? He set his jaw harder. They wouldn't have the chance.

John stole to the left side of the boulder. He had a good bit of room before the edge of the bench. It dropped to a steep incline, more like a cliff. Stepping quietly back, he raised his gun and carefully peered around the boulder to the right. If he could get off a shot—

Stones crunched under a boot. One brother was running to a rock near the horses. John quickly drilled a bullet at him. Jeb yelped and dove for cover.

That instant another gun barked but John had instinctively dropped, the bullet whizzing past his ear. If he'd been a little slower—

He'd scored on Jeb, but where, he wasn't sure. The men's horses weren't far away, and Jeb was behind the rock near them. Hob—John was sure he was hiding behind that large boulder to his right front. Before John gave himself more time to think, he bolted to the horses to use them as cover, and saw not ten feet away, Jeb hunched behind the large rock, holding his shoulder.

Jeb startled and groped for his gun with his good hand, but John rushed him, pistol whipping the hand just closing over the gun. Seizing the firearm, John threw it back in the direction he'd just come. "Don't try anything," he warned Jeb in a low voice. He crouched behind the big rock and raising his gun, pointed it at the boulder he felt sure Hob was hiding behind.

A gun came into view, and John fired, nicking the gun so that it twisted away. A quick second shot dropped the gun from Hob's hand, and John rushed from behind the boulder to press his advantage.

A movement at the trail caught his eye. Sarah? Just as John saw Hob swing up a rifle, he struck Hob running.

———— ◦◦◦◦◦ ————

`Sarah saw John's gun fly as both men sprawled to the ground. She slid off her horse, gripping the derringer. Had two men fired at John? She wasn't sure and scrambled for cover behind a large rock. Catching her breath, she could hear men grunting and scrabbling around in the dirt.

She must help John. She ran to another rock, looked around it, and now saw a third man standing over the two wrestling men. He had a rifle in his hand and was trying to train it on John, favoring his left shoulder.

Sarah came out from behind the boulder, pointing the derringer. "Drop that rifle!" She moved in quickly, setting a cold, hard look on her face. "I said put that rifle down!" Her tone of voice brooked no argument. When the man didn't move fast enough, she shouted, "Now!"

"Wait! My shoulder is injured! I'll set it down!" The man slipped the rifle to the ground then raised his hand, the other at half-mast. "This is all I can do with the left. Took a bullet in the shoulder."

"Stand and be quiet!"

"Yes, Ma'am!"

Both opponents were now on their feet. John caught a wild right that glanced off his jaw. He quickly reset himself and hit a left to Hob's face, then jabbed two more in quick succession. The man reeled back, but swiftly regained his footing. As John lunged forward, the man feinted to one side and jerked up his leg and kicking hard, sent John to the ground near the precipice. Sarah felt herself jerk with fear.

Hob charged John, meaning to pounce on top, but John thrust up his legs, catching the man on the belly. For a few seconds he was poised over John, then John neatly lifted him over his head and onto the ground. Hitting the dirt, the man rolled. And rolled right over the precipice, yelling. Sarah stared, unbelieving.

Jeb swore and rushed to the spot where his brother had disappeared. John jerked up to a sitting position and stumbled to the edge of the cliff.

Both men craned to see below.

Sarah's stomach clenched. Stunned, she still gripped the gun.

Jeb just stared over the cliff. "Hob! Hob!" he called, his voice shaking.

John shouted, "Hob, can you hear me?"

Sarah thought she heard a faint groan. She, too, stepped near the edge and peering over, saw dirt punctuated with rock, scrub, an occasional tree. No one could be seen. Looking down made her dizzy, so she backed away.

John kept scanning the area below. "I see him! I think he's alive." He looked around. "Sarah!" Saw her holding the gun. "Good! Keep that on Jeb."

He turned to the brother, jerking his head in the direction where the two men had slept. "Which horse is yours? And which saddle?"

"The roan and the darker saddle."

John strode to the campfire, lifted the saddle and walked to Jeb's horse. He saddled it and then securely tied one end of Jeb's rope around the pommel, forming a lasso at the other end.

"Jeb, I'm going to need your help to rescue your brother."

"I can't go down there, not with my shoulder."

"Not asking you to. I'm going down. You hold your horse. Let's first back him up." He took the roan by the bridle and led him to the trail's entrance. "I hope this will do it. Come here."

Jeb walked over.

"Here, use your good arm to hold onto the pommel." John circled the lasso around his chest and tightened it. Stay here and keep the rope tight. I'm going to let myself over the edge. When I say 'ready,' slowly move the horse forward, letting me down. Listen for further instructions."

Sarah watched as John let himself over the edge, holding onto the taut rope. "Ready!" he shouted.

Jeb nudged his horse slowly forward, talking quietly to her. Little by little the distance to the cliff shortened.

Sarah felt impelled to approach the precipice and look down. She saw John gripping the rope, slowly stepping backward down the steep incline. She said a silent prayer. When the horse had just about reached the rim John called out, "That's it! I have him."

Jeb yelled. "We're about to the edge."

"Okay!" John shouted. "Hold it there. Wait till I tell you what to do."

All was quiet. The sun had risen to near noon. The air was clear, and Sarah could see across the valley to the distant mountains. *Strange, so lovely, yet all this hatred here.*

John was talking. Sarah's attention turned back to him, trying to hear what he was saying. Just barely, his voice carried up the rocky incline. He asked if Hob could hear him. Sarah didn't hear a response, but then John talked as if the man could. "Let's try to make it, Hob. I'll put this lasso under your arms." Silence. "Hob, try! This rope is tied to your brother's horse; he's ready to lift you to camp." Sarah heard a murmur.

There was a long silence before John shouted up, "Jeb, your brother doesn't think he's going to make it. I'm going to pray with him."

Sarah strained to hear. Now John's voice was low and comforting. He was praying so quietly she couldn't make out the words. But his voice broke, then she heard a quiet *Amen*. Somehow, she felt comforted.

After a minute of silence, Jeb called out, "What's happening, Preacher? How's my brother?"

"He's gone, Jeb. Give me a minute and I'll send him up. I need to tie him securely, then you can back up the horse."

Hob's body was raised slowly, then finally dragged over the edge. Jeb motioned to Sarah, "Come here, Ma'am." He nodded at the gun. "I won't do nothin' bad. You hold my horse while I get my brother, then we'll let the rope down for the preacher."

Sarah walked to Jeb and his horse. The gun was feeling cumbersome and she tried to steady it on Jeb, even as she held the horse.

After John had been hoisted up, she lowered the gun with relief. John asked what Jeb wanted done with the body. Jeb choked back a sob. "It should have been me going over that edge."

They waited while Jeb collected himself. He wiped his face with the back of his good hand. "Can't do much with my arm. Best bury him here. Would you have another prayer for my brother?"

John nodded assent.

"I appreciate you risking your life, going down there, especially after we tried..."

"That's okay. Here, let me look at that arm."

A couple hours later, Jeb's shoulder patched and the body buried, Jeb announced he wanted to go south to Cañon City.

John and Sarah helped him pack up camp.

"Jeb, you go on now. Miss Whittington and I will stay a little longer."

After Jeb had ridden out of sight, Sarah looked at John. "Shouldn't he have been brought to a sheriff? Not that I was eager to spend more time with him."

"Ordinarily, yes. But he's suffered enough, losing his brother. Besides, I figure you're my first responsibility. You need to get back to the trading post. Your friends will be worried." His eyes flashed a smile. "Besides, I don't cotton to the idea of spending more time with Jeb either. And say, you surprised me. For an Easterner, you handled yourself pretty well."

"Fortunately, I always seem to be able to carry through in an emergency. But I can't guarantee what happens later."

John looked at her closely. "I can see you're tired." Then a full-blown grin came over his features. "Not saying anything about myself, of course. It's not every day I have a shoot-out, climb down a cliff to perform a rescue, and dig a hole for a burial."

John walked to his horse to retrieve the blanket. "Before heading down the trail, we both need to rest. We'll set ourselves over there in front of a boulder and enjoy that view I talked about."

"Can we make it back tonight or...." Sarah's voice trailed off.

"It'll be after dark, but we'll make it." He took her arm and led her some distance from camp to the far end of the bench. "Now, just look west...over the valley to those mountain ranges. *This* is what I wanted you to see."

CHAPTER 16

They stood some moments, looking over the rolling hills which led to a vast open valley with majestic mountains rising from it. Then John folded the blanket and placed it near a boulder and helped Sarah sit. He drew himself down beside her.

"Thank you," she whispered. "This is all so beautiful."

He'd hardly heard what she said before her shoulders started to quiver. The reaction was settling in. Another storm was coming.

"You've been through a lot," he said softly. She shook harder, and he put an arm around her. She leaned toward him, and he steeled himself to hold her protectively without going further in his thoughts. When she started to heave, he reached out his other arm to steady her. "There, let it all come out."

Her head fell, resting against his neck. *The second time in two days.* Crying, she huddled against him.

He could have spared her this if he'd just taken her straight back to the post. Mentally, he kicked himself for being a fool, but he'd wanted to show this to her. He felt worn down himself, and for a few moments his lowered face rested on top of her head, the comforter needing comfort.

Her sobs began to quiet, then started up again.

At last, it seemed she'd finished and she let out a huge sigh. But her cheek nestled against his neck. The tight figure in his arms began to relax. Finally, her body softened, alerting him to her womanliness.

He was smack in the middle of temptation before he realized it. For a few seconds he closed his eyes and stared it in the face. He wanted to hold this woman for as long as she would let him. For some moments longer, his arms encircled her—then he looked up to the heavens.

God! He shouted silently.

But no assurance came to him other than the fact that he had come to rescue her, not to complicate her life. She belonged to another world and another man. He had to keep reminding himself he was just her shepherd, rendering help in time of need.

He purposely loosened his hold and encouraged her to move away from him. "Do you feel better now?"

"I think so. All this fighting and killing is so completely outside my experience. First the Indians and now this."

They sat without speaking. A breeze was blowing from the west. Then he said, "I'm sorry you had to go through this last. I brought you up here to see this beauty, to give you something to think about besides what you went through yesterday. Hob and Jeb...if I'd had any thought they were here, I'd never have brought you."

"I know that." She was silent for a few moments, then asked, "But why did they want to kill you?"

An exasperated sigh punctuated his next words. "Jeb and Hob have been selling whiskey to the Indians for years, and I've tried to stop them. At first I talked with them. That didn't work. I exerted more and more pressure. Finally, I roughed them up and told them to leave the country."

"But they didn't."

"Nope." He drew up one long leg, clasped his hands around the knee. "They continued to do just what they wanted, no matter how it affected others. The Indians provided a ready market, and if whiskey impaired the Indians' judgment toward white settlers—that was just too bad."

"And you got in their way?"

"Yes. I've suspected for some time they were spoiling for a fight or something worse. I didn't know until today—how much worse. One thing is almost sure, though. With that pile of Indian knives I saw, and the fact those two men had been selling whiskey, pieces of this puzzle have been falling into place."

"I can't imagine men being that bad."

"Oh, I'm sure they didn't start out that way. At first, they just wanted some extra money, some fun, some thrills. Then they got set on doing things their own way. They believed a lie, the lie the devil told them. Whenever I spoke of God to them, they replied that He was some kind of a killjoy."

Sarah smiled sheepishly. "I have to admit, I've thought that."

"Well, I think most of us have, at one time or another. We doubt God and go our own way. There's a verse in the Bible. 'All we like sheep have gone astray; we have turned everyone to his own way...'" He looked at Sarah. "And you know what? Sheep are incredibly dumb. Left to themselves they lose their way and get into all kinds of trouble. That's why sheep need a shepherd."

She looked up at him. "Just like people?"

"Yes." He smiled back at her, stretching out his leg. "There's a reason Psalm 23 is a favorite of so many."

"'The Lord is my shepherd...'" she said quietly. "You know, you were like a shepherd to Hob—risking your life to rescue him."

"I tried. I'm just grateful he prayed at the end—asking forgiveness. Sometimes a person has to hit bottom before he realizes his need of God. That's where Jesus the Good Shepherd comes in...our Savior."

Gently, he reached over and covered her hand. "And as a minister, that's where I also come in. I'm called an under shepherd. I came to rescue this lamb from danger."

He squeezed her hand, then let it go. "And now I want you, want us—to rest. Feast our eyes on that vast plateau and the grand mountains. It's a gift from God."

They rode downward from the bench, the horses carefully picking their way on the faint trail. At its bottom, the country was still rough, rocky with scrub bushes and clumps of trees, but the riding was easier. After a couple of hours in the saddle John held up his hand, signaling them to stop. "This is a good place with plenty of water for ourselves and the horses. I'll build a fire for coffee and supper. We won't stay long, but we need nourishment and a little rest. There's a rather long ride ahead, but after the next pass it should be fairly easy going."

"While you build the fire," Sarah said, "I'll walk to the stream to get water for coffee."

"All right. But be careful."

John surreptitiously watched her as she held the coffee pot in one hand and her riding skirt in the other, gingerly stepping from rock to rock. She collected the water and triumphantly turned around when, unexpectedly, a stone rolled under her foot. "Oh-h-h!" she cried out. He saw her fall, tenaciously holding onto the coffee pot until she hit the ground.

John ran. He found Sarah on her elbows, trembling with pain. He grasped her arm. "Hold on! Where does it hurt?"

"My ankle," she burst out, her head bent. She had barely gotten out the words.

"Which one?"

"My right." She gritted her teeth, looking faint.

"Breathe deeply, Sarah. Here, grip my hand."

After a minute, he saw she was past the first severe pain. "That shoe must come off, and your ankle needs to soak in the stream. The cold water will keep down the swelling."

"No-o-o." She talked with effort. "I can't do that."

"I'll help you. Lie down now and straighten your leg. I'll take your shoe off as gently as I can."

"No! Please!"

She was so adamant, he sat back on his haunches.

"I need to lie here and get my breath. Please!" she begged. "Go water the horses. Afterward we can think what to do."

"That shoe needs to come off as soon as possible." He had judged her as pretty game—the way she'd handled herself with the Indians and all. Now he was at a loss. "Is it the cold water? I know it won't be pleasant, but believe me, it's for the best."

She was still a few moments, eyes closed. Then she seemed to come to a decision. "All right. But I can get my own shoe off. If you'll just go back to the horses—and bring the blanket so that I can dry my foot after I've soaked it."

"Bending over to unbutton your shoe will only aggravate the pain." He looked at her. "You know, this is no time to be prudish. You need help."

"Please! If you'll just get the blanket—I can do it myself."

Why had she become so...stubborn? But when he saw her pinched face, he softened. "All right."

He touched her shoulder, trying to give a little comfort before he left to get the blanket. When he came back, he put it on the ground. "All right, I'll attend to the horses."

However when he returned, he saw she was white from the pain of bending over to unbutton her shoe. "Miss Whittington! I'm not taking *no* for an answer. Now lie down and let me handle this."

Without another word, she lay down, hiding her face in her crossed arms.

He lifted the skirt of her riding habit, pulling it out of the way and exposing her leg as little as possible. Gingerly, he unbuttoned the shoe. He felt her stiffen again and again each time her foot was moved. But she didn't cry out. He had to give her that.

Finally, after carefully loosening the shoe, he said, "Now grit your teeth while I take it off." He hated making her hurt, but it had to be done. She tensed and gave one sharp cry as the shoe came off. He let her rest a bit.

"Now I'm taking off your sock...or stocking. Don't worry. I've seen a woman's ankle before. Remember, I was married." He said it with levity, to put as light a face on things as possible.

He rolled down her stocking. As he did so, he felt her stiffen again. Then he saw it. A scar curved up her slender ankle around her shapely calf, and an unexpected feeling took hold of him. He didn't let himself look farther. He drew in a deep breath.

"I'm sorry, it's so ugly," she said. "I didn't want you to see it."

"It's not ugly. Not at all." If she only knew how seeing that serpentine scar curve around her calf affected him—

But her voice had brought him a measure of steadiness. He made himself concentrate on the job at hand and finished removing the stocking from her foot. "Now we're going to ease you to the stream." He helped her sit, then inch nearer to the water's edge. "I'm going to lower your ankle. Relax as much as possible." He supported her leg in both hands. "This will feel extremely cold, but just tell yourself it's good. Your ankle will be better in the long run."

He couldn't have been more professional, she thought, as afterward he wrapped her foot and ankle with strips of cloth he kept in his saddle bag for emergencies. Gently, yet firmly, he finished the task. He felt very much like her doctor at home.

"Now, rest while I take care of things. We'll have something to eat with coffee in no time. On second thought, I have some herbs wrapped in my saddle bag. One helps alleviate pain. I'll make you a tea out of it."

She watched him and her thoughts went back to what had just happened. Those moments with her ankle uncovered and the scar exposed had passed without much fuss. True, for a few seconds he had been very quiet, but he had assured her he hadn't found it ugly and then proceeded in a business-like manner. What a relief. She had always wondered how someone like him—a man—would react to her scar.

She wanted to be beautiful—for a man.

Of course, John Harding had a pastor's heart. He was compassionate. He'd seen a lot of suffering in the Civil War. Even had a scar himself. Maybe he was different from most men.

But what about Prescott? That was who worried her. Most of the time she didn't let herself think about it. Those times she did, she would think of some way to get around Prescott seeing that scar when he became her husband. On their wedding night—maybe the room would be dark. She could wear an extra-long nightgown and robe. Prescott might not even see her scar. Not for a long time. She might be able to manage it. It wasn't like husbands and wives were necessarily naked in front of each other, were they? Maybe she could make this a condition of their marriage. When they did have—relations—it would be in the dark.

Could she ask Mother about this? She was quite sure mother and father hardly ever—well—they were always so cordial. She was sure this extended to the bedroom as well.

She hoped Prescott would be much the same. He was so similar to her father, both were pleasant and somewhat distant. Well, Prescott was a *bit* warmer. Flirted a little. But he was always careful to treat her respectfully. Respect was a very real part of their relationship.

So why would he cross that line when married? He was careful and methodical in everything he did. Admirably so. She hadn't felt the least pressured by him.

Yes, maybe it was all to the good this ankle thing had happened with the minister. Breaking the ice of someone seeing her scar. She'd even feared Jean seeing it, because her cousin would never let a thing rest. Yes, it was a relief that Mr. Harding had treated it so matter-of-factly. Of course, that first awful silence when she was looking down at the dirt beneath her folded arms, she had wondered what he was thinking. But he had assured her he didn't find it dreadful at all. He understood about such things, treated it as nothing. That had been a relief.

Not that she would show it to anyone else. No! One man was enough. Yet, some edge of fear had been blunted.

Sarah watched John as he doused the fire and tightened the horses' cinches. He walked over to her. "Are you ready to leave?"

"Yes, I am."

He helped her stand on one foot and assisted her to the horse. "All right, take hold of the pommel and I'll lift you into the saddle." He laughed. "Now we'll see how strong I really am."

She grinned. "Or how heavy I am. I'll jump up as best I can."

"You do that," he encouraged. "I wouldn't want to be embarrassed not getting you up there."

He bent to place his hands on her waist and hoisted her up.

Once in the saddle, she sat straighter—to show him and herself she was all right. The herbal tea he had given her helped with the pain.

An hour later they rode over the pass without much trouble, but she could tell she tired more easily. It had been a long, strenuous day. Fighting those two brothers and now her ankle.

They entered a plain of sorts, a high plateau he called it. Pikes Peak was ahead, off to the right. And sunset was coming. John bade her stop. "Look! The next few minutes the Peak will redden. I'm not often this way, so I'm glad we can see it."

It felt good sitting quietly in the saddle as she looked at the mountain. It began to flame. "Beautiful—such fire!" The exclamation burst out of her. The scene warmed and energized her soul.

"That fiery beauty—it shows a little of the glory of God..." He sat relaxed in the saddle, gazing up at the mountain..."yes, the glory of God."

In that moment it struck Sarah how different John was from herself, how far above her. He knew God in a way she had never even considered. Was this because he was a minister?

As an artist, she felt deeply about the beauty spread out before them. These feelings about this scene, about the west, would be difficult to capture in paint. It would be a struggle to do so. Yet, if she could put her feelings on canvas, oh, how she'd love to share this with others.

They watched a few minutes longer. "We best move on," he said. "This light will last a bit longer to make traveling easier, but we've some miles ahead. We can continue to glance at the mountain while riding."

"No wonder the Indians love that mountain. I think I love it, too."

He looked back, his eyes glinting his approval. He didn't have to say anything. She knew he felt the same way about the mountain and its glory. On the subject of beauty, they had a wonderful, comfortable agreement.

It was almost dark when he encouraged, "We're on the last leg now." Suddenly he smiled. "I know *you're* on your last leg."

Responding to his sally, she said, "You, sir, are the most unfeeling man—to joke so." Actually, she mused, he was kindness itself in the gentle way he treated her, then with humor helped her take things more lightheartedly. She added,

"Although, you *have* been rather handy— rescuing me from the Indians, fighting Jeb and Hob, doctoring my ankle, and now bringing me back to the post." She couldn't help adding, "I might consider taking you along on my next trip out in the wilderness."

"Do that," he said lightly. Then he laughed. "You flatter me. I'm surprised you'd even consider having me along—after that Jeb and Hob incident *I* got us into."

A mile or so farther, her injured leg began to ache dreadfully. Her other leg didn't feel so well either. All of her, in fact, felt rather unwell. Finally she asked, "How much longer do you think?"

"If we keep on at the present rate an hour, maybe an hour and a half. Are you very tired? Should we get down and rest?"

She was quiet a long moment. "I can make it a little farther."

She put off stopping, because deep down she wanted it so much. Not only because she was tired, but because she wanted to feel him helping her. Wanted to feel his strength as he lifted her from the saddle. Had begun to yearn for it.

She wanted his arms around her. Longed for them.

Suddenly she was confused. She was engaged, or as good as engaged, to Prescott. Why was she yearning for this other man to hold her?

She couldn't answer that.

Well, she would hold off on stopping until they reached the trading post.

But feeling the rhythm of the horse beneath her, a rhythm that had begun to be unbearably jarring, she wondered how much longer she could ride. Was it just yesterday morning they had left the trading post? It seemed an age ago.

Fifteen minutes later, she said, "I think I need to rest."

"Of course. It won't hurt the horses either. It's almost a full moon. It'll be easy to find a good spot."

When they stopped, he came to her horse and lifted his hands. She wearily swung her right leg over the pommel. He put his hands firmly on her waist. When she came down, her good leg crumpled under her and she fell against him. He quickly encircled her, holding her. Night sounds surrounded them. He finally asked, "Can you walk at all?"

"I'm not sure. Can you give me a few moments?"

For an answer, his hold tightened.

She was not sorry, not sorry at all that her leg had given way. She leaned into him, grateful for his strength. His compassion.

After a minute, he said quietly, "Why don't I carry you to that patch of grass. First, let me remove the blanket from behind my saddle."

Holding her with one arm, he reached for the blanket with the other. "Can you hold this?" As soon as she grasped the blanket, he lifted her and walked to a small plot of grass.

"Here," he said, gently putting her down on one foot. "Steady yourself against me while I spread the blanket." With the blanket unrolled, he helped her lower herself. "We'll take some time here, enough for you to feel at least somewhat refreshed." She could hear the gentleness in his voice. It warmed her very soul.

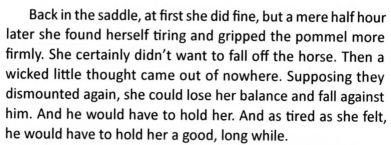

Back in the saddle, at first she did fine, but a mere half hour later she found herself tiring and gripped the pommel more firmly. She certainly didn't want to fall off the horse. Then a wicked little thought came out of nowhere. Supposing they dismounted again, she could lose her balance and fall against him. And he would have to hold her. And as tired as she felt, he would have to hold her a good, long while.

Then she felt her face go warm. She was ashamed of her thoughts. What did they say out west? Horsewhipped—that's what she should be. She should be *heartily* horsewhipped.

It was near eleven o'clock when they saw the lights of the post. She was more tired than she could say. This last while, she'd been hanging on by sheer grit.

When they reached the hitching post, all was quiet. No one came out to greet them. They were just beyond the light of the windows. He slung the reins of their horses over the rail and stepped to her horse's side. Truly, she was so fatigued she could hardly think. That last mile in the dark, with her slumping in the saddle, he had long since guided his horse to walk beside hers, telling her they were almost there, extending a hand to steady her.

When he lifted his arms to help her descend, her eyes blurred. She felt lightheaded, her strength gone. As he reached to grasp her waist, she suddenly felt herself falling. Felt his arms grasp and hold her. Then all went black.

——◦◦⟨◦⟩◦◦——

John clasped Sarah close. His thoughts flashed back the last couple miles of their journey when he had looked at her again and again. She had been very tired. He tried to gauge if they should stop to rest, wanted to do it, wanted to lengthen this time with just the two of them.

Maybe that's why he'd pushed a little harder than he should. He was trying not to give in to his desire to touch her again, to lift her down from the saddle and hold her.

So he made himself suffer, and maybe her, too, by staying the course. Forgoing another rest period when it might have been good for her.

Finally, though, he'd had to admit Sarah's need of help was more urgent than his need to deny himself. She had swayed, then righted herself from a dangerous lean. He mentally scourged himself for being self-centered—he'd not been looking out for her true welfare. From then on he'd helped hold her in the saddle.

157

When they arrived at the trading post, he could better see her face in the diffused light from the windows, and quickly dismounting, slung the reins over the hitching post, not taking time to tie them. He had turned to assist her, but her face looked so wan, so disoriented, he immediately raised his hands to help her, only to have her fall against him. He tightened his hold.

"Sarah," he said softly. No answer. She was a dead weight. He hoisted her up in his arms. Before taking a step toward the building, he bent over and whispered close to her ear, "Sarah." He could hear her regular breathing. She had fainted and now rested quietly. If he had the strength, he'd like to hold her forever.

He bent his head so that his cheek brushed hers. Let it rest there a moment. His lips touched it. Gently.

Then his lips touched hers. Gently, again. How soft they were.

Kissed them.

For a few moments his lips clung to hers. Desire flamed up.

He stopped, shaken. He made himself straighten, and stand some moments, mastering himself. Then he carried his precious burden to the door.

He knocked as best he could and Frank Castello opened it. Aunt Martha looked over his shoulder. She took one look at John, then the way her eyes dropped he knew she'd seen something. Were his feelings so obvious?

"Where is Miss Whittington's bed? She's had a hard day of riding, and she's fainted."

CHAPTER 17

Sarah awoke, but kept her eyes closed. How comfortable she felt—unlike last night when she'd been cold and the bed lumpy. Here, the air around her face was warmer. Where was she? She certainly wasn't in her own bed.

Finally, she opened her eyes to a room lined with canvas and adorned with copies of illustrated newspapers. The trading post hostelry. The last two days came back in a rush: the Indians absconding with her, sleeping outside in the make-shift lean-to, meeting up with those wild whiskey brothers. Stretching her leg, she remembered her sprained ankle and its scar—and John.

All the emotions of those incidents surged back. How frightened she'd been. Yet comforted, too.

Raising up on her elbow, she wondered where John was this morning. Almost, she was embarrassed to see him. He'd done so much for her. Last night she'd come out of her faint as he put her down on this bed—and looked up at him and mur-mured her thanks. His eyes had been dark, and—she couldn't put a word to it. Maybe his look had been that of a loving shepherd who was putting a favorite lamb down for the night. She had felt very much like a helpless lamb. But one deeply cared for, too.

She turned and looked at the bed next to hers. Jean had already arisen. Sarah stretched to better see out the window. The sun shone brightly, the morning advanced. Obviously, she'd had a good, long sleep, so there was no sense in wasting any more time.

She carefully lowered her injured leg over the edge of the bed. At the wall near the foot of their beds stood a basin of water and a towel. If she took it easy, she could hop over to the pitcher and basin. Nearby, a fresh dress hung on a hook. They'd let her sleep in the one she'd worn for two days. That was probably Jean's idea. For once, Sarah was thankful for the tomboy in her cousin, in not being overly concerned about clothing.

She hopped lightly, her ankle throbbing with each one. However, she was determined to keep going. Keeping her weight on one leg, she performed her ablutions quickly. This was not the morning to fuss. Besides, John had seen her in a much worse condition. She was eager to see him and discover how he fared. During the last of their trip, she'd hardly spoken because of fatigue, just grateful for the hand steadying her in the saddle, first on her arm, then later at her waist.

A quick knock sounded on the door and Jean bounded into the room. "You're up! Here, let me help." She placed her arm firmly around Sarah and half carried her to the one chair in the room. "I'll get your shoes, or rather one shoe. Mr. Harding thought you should leave your ankle wrapped for the day."

Next Jean helped her to the main gathering room. Sarah looked around to see the table cleared. "Is there still time for breakfast or should I wait until noon to eat?"

"Just another hour until lunch, I'd say." Jean nodded toward the coffee pot sitting on a stone in the fireplace. "Why don't you have a cup of coffee and tell me all about your adventures. My gracious, taken by Indians! When Sid and I finally returned to the post and told Mrs. Castello our predicament, she said everyone who could help was away—and with only one horse on the premises—I was fit to be tied. But Mrs.

Castello assured us if Mr. Harding said he'd do it better alone, he was up to the task.

"By the way, he said very little about how he rescued you, so you must tell me all about it."

Jean grabbed Sarah's arm. "And what did you do at night? Did you sleep with the Indians? I would have been petrified! And I'm the tomboy. With all you've been through, no wonder Mr. Harding said we should let you stay in bed this morning."

Gratitude surged through Sarah. So he was the one who had arranged for her extra sleep. She asked the question uppermost in her mind. "By the way, where is J—Mr. Harding? I hardly thanked him last night. Jean, I wouldn't be here but for him—"

"Oh, he left already. Got up early to ride to the Springs. Said he was a day late getting back to his duties."

"Oh..." Disappointment shot through Sarah. She'd counted on seeing him this morning—recounting—sharing some-thing of what they'd experienced. Telling the others about it *together*. Now—

"He said to tell you good-bye. He insisted I go in and check on you before he left. Said you'd been through a lot. That you were not to be awakened." Jean sighed. "I wish he was so con-cerned about me. No, I'm just good old Jean, somebody's sister or cousin, able to take care of myself. Maybe I should sprain my ankle." She held out her foot and wiggled it suggestively.

Then she leaned over and lowered her voice. "He carried you so close. How did it feel to be in his arms?" She looked at Sarah more carefully. "You're blushing—well! Some people have all the luck." She gave a dark look then rose quickly to get the coffee pot by the fire.

Sarah let her cousin rattle on while she poured coffee. She didn't feel particularly lucky at the moment. So he had asked about her. But then had left.

"There!" Jean handed her the cup. She had already put in cream and a little sugar. "Now, tell me *all* about your adventures."

"I've decided what to do," Aunt Martha, said, determination steeling her voice. "We're going back to Philadelphia as soon as possible. I'll not be responsible for you any longer. It's a wonder you weren't killed out there. Indians!"

Sarah stared at her aunt. Jean had let the cat out of the bag. She couldn't believe it—to leave so suddenly. Wouldn't they have a going-away party or something, she asked.

"Absolutely not! When you didn't return when expected, I was sick. Sick with worry. Never will I go through that again. And I certainly won't tell your parents every detail. They'd wonder about *me*. I've got *some* sense left. I'll let them know just enough as to why I decided not to stay the winter."

Aunt Martha leaned over to her niece. "Where did you say you slept that night? And where was the minister?"

"I didn't say, but it was perfectly all right. He looked after me like I was one of his flock."

"Did you find some ranch house to sleep in? There are ranches out there, aren't there?"

"I suppose there are, but the Indians took me so far back into the wild, I didn't see any. But Mr. Harding did so much for me, I wouldn't feel right—"

"You thanked him at the time, didn't you? And last night. Well, then. If you want to do more, send him a note or short letter. Or you can write to him on the train."

Her aunt was folding Sarah's clothing for the return trip to the Springs. "And maybe send him a gift from Philadelphia. He's originally from Philly, isn't he? That would be appropriate."

162

Sarah was too weary to argue with her aunt. And she felt she'd dodged a bullet in not telling Auntie how she had slept that night in the wilderness.

The day after their party returned to the Springs, Sarah felt her ankle was feeling better. The family doctor thought it a light sprain. It was good she'd applied cold to it so quickly, he said. And her aunt assured him that once on that train, Sarah could just sit and rest.

Back in her bedroom, trying to pack for the trip to Philly as best she could, Sarah felt rather confused. She wasn't back to her old self yet. To tell the truth, she was surprised by how much she wanted to see John, and here she was, all but engaged to another man. Maybe it would be better to leave right away.

Yes, she would be sure to write him on the train. Keep the tone warm, yet slightly impersonal. She didn't want to appear the fool—for would she actually have considered staying here to live, if there had been something between John and herself? He had been the perfect gentleman and he hadn't said anything—so there must have been nothing. And she had always planned on living in Philadelphia, being part of its society.

That was her place, surely, and marriage to Prescott was already expected. No, it would be foolish to consider anything else. The way she had started to think about the minister, it would be best to break it off now.

Yes, she would write a nice note, thanking him for all he'd done—and particularly mention his talks about God. That should make him feel as if he hadn't wasted his time with her.

John strode into the kitchen. The Garland buggy had just passed with Jean and Ben. He had stopped it and asked about Sarah, and Jean had told him Sarah had taken the train for parts east that morning. After that he had waved the two on, not interested in making any kind of conversation.

Sarah had left. He stood, stunned, in the middle of the kitchen. *Why hadn't he been told?*

"John, you look—can I do anything for you?"

"Excuse me, Hannah." He left her and marched down the short hall to the back study. He paused in the middle of the room, his hands clenched.

He couldn't stay in the house. He felt penned up.

Bursting through the back door, he charged over the lawn to the workshop in the corner of the lot, the place where he kept his tools, odds and ends. And wood.

He slammed the door behind him, feeling physically at odds with himself. He grabbed a slender board. Bending it fiercely, he broke it in two. Then seized a chunk of wood and hurled it into the corner.

How could she do this? Leave without telling him? With all they had gone through—had it meant *nothing* to her?

Suddenly he bent over, trying to ease the terrible pressure inside him. What was happening?

He didn't recognize himself. Where was the godly man he supposed himself to be? *Where?*

He fell to his knees on the rough-hewn floor, shoulders slumped, his arms wrapping around his lowered head. From somewhere deep in his gut he felt a horrible mass. The heaviness pushed up through his chest and came out, first in a groan, then in a great wounded cry. "Oh, God! God!"

Minutes passed. He remained on the floor. Knew, if pushed, he would do something terrible. He could take her body and—he could crush her to himself, crush and bruise her lips beneath his. He could do something he'd regret in years to come.

"Oh, God!"

At the moment, he knew he couldn't say or do anything good.

"Help me! *Help me!* I don't want to be this way."

Tears formed. His eyes ran awash with them. He didn't try to figure out the ins and outs of the situation. For once in his life he *just felt*.

After a while he quieted. A sigh burst from him, then he stayed immobile, silent, eyes closed.

Unexpectedly, Rosalind came to mind. So clear, it was as if she was standing beside him. She wore a favorite misty-blue dress, the one she chose for special occasions. The dress showed her trim figure, brought out the softness of her brown hair. She looked as gentle and sweet as he remembered her.

He opened his eyes to better see her. But, of course, she wasn't there.

She was gone. She had died so quickly he hadn't had a chance to say goodbye. When he had returned from that trip to the Utes, she was dead. The cholera had taken her before he even knew she was sick. His hands clenched. He'd felt sorrow, sometimes overwhelmingly so, and here it was back again—unexpected and sharp.

He thought all this sorrow and anger was about Sarah. It *was* about Sarah. Now he wondered, was it about Rosalind, too?

He slumped down on the cool floor. He felt bereft. Absolutely bereft.

An hour later, he heard a knock on the workshop door. "John!" It was Hannah. "You've a visitor. I put him in the parlor. Can you see him?"

His soul shrank from the encounter. Some moments passed before he said, "I'm coming, Hannah. In a minute."

He rubbed his face with his hands, wiping off the outward show of sorrow, willing the role of minister to take charge. He would *down* this confusion, this grief, and attend once again to another soul. But for once, he wanted someone to minister to him. How he needed it.

CHAPTER 18

John ushered the man from his congregation into his study. He felt well-nigh incapable of talking with him, praying with him, but he soldiered on. Afterward, accompanying him to the seldom used front door, he bade him farewell. Feeling completely drained, he now just wanted to be alone.

He walked to the kitchen to inform Hannah. As he entered, he heard her talking to someone at the back door. "You know he hasn't been himself tonight," Hannah said. "He's tired. Why don't I just give this to him."

Too late. The woman at the door saw him—Jane Tippet with a pie in her hands. Her eyes lit up, with more than an "I'm glad to see you" look. Maybe because he'd been thinking so much about Sarah, he saw something else in her eyes. The look of a woman—

Those few seconds decided him. He would *not* encourage this woman. This sweet, little mouse of a woman—because she could never be Sarah—beautiful, vibrant Sarah. No, he would rather do without a wife than substitute someone so sweet as Jane—and mousy. He was spoiled, he feared. Spoiled after spending those heart-stirring days and night with Sarah.

He made himself walk to the door and stand beside Hannah. "Thank you, Miss Tippet." He tried to inject warmth in his voice. "It's kind of you to bring me cakes and pies, but I do have a very capable housekeeper. She takes care of all my needs along that line." He forced a smile. "I'm going to make a suggestion now. In the future when you bake something, I want you to think of someone needy in our congregation and take it to him or her. Or to a family who doesn't have much, like Mr. Riley's. He was just here and can hardly support his family."

He reached out and took the pie from the little woman. "Thank you. Both Hannah and I will enjoy this. But from now on I'd like you to do as I suggested. You understand, don't you?"

Her eyes pleaded with him. "We're all so fond of you, Pastor. We want to do *something* for you."

"Yes—I appreciate that. But from now on I would like you to do what I've proposed. Please, Miss Tippet." He didn't want to hurt her, yet felt the need to be firm. To give her no hope whatsoever—of anything more between them.

She backed away from the door. He could see she was hurt, but felt he could say no more. He just wasn't up to comforting anyone else just now.

As soon as the woman left, Hannah looked at him strangely and said, "Well! You turned down one of the best bakers in the congregation, but you're finally wising up. That woman has had a thing for you the longest time." She threw up her hands in relief. "Let the blind man see."

John winced. "I have been rather blind, haven't I? If more should be said to her, would you be so kind and do it? I'm out of my depth." He tried to smile, but failed. "I need to get away for a while, Hannah. I need to think—and I need my old mother housekeeper to support me—with people like Miss Tippet. For now, I'm going to bed."

The next morning he woke with an overwhelming sense of loss. He couldn't face seeing anyone. When he went to breakfast, he quietly told Hannah he was leaving for the day. She asked him where he was going. He wasn't sure. Said he'd try to be back by nightfall. Could she pack him some food?

Surely she could. Her eyes showed her concern, her puzzlement, yet she didn't say more—for which he was grateful.

He rode south out of Colorado Springs; he didn't want to go anywhere near where he and Sarah had been. New terrain was what he needed. Maybe then he could think straight.

He passed Cheyenne Mountain and continued south, then suddenly turned his horse east onto the plains. Before him stretched mile after mile of wide open space. The ever-present prairie wind hit his face—a wind that dried out a body—yet now felt good, touching him more gently than a person ever could.

Clumps of gray green brush dotted the semiarid landscape. Much of the land supported grazing cattle. Here and there a little tilled land and trees surrounded a small ranch house, but mostly what he saw was wide, open sky over wide, open land. Just what he needed. He chose a route away from any dwelling, where no human would conceivably cross his path.

The simplicity of the land fit his frame of mind. Keeping his horse east on the plains, he refused to look back at the mountains where *it* had all happened. He felt numb inside and this open nothingness of the plain suited his outlook. Just now he didn't feel he could reach out to even God. And didn't have the energy to try.

Noontime he stopped near a creek fringed with juniper and cottonwood, trees that gave welcome shade from the hot sun. Maybe he'd rest here awhile. He was tired, tired to the marrow of his soul.

He led Flossie to the stream then staked her near clumps of grass. With his back against a tree, he took out a sandwich and chewed it absent-mindedly. He wasn't much hungry, yet he knew eating would be good for him. Besides, he had enough feeling in him not to upset Hannah by bringing back her food untouched.

After eating he thought he felt some better, yet was still so tired he could hardly think.

Being alone on the prairie soothed his soul. Here, he could be *nothing*, nothing to his congregation, nothing even to himself.

He spread his ground cover and blanket, lay on his back and placed his hat over his eyes to block the sun's reflected light. The darker shade beneath his hat was a relief. Closing his eyes, he saw nothing, felt nothing, and drifted off.

On awakening, he was stiff. Rarely had he slept so hard. He was in the same position as when he lay down, his hat still covering his face. With half-closed eyes he gazed into its brown closeness.

Nearby, Flossie stood quietly. If someone had approached, she would have let him know. A glimmer of thankfulness rose from his heart. Yes, he was thankful for a good horse. His mind wandered around that thought.

However, on becoming more awake, sorrow welled up. Underneath the dimly lit circle of his hat, his face scrunched up. Tears began, and suddenly, a cry burst out from him. His arms clutched his chest. He wanted to hold something, if only himself.

After a while, calming some, he turned over, positioning his knees under him. He pressed his forehead to the blanket. His hat had fallen off, so he placed the blanket over his head.

The wind gusted, billowing out the blanket, cooling his face.
I will never leave you, nor forsake you.

God could have spoken audibly, so clearly had the words of Scripture come to mind. He ran a hand over his eyes, then his cheeks, wet only a few moments ago but in this climate already dry.

How he needed God's help to figure out this mess. And to bring him comfort.

He tried to look the problem full in the face. What had been happening? Last night in his workshop, he had never felt so violent. Or felt so deeply. It scared him. Were his feelings for Sarah that intense? But Rosalind had come to mind, too. Somehow, his passionate reaction had been bound up in Rosalind as well.

He'd always been the one to comfort others, to take the words of Jesus to the grieving. Where were those words for himself?

But he didn't want words. He wanted flesh and blood. Here and now! He thought back to the night with Sarah. At first he thought it was Rosalind he held, so much he'd been between dreaming and waking. How wonderful to hold her, just as if she had never gone. Oh, her warmth and softness.

Then it slowly began to dawn on him this wasn't Rosalind. Still in a half dream state a full minute must have passed while he held the woman close. Then he realized it was Sarah. He was shocked at himself.

No! He would not compromise Sarah in any way. So he slowly turned over, and, to make perfectly clear he would keep his word to himself, he left a space between them.

He took the blanket from his head and looked up—stared across the arid miles at the prairie stretching beyond the stream. The emptiness of the wilderness mocked him. The aloneness he had craved these last hours now changed suddenly to a longing for this woman.

In the clear light of the bright prairie sun, he saw how much Sarah had come to mean to him. It had been building in him all these past weeks, his wanting her. But with his hardly realizing it. He had kept arguing she belonged to another, to a different world than he could ever give her.

However, in his heart of hearts, he now saw he had hoped something would work out between them. That what he felt for her, she also felt for him, and before she went back east, they would reach some kind of understanding. And she'd sever her tie to that lawyer.

But that wouldn't happen now. She was gone. Gone! And he'd never had a chance to say goodbye. Just like with Rosalind. His mouth had a bitter taste, a bitter taste that went right down to his heart. He felt bitter and angry. Angry for losing Rosalind so unexpectedly. Angry at Sarah for going away without saying goodbye. Angry at himself for not telling her how he felt. Angry at God—for the whole business.

He rose suddenly from where he'd been kneeling. All this thinking, where was it getting him? Somehow this didn't fit together. How could he feel so strongly about this woman and not have it work out? What was the purpose of it all?

He strode to the stream, splashed through it to the plain beyond and started running. He had to *run*.

"God! I want her!" He wanted his arms around her, feeling her close.

He thought back to the time he had steadied her as she fell from the horse, holding her. He imagined her arms encircling his neck.

How he craved her embrace.

But here on the plain, all he felt was air. Hot empty air.

He couldn't stand this emptiness. Shouting, he told God again what he wanted.

A protruding rock caught his foot, and he stumbled, falling to his knees. He stayed there staring at the prairie—for how long, he didn't know.

Overhead, something caught his eye. Up from behind had come an eagle...from the mountains. Gliding with the wind current, it dipped down, then soared up.

He gazed at the bird, remembering the eagles at Glen Eyrie that had given the place its name. Remembered the kindness and hospitality of General Palmer and his wife Queen. Something in him softened.

He stared at the soaring, majestic bird. Another living being out here on the lonely plain. Almost, he felt as if it had come for him.

In his mind's eye he could picture the beautiful design of its body and wings, the intricacy of its overlapping feathers. A creature wonderfully fashioned.

His thoughts went to God who had created such beauty and strength, this creature that reflected a little of God's own beauty and strength.

And how suited the eagle was to its place in the mountains. How wonderfully it mated and cared for its young. Surely, there was purpose in its existence.

And if there was design and purpose for the eagle, wouldn't there also be the same for other living things?

He sat without moving, his mind prompted into contemplating his own life. Didn't it follow there was purpose to his life? Purpose in his marriage to Rosalind? Purpose in meeting Sarah?

He had trusted before, could he not trust God now?

He *had* trusted God, all these years. But somehow Sarah's leaving had knifed open a wound. Ripped open the scabbed-over lesion of Rosalind's death, a wound which he now wondered had ever been fully healed.

What was he to do?

He looked over the prairie. "God, I need Your help!" If he couldn't resolve this, he feared his soul would become like that dry, scrubby landscape he saw before him.

Be still, and know that I am God.

I have loved you with an everlasting love. Words from Scripture came to mind as suddenly as the other had earlier.

Somehow, he knew God *did* love him, even though He had allowed these devastating partings. Knew, too, one of the results of Rosalind's dying was that he was a better minister. He now wept with those who wept. He had the heart of a pastor, whereas before he had just been merely sympathetic.

Rosalind...then John realized something else, knew in the deepest part of him he had questioned God for taking Rosalind and questioned the manner of her taking. Saw he had not let her go, not fully.

He looked up to the sky, beyond the few scattered clouds into its wide, blue expanse. What had he been wishing, that Rosalind come back to him? That she exchange the glories of heaven for the mixed joys and sorrows of this earth? How short-sighted and selfish of him.

No, he must let her go, completely.

He thought he'd been over the grief of his wife, yet when Sarah had left without a goodbye, the sorrow of Rosalind had resurrected with a sharpness he hadn't thought possible.

Staring up to the heavens, he imagined Rosalind there. He *would* let her go. Let go of any wanting, any thinking she should return.

He flung up his arms. "Rosalind! Stay! Stay there in that beautiful place!"

He sat back on his heels, letting the finality of what he said soak in.

Then what about Sarah?

Staring over the plains once again, he was silent. He didn't know about Sarah. Could he let her go, as he'd just done with Rosalind? His chest tightened just thinking of it.

Was there any hope for him and Sarah? Considering the way she had left without saying good-bye, probably not. She obviously didn't care in the same way he did. And once she returned to her life in Philadelphia, he would become a dim memory. And anything they'd had together would become part of that same memory.

It was a hard thought to feel so dismissed.

Jane Tippet came to mind. Now, he saw how careful he must be of her feelings, must make his position clear without hurting her unduly. He had learned that today, at least. He was thankful—as he always was when a new insight broke through.

Yet he still felt bereft. He was a man in mourning. He ached for Sarah. Could he trust God without knowing the end?

But God did love him—that he knew. He caught up Flossie's reins and mounted. Then he turned west to face the mountains.

CHAPTER 19

As the train engine blew off a last spurt of steam in the station, Sarah drew away from Prescott's embrace. How nice and solid he felt. These last days on the train she had wondered about their initial meeting, partly because she kept thinking back to Colorado. Her time in the mountains had confused her.

On the train she had ached for another's arms. She would never forget how they had comforted her after the Indian kidnapping, holding her as she wept after the whiskey brothers' fight and keeping her warm at night.

Something sweet and close had developed between John and herself. He was anyone's ideal of a man. But now she was hoping to share that same closeness with Prescott.

At this moment Prescott's sure arms had done much to restore her equilibrium. How like her father he was. He was good and right. And, surely, those other memories would fade with time.

Her mother stooped to grasp Sarah's satchel. "Dear, it's good to have you home. We've missed you. Your father was unable to come, occupied as he was with an important client. Of course, Prescott has been busy, too, so it was most thoughtful of him to accompany me."

"Yes, I've been working hard for us, for our future," Prescott said. "I want everything to be just right."

"Sarah, don't forget your paintings in baggage," Aunt Martha reminded.

"I won't. They were difficult enough to acquire."

Her mother glanced at Aunt Martha. "I'm surprised you came back East so early. I thought you were considering staying the winter."

"On thinking it over, with Sarah separated from Prescott, I thought it was time to come home. It was *time*," Aunt Martha repeated with decision.

Sarah turned to her mother. "I trusted Auntie's judgment in coming." For now that's all she'd say. The time didn't seem right to relate her encounter with the Indians. Besides, Auntie had warned her to tone it down when she did tell.

"Well, Martha, I trust your decision. Now, about the paintings. Prescott, would you see to them? Then afterward, you and Sarah can talk. And why don't you come to dinner tonight."

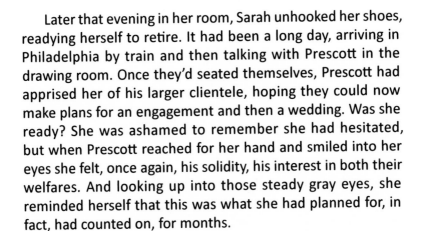

Later that evening in her room, Sarah unhooked her shoes, readying herself to retire. It had been a long day, arriving in Philadelphia by train and then talking with Prescott in the drawing room. Once they'd seated themselves, Prescott had apprised her of his larger clientele, hoping they could now make plans for an engagement and then a wedding. Was she ready? She was ashamed to remember she had hesitated, but when Prescott reached for her hand and smiled into her eyes she felt, once again, his solidity, his interest in both their welfares. And looking up into those steady gray eyes, she reminded herself that this was what she had planned for, in fact, had counted on, for months.

So she said "yes" to an engagement. They both thought Prescott could beard her father after dinner when the men habitually remained at table while the woman adjourned to the drawing room. And things had gone according to plan. After the men rejoined the ladies, both had wide smiles on their faces.

Sarah slipped down her stocking, feeling the scar on her right calf. A momentary twinge coursed through her. How would Prescott react to this, he who wanted everything *perfect*? She wanted to be beautiful—especially for her husband—but invariably she felt mortified by this one thing.

She sat up, gazing around her familiar bedroom, trying to take in these last hours, feeling a little dazed. Here she was, officially engaged. No ring rested on her finger, yet the thing had been settled.

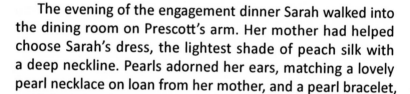

The evening of the engagement dinner Sarah walked into the dining room on Prescott's arm. Her mother had helped choose Sarah's dress, the lightest shade of peach silk with a deep neckline. Pearls adorned her ears, matching a lovely pearl necklace on loan from her mother, and a pearl bracelet, a gift from her fiancé.

Prescott was dressed in a well-cut tuxedo. Sarah supposed every man looked to best advantage in such attire.

He gazed down at her appreciatively. "Exquisite! You are flawless, Sarah." He pressed her hand resting lightly on his arm. She was glad she met with his approval, that he was proud of her. For wasn't that one of her roles, to be beautiful for him and to be a gracious hostess to his clients, adding to his standing in the world? She knew he would want his home life to be perfect. He would expect the perfection he now saw walking into her parents' dining room.

The table with its silver and china shone festively in the candle light. Extra candelabra had been brought in for the occasion, so that everything sparkled brilliantly. The bouquets of red roses stood out richly against the white damask dinner cloth. Mother had spared no expense for what Sarah knew would be a sumptuous meal. Once Father had given his blessing to the engagement, her mother had gone full steam ahead. Mother was in her element. She actually glowed, executing a flawless dinner party for an engagement she had long awaited. Members of the two families had been invited along with their closest friends. In all, eighteen were at table.

Prescott's mother came up to Sarah as the guests looked for their place cards. "My dear, you are absolutely lovely. You are perfect for my son. You'll be such an addition to our family." She leaned over and gave Sarah a quick embrace. "When would *you* like to get married? Have you thought about a month?" Her eyes gleamed in a conspiratory look. "Of course, we can talk about it later."

Prescott drew back Sarah's chair then stepped to his seat beside hers. This was the first time he had been placed next to her. He had previously been placed on the other side of the table. Sarah couldn't help thinking of Aunt Amelia's more casual seating arrangement where a favored guest such as Prescott would have been seated beside Sarah from the first.

Tonight, the apex of the seven course meal would be crown roast of pork, succulent sausages in its crown to flavor and moisten it. There would also be creamed potatoes and caramelized carrots. Looking around the lavish table with the guests resplendent in evening dress, Sarah knew this was the evening she had visualized when she had dreamed of her engagement dinner.

Yet, for some reason her mind flashed back to her time in the mountains—eating beef jerky with dry biscuits dipped in coffee. While far from tasty, the food had been celebratory in its own way. She had been rescued, and hadn't minded the food or the hard conditions. And she had felt cared for.

"So when is the wedding?" Prescott's aunt asked. She smiled at the couple situated at the center of the long, elaborately dressed table.

Sarah looked at Prescott, unsure what to say.

"Well, negotiations are underway," Prescott offered with a try at wry humor. He turned to Sarah. "We've discussed it, but as of yet, a date hasn't been set. I want everything perfect for her."

"Yes," his mother added. "We want to look for a nice house for them. Prescott's grandfather has set aside money. And, of course, my husband and I will do our part." She looked at Sarah's father, encouraging him to give some sign of support. However, he just smiled, saying nothing. For some reason, Sarah felt relieved. Everything was moving so quickly.

"Well, this will all work out," Sarah's mother assured everyone. She looked across the table at Prescott's mother. "We two mothers will put our heads together—for the parties, and later helping with the house and its furnishings." She turned to Prescott's father who sat on her right. "You men are so busy with your work, you don't have time for this type of thing anyway."

Prescott's father laughed. "Yes, but we'll need to make time to withdraw money from the bank, eh, Mr. Whittington?"

Everyone laughed, then talk drifted to other topics.

"What do you think of electricity coming to New York streets?" Prescott's father asked. "The powers that be say they'll have it by next year."

Mr. Whittington set down his glass. "When I see it, I'll believe it."

"Well, you know Philadelphia won't be far behind."

"That I *can* believe."

Sarah sat relaxed, enjoying the general flow of conversation, relieved it wasn't centered around the upcoming nuptials. But it wasn't long before Prescott's mother brought the conversation around to her. "Sarah, we're so proud of you.

An artist—and someone who has acquired paintings from the West. Did you have much success in purchasing art?

"I came away with five rather good paintings. Two for the Academy and three for a friend who owns a gallery. Of course, with the connections I acquired out West, I hope to obtain more western art in the future."

"You're an unusual lady," Prescott's father said. "I hope my son appreciates that. Will you return to your studies at the Pennsylvania Academy?"

Sarah hesitated just long enough for her father to intervene. "No. We've heard disturbing reports about Thomas Ekins, one of their instructors. So, we think it best Sarah settle down to running a household."

"I'll say Amen to that," Prescott said.

Prescott's cousin leaned over to whisper, "What about Thomas Ekins?"

Someone shushed him, saying in an undertone, "Too much nudity in the drawing classes."

"Furthermore," Sarah quickly picked up the conversational thread, "I obtained one interesting sketch of a Ute Indian. They're the principal Indians of the Colorado Rockies. Like most other tribes, they've been relegated to reservations. However, at times small groups of Utes still roam about, with government permission for hunting trips—but sometimes without."

"We've all heard about the noble savage," Prescott's mother said. "I suppose the sketch conveys that?"

"Noble? I think you've wrong there, Mother," Prescott said. "With what we've read in the papers, it's my opinion Indians who don't remain on their reservations should be shot. Surely you've heard about that Geronimo fellow loose in Arizona, terrorizing settlers—"

"And just think back to '76," his father interjected, "Custer and all his troops losing their lives at the Little Big Horn. I agree with you, Prescott. Indians need to be contained or killed off."

"Well," said Sarah's father, "it's always been the way of the world that the strongest wins—it's the practice of the conqueror. I maintain the West is a big place, too large for the number of Indians who roam it. They need to share it. Besides, people in the East dream of a better life, of making a new start out West."

"What do you think, Sarah?" Prescott's father asked. "After all, you lived there. You'd have an informed opinion."

Sarah glanced at Aunt Martha and caught her aunt's cautioning look. She'd been home almost three weeks and still hadn't said anything about her abduction by the Utes. How was she to ever tell Mother and Father now? And of course, her engagement party was not the place to do so.

Sarah smiled at her future father-in-law. "A minister friend of ours who brings medicine to the Utes, said Indians could be of two minds—either to be your friend or to take off your scalp. But above all, they are a people to be respected."

She chose her words carefully. "Many white settlers have lost their lives. But the Indians have lost their lands and the buffalo they've depended on for food, shelter and clothing. If you were them, wouldn't you fight back, too? The West was their home long before we arrived."

Sarah took another bite of food giving herself time to think. "The West can be both safe...and dangerous. One thing I will say, there are courageous people who make the place better and safer. One of them is Aunt and Uncle's pastor, John Harding."

"John Hardin!" Prescott's cousin exclaimed. "You can't be talking about the gunfighter—John Wesley Hardin?"

"No, it's John Hard*ing* and as I said, he's my aunt and uncle's minister—but he *is* good with a gun. He once fought an Indian." This last popped out of her without thinking. But as soon as the topic of the West had come up, she'd been wanting to talk about John.

"A fight with an Indian!"

Sarah hesitated. "Well, yes."

"Tell us about it!"

There were a few moments of silence with Sarah glancing at Aunt Martha, but the same young man urged her, "Go on! Please!"

Sarah shifted in her chair. "Well, it was back in the wilderness and this Indian—the leader of four braves—got into hand to hand combat with the minister. They fought with knives, slashing at each other. First, Mr. Harding sliced the Indian's face, then the Indian's knife caught the minister's shirt, ripping it open—the second time drawing blood. It was terrible!

"They jerked this way and that, trying to avoid each other's knives. Suddenly the minister stuck his knife down hard into the Indian's shoulder. Then before the fight could go any farther, a chief arrived, shouting them to stop."

"Why?" the cousin asked.

"As it turned out, the chief stopped the fight because he had a great respect for the minister. John Harding had brought medicine to the chief's tribe. In fact, one time he'd saved the life of the chief's daughter. But if that chief hadn't come, I'm afraid someone would have been killed."

Prescott's young cousin leaned forward, his eyes bright. "Wow! I wish I could have been there."

"No, you wouldn't have!" Sarah burst out. It flashed through her mind how brave John had been. The fight had been so fearful she hadn't allowed herself to dwell on it, all but blanking it from her memory since returning home.

"You sure know how to tell a story, just like you were there," the cousin exclaimed. "Was this person who witnessed it a friend of yours, or something?"

"Not a friend of mine—but—this lady had been captured by the Indians and saw it all."

"You're kidding! What else did she tell you?"

How could she relate the story without telling the truth about herself? She felt a blush rise up her throat.

"Please! Go on!"

Suddenly she made a decision. *This person would have to be someone else other than herself. She couldn't tell the truth, not without first telling her parents and Prescott. She just couldn't.*

"Well, this woman had been alone for a short time in the wilderness—her friends had gone off for a bit—and these four Indian braves came on her unexpectedly. They told her to get on her horse and come with them."

"Didn't she try to escape?"

"She didn't know the country. Also, the Indians were four strong, muscular young men who didn't particularly care whether they took her alive or"—Sarah paused—"took her scalp...."

The other guests had already left when Sarah led Prescott to the foyer. He stopped near the entrance door. "That was quite a story you told about that woman's abduction. You must have known this friend rather well for her to confide in you. Why didn't you tell us this before?"

Sarah felt guilty. Was Prescott looking at her closely, examining her like a lawyer? She felt her chest constrict. She wouldn't tell her fiancé anything more. She *couldn't.*

"It just never came up in conversation." She grasped his arm lightly. "There! I didn't realize I was such a good storyteller. And at our engagement party, too!" She made herself smile brightly. "But I don't want to talk about it anymore. After all, everything turned out fine."

"All right, my dear." He reached for the door knob to leave, then turned and drew her through the glassed door into the vestibule. "This gives us a measure of privacy," he said smiling. He took her shoulders and she suddenly realized he was going to kiss her as he lowered his head. Instinctively, she moved her face so that his lips touched her cheek instead. Then she buried her face into the neck of his coat.

"You're not ready for more?" he asked.

"No." Her voice was muffled, so she raised her head to look over his shoulder. "Not yet."

"All right. I can wait, as long as I know you are mine. The engagement dinner your parents gave us tonight was something I appreciated. My family did, too." He tightened his hands on her shoulders and held her away from him. "I'm working hard at the office. It won't be long before we can set the wedding date. I promise."

After Prescott left, Sarah stood for some moments in the vestibule, thinking back on their conversation. He had commented on the Indian abduction story. She had described it as someone *else's* story. But it was hers. *She* had been rescued. This was something she had pushed to the background of her mind, it being so outside her normal world. In fact, now that she had returned home, she could almost imagine it had never happened. But it had.

And John had rescued her. John! For a moment she visualized his tall form. Strong. Athletic. Fearsome, in a way, with that scar. Would Prescott ever do such a daring thing, be willing to fight to the death for her?

But to ask if Prescott would ever do the same was a bit unfair. Life in the East was so different from the West. Prescott said he was working hard for her. Practicing law had its own challenges. Building a practice was a large undertaking in itself. She shouldn't compare him with...but something stirred in her. Something strong and... fervent. She opened the glassed vestibule door, meaning to join her parents in the drawing room.

She felt restless. The whole evening was bearing down on her. She no longer felt the young, carefree girl she'd been before going west. There was a life beyond what she'd experienced here in Philadelphia. Life—and death. Beauty—and ugliness. In the polite society of Philadelphia she hadn't seen this.

She walked across the entrance hall to the drawing room, and then paused. She couldn't stay and make small talk with her parents. Her lack of gratitude toward John and what he had done now pressed down on her. She needed to be quiet, by herself, and think about what had happened while this realization was fresh. It couldn't be swept under the rug any longer. She would go to the drawing room and make her excuses. Then retire to her room upstairs.

CHAPTER 20

Sarah poked her head in the doorway of the morning room. At the table Mother and Aunt Martha were cozily ensconced next to each other, looking over the latest fashion magazines. When Sarah looked a question, her mother blithely said, "For the wedding, my dear. We want to be up-to-date on the latest styles."

"And, for once, I'm paying attention," Aunt Martha added. "I know I haven't been too modish in the past—but for your wedding, my dear, it's going to be different." She gave her niece a mischievous smile.

"We haven't set the date, yet," Sarah objected.

"It's never too early to start planning," her mother said. "Your wedding will be one of the social events of the season. I think we should start thinking of when it might take place. Let's see, it's fall now. Might it be as early as next summer or maybe the following spring? What do you think, dear?"

"Mother! I've just become engaged. I've hardly thought of a wedding date."

"Sarah, most young women automatically think of the one with the other. Let's get busy on that. You know me, I'd like everything flawless. Prescott agrees on that, at least." She turned back to her magazine. "By the way, there's a letter from Jean in the foyer."

"Oh! Thank you."

Sarah hurried to the hall table. How hungry she was to hear news from the west. She ripped open the letter.

Dear Sarah,

I know you'll be interested to hear this first piece of news, especially after your experience with the Ute Indians. Things have been heating up with them. The *Denver Post* has reported some have been traveling off their reservations without permission, even setting fires. They just don't want to become farmers or be contained the way the government wants. I will have to say if I'd been free-roaming, it would be hard for me to stay in one spot. John Harding, who has more perspective on all this, has said he wonders how it will all end.

I have other news. Sid has been very attentive. I can feel it in my bones, Sarah—that he might pop the question. Whatever became of John Harding? Well, nothing. He always treated me nicely, like the rest of the girls in our circle, but that was all. And after you left, we've hardly seen him except for Sundays. He has disappeared from social life, except for the church's. Can you fathom that?

By the way, I never felt satisfied with what you told me about your time in the mountains. Suddenly, you left for Philly—with Aunt Martha so upset. Did something happen of which I was unaware? That night in the wilderness—I asked if you spent it with the Indians, but you never said much. Did you spend it with the Indians or with Rev. Harding? Now I'm beginning to wonder. Please, cousin, fess up. Now that I'm no longer casting out lures for the pastor, you can tell me with a clear conscience. To tell the truth—you can see I'm being completely honest, so you be must too—in my heart of hearts I didn't think I was a good match for him. You'd have been much better. But of course, you had Prescott.

Speaking of Prescott. Did you ever compare him with the pastor? Now, I know you think you're destined for Prescott and all, but did the pastor strike a chord in you? When you were here in the Springs, you both talked about art and such—and then to be alone with him on the trail! If it had been me with him, I'd have died—and gone to heaven. I'm laughing as I write this. Despite the fact I'm a tomboy, I have a bit of the romantic in me. You must be honest with me! Especially about that night you were in the mountains.

Well, anyway, I'm excited as anything about Sid popping the question. And Mother is, too. Of course, mum's the word. Father said he wouldn't consider any proposal until I turn twenty. My one consolation is that until then, I'll have fun at all the parties this winter.

Do write soon!

Love,
Jean

Sarah sat back in her chair and smiled. All that scheming for naught. It figured. As time went on, Jean hadn't seemed such an ideal mate for the pastor.

And what of herself? Last night when she'd felt restless after the engagement dinner, she had worked her way into realizing that she was engaged to a fine man. Wasn't that enough for her?

Somehow she had to settle down, get back into her old life here in Philadelphia.

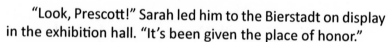

"Look, Prescott!" Sarah led him to the Bierstadt on display in the exhibition hall. "It's been given the place of honor."

"It's certainly big enough. Takes up the whole wall."

"That's Bierstadt! Grand, isn't it? His paintings were the reason I was so bent on seeing the West. I'll never forget my time there." Seeing the Bierstadt brought a familiar quickening, a rush of pleasure.

She looked up at her companion. "You see how light comes through that opening in the mountains and shines on the lake? And the way the figures of the deer are outlined against the water shows Bierstadt's use of light. It's genius. That's my humble opinion, of course."

In her eagerness, Sarah pulled on his arm. "What do *you* think?"

"I'm sure you're right, my dear. I think it's fine."

"What about the artist's use of color?"

Prescott paused. "Looks fine to me."

A little flame of impatience flared up in her. Everything was just *fine* to Prescott. She had hoped for more in the way of a specific comment or reaction. That night at the Bell's party— she couldn't help remembering how she'd waylaid John and the thought-provoking conversation they'd had about Bierstadt. How that talk had fed her artistic soul.

"What are you smiling about, Sarah?"

"Oh, just a memory."

"It must be a pleasant one."

"It is."

He chucked her chin like she was a little girl. "No secrets now."

"Oh...I was thinking of a party in Colorado Springs. You remember me telling you about the railroad developer, General Palmer, the man who founded the town? Well, his associate, Dr. Bell and his wife Cara, are the social center of the Springs and give wonderful parties. I was remembering one of them."

She wouldn't say more. It was no use pitting the memory of one man against another. "We can see these other paintings rather quickly," she offered. "I can always come back to examine them later."

"Don't worry, dear. When I make enough money, I'll buy you one of these for our home. You take care of the artistic endeavors, and I'll manage the finances."

Sarah looked up at Prescott. He *was* trying to enter into the spirit of things. Always he'd been a good escort, and she appreciated that in him.

After climbing into bed, Sarah looked up at the ceiling. She thought back to when Prescott and she had arrived home after the exhibit. They'd stood in the vestibule, and Prescott had put his hands on her shoulders as he had the night before. When she held back, his voice took on a note of pleading. "Sarah!"

How foolish of me. Here we are engaged, and I'm acting like a ninny. Of course, he wants to embrace...and kiss me. So, she'd moved closer and Prescott's arms had encircled her. He did feel solid and reassuring. Then he'd lowered his head.

The kiss had not been too bad. He had placed a light one on her lips, the way her father kissed her mother mornings before he left for work. Since arriving home Sarah had been careful to note this. She was relieved Prescott already knew the proper form, understood what was expected. There was security in that.

But now Sarah felt she must think through something else. She drew the covers up closer under her chin. In the hansom cab on the way home, she'd persisted a bit, talking about art. "Prescott, did the beauty of nature depicted in those paintings bring anything to mind? Arouse anything in you?" She waited, looking at him. When he remained silent, she added, "Have you ever thought how all this beauty came into being—how God must have delighted in creating it?"

"God?" Prescott looked as if taken off guard. "I've never connected a nature painting with God. Or nature much with God, for that matter."

"At one time, I wouldn't have either, but a friend out West challenged me to see nature and its beauty as a creation of God."

"Of course, God comes to mind when I'm in church."

"Yes...but do you ever think about God—outside of church? How He might have something to do with nature—and with our everyday lives?"

"I'm afraid you're out of my depth, Sarah." Even in the semi-darkness she could see a broad smile. "I didn't know you could have such weighty thoughts." He reached over and took one of her hands in his. "But I think we can leave such musings to the minister. Isn't it his job to bring us sermons and such about God? My job is lawyering. And your job is to look pretty and do the socializing you do so well...something ultimately benefiting my law practice, and our life together." He then squeezed her hand and changed the subject.

As she lay in bed, an aspect of Prescott dawned on her—while he appreciated beauty, it was hardly a real love for beauty itself. It was more a love of perfection.

190

She thought back to John and their time in the mountains. She could picture, again, that brisk, beautiful morning when she'd heard him singing.

John. His love for beauty was genuine. But it was more than that. It had something of God in it. He saw earthly beauty as something God had created. And even more, saw beauty as showing a bit of God Himself.

She was realizing, too, that something had happened out West. Those conversations with John had touched her soul, her heart. They had started *something* in her.

How wonderful it was to share with someone what she really thought and felt. And to have that someone challenge her to think even deeper. At the moment, she longed for just such a talk. But the person who had brought this to her was far, far away. And the likelihood of seeing him in the foreseeable future, of having the talk she so longed for... well, did she even figure in his life?

She stared absently at the brass fittings on her bed as her mind turned over and over. Had John ever indicated a preference for her? He'd always treated her kindly, with respect—even tenderness.

But if he did feel something for her, what chance was there of anything coming of it? They were half a country apart, separated by miles and miles.

Her hand balled up. Thinking like this, she was beginning to feel very foolish. She turned over and buried her face in the pillow, then a minute later, rolled over on her side. Feeling foolish like this—was very uncomfortable.

CHAPTER 21

Sarah stepped out the door of the elegant dress shop her mother had recommended. She'd come to see what might appeal for her trousseau. Something inside her had lifted when fingering the beautiful materials, envisioning the gowns that would bring additional loveliness into her life and that of her husband.

The shop was located on one of Philly's busiest thoroughfares. Here and there, trees with their stark, dark branches, etched patterns against the gray and buff-colored stone buildings, reminding her that fall had all but passed.

She crossed the sidewalk to catch a cab.

At that moment a newsboy strode down the walk shouting, "EXTRA! EXTRA! Read all about it!" He held a newspaper high above his head. "Indian massacre in Colorado! Buy your paper right here and read all about it."

Sarah's heart lurched. *Indian massacre?* She rushed to the newsboy and searched frantically in her purse for the correct change. "Here!" she said, and grabbed a paper. She stepped back across the sidewalk to the dress shop window, out of the way of oncoming strollers.

She found the article. At the Meeker agency, Ute Indians had massacred the local Indian agent, Meeker, and six other white men. Wives and children had been taken captive, the Utes disappearing with them into the mountains. The terrain was rough country, little traveled. Prior to the murders, Indian women and children at the Agency, fearful of what might happen, had fled the scene, escaping to the surrounding hills.

Where in Colorado? John was always going out somewhere among those Utes.

She scanned further down the article. White River country. How far was that from Colorado Springs or the back country where he'd rescued her? Her father had maps in his study. Would there be any indication on one of those where this had taken place? She must get home as soon as possible.

A hansom cab was traveling down the street at a good pace, and Sarah stepped to the edge of the pavement, hailing it. The cabbie seemed not to notice her, so she darted into the thoroughfare waving her paper frantically, all but stepping in front of the cab.

The driver reined in his horse sharply. "Hey there, Miss! 'Bout run you over."

"I must get home as soon as possible. I'll pay you extra." The driver jumped down to assist her into the cab. "Drive as fast as possible. Please!"

All the way home, she visualized again her kidnapping—the threatenings and ill-treatment, the thirst and hunger and absolute fatigue of the journey. But most of all, the fear. The stark terror she'd felt at times, not knowing what her fate would be. It had been horrible. Horrible!

And the place where the Indians had stopped to make camp—where they had started rushing by her—she remembered trying to keep from falling as one Indian after another plucked at her dress, her hair, yelling and gesticulating in the most dreadful way.

Then without warning John had stepped from behind a huge boulder. She thrilled again at his commanding figure, his voice ordering them to halt, claiming her as his woman.

His woman? Had he meant anything by that—or was it just to stop them?

She had blanked even that from her memory, but now it was all coming back with a vengeance. The fight! That terrible fight. She gripped the seat of the cab, looking anxiously at the buildings, the houses speeding by, more than ever eager to arrive home.

The cabbie finally handed her out, and after she paid the fare she raced up the walk and flung open the front door to the vestibule. Beyond the glassed door, she saw her mother checking her hat at the hall mirror.

"Mother!" The cry burst from her as she opened the door into the foyer.

"Sarah, what has happened? You look—beside yourself!"

"Oh, Mother! This newspaper article. I feel terrible. There's something I have to tell you—something that happened out West—" Minutes later, Sarah, weeping in her mother's arms, finished her narrative.

"Sarah, why didn't you tell me this before? Your father and I never dreamed of this. Why didn't your Aunt Martha inform us?"

"She was waiting for the right time. But it never seemed to come. That was the real reason we came home so suddenly. Aunt Martha was that upset."

"And this minister, this John Harding, rescued you?"

"Yes, Mother! And he was wonderful. Absolutely wonderful!"

"Well, I'm grateful to him. Most grateful! I don't know what my sister Amelia is doing, living out there."

"It's perfectly safe in Colorado Springs. I was in the back country."

"The back country! What were you doing there? Oh yes—painting. Oh dear! However, you are *here now*, safe and sound."

"But Mother, this newspaper article I just read—I'm concerned the minister might be involved. He was always doing something for those Indians. I have to know where this Meeker

Agency is. I want to see what maps Father has." Sarah handed the newspaper to her mother and rushed to her father's study.

She located a group of maps, laid them on the desk and flipped through them to find one of the West. Finally, she found one marked Colorado Territory. But, she thought, Colorado is now a state, has been for a few years.

The map had just the sketchiest of markings in the western mountains. Her eyes were immediately drawn to a town in the southwest part of the state—Animas City. But that hadn't been mentioned in the article. It happened in White River country. Her eyes scanned upward. The White River! In the northwest part of the state. Was it there? It must be.

The area in question was a good distance from Colorado Springs. That brought a measure of relief. But who knew where John was? She hated not knowing. Hated it!

Sarah put down the map, trying to think through the situation. But John had his church to attend to. Wouldn't it be unlikely for him to travel so far west again? Reason told her in all likelihood he was safe.

Then why was she so concerned?

Because she knew what could happen. Those Indians had terrified her.

She sat back in her father's leather chair. John had saved her, risked his life. And how had she expressed her gratitude? A note sent from the train.

Did she expect such service as her due? Expect life handed to her on a silver platter?

She felt sick. Sick of herself.

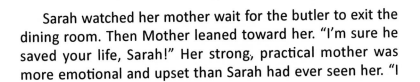

Sarah watched her mother wait for the butler to exit the dining room. Then Mother leaned toward her. "I'm sure he saved your life, Sarah!" Her strong, practical mother was more emotional and upset than Sarah had ever seen her. "I can't believe all you did was send him a brief thank you note. Something more must be done." Her mother looked pointedly at her husband. "Don't you agree?"

"He has a mission board, doesn't he?" her father asked. "Maybe we could give through that." He sat back in his chair. "As soon as you find out, I'll write a letter of commendation, gratitude for his service. Mention that his work among the Indians has come to my attention and I want to make a donation—a sizable one—to the mission on his behalf. If I'm any judge of men, that gesture will say as much as anything."

Her mother leaned over to Sarah once again. "You said he's originally from this area? Has family here? Write him that he must be sure, if he's ever in Philadelphia, to stop here. For dinner," she said emphatically. "We want to meet him. Risking his life like that—for one of his parishioners. And you were hardly even that. I'm sure I've never heard the like. He must think you—and us—ingrates." She shook her head. "And then, just think of a cleric being able to make a rescue like that...."

"A minister in a white collar and black coat?" Her father smiled. "A scholar?"

"Well, yes! That makes it all the more incredible, doesn't it, what he did for our Sarah?"

Sarah didn't have the heart to disabuse her mother of her fondly painted picture. John Harding was certainly more than a scholarly cleric in a white collar. Did her mother also picture him as someone with a balding head, a little rotund, maybe?

But the momentary, light thought quickly dissipated in the increasing guilt she felt. The more her parents talked, the more she felt ashamed in showing so little gratitude. What a self-centered—

Father interrupted her thoughts. "Why don't you first telegraph your aunt—to ascertain whether the minister was present at this Meeker Massacre."

"Thank you, Father! I'll write Jean, too—she might know more details."

Sarah stepped inside the Church of the Holy Trinity. She had come alone this service and had chosen a seat at the very back, not her family's usual pew near the front. Somehow she had to rid herself of this guilt she felt over John. Had he ever seen such ingratitude? Had it sickened him toward her? She hoped not. In his eyes she wanted to be a person...of worth. Cherished...as a friend.

This was the church she hoped to be married in. The beautiful dome, high in front, reflected the light from the sun. However, she had taken a seat far from the light, a place in the shadows.

This feeling of unrest, of shame, had been building in her since she'd told about the rescue—her rescue—at the engagement party. As much as she'd tried to hide, escape from it, a feeling of wretchedness, unworthiness had been growing in her. Sarah bowed her head and closed her eyes. She wanted relief. Wanted something to salve her suffering, guilty heart.

People passed by and she lifted her head. The vast, beautiful sanctuary was slowly filling, everyone fashionably attired with women in beautifully tailored dresses and ensembles, men in the finest black broadcloth suits. She had hardly bothered with her clothing this morning. Oh, she was acceptable enough—but she had put on the first thing at hand. It hadn't seemed important.

For the opening hymn, she stood and sang the familiar words, "Rejoice, ye pure in heart, Rejoice, give thanks, and sing..." But she felt no rejoicing, or anything like the pure in heart. This sense of guilt, this shame—she wanted to be rid of it.

Would the minister...would he say anything to soothe, lighten her soul? She was determined to listen, really listen to him this morning. Surely there must be some help for her.

He began with a Psalm... *O God, Thou art my God; early will I seek Thee: my soul thirsteth for thee, my flesh longeth for thee in a dry and thirsty land, where no water is..."*

John didn't think or talk about God the way most people did, she'd noticed that from the first. But she'd attributed it to the fact he was a minister. However, she'd discovered he was someone with thoughts and feelings like the rest of humanity. How he'd fought that Indian. Fiercely! No, he was a man. All man.

God was near to John in a way she'd never realized a person could be. He appreciated things about God she was sure no other person of her acquaintance did. She found herself longing for more of God, the way John knew Him.

The pastor directed the congregation to a New Testament passage. "John chapter 10." On hearing the name of the book, Sarah felt warmth wash over her. The choice of this particular book, was it a hopeful sign?

"Starting with verse 11," the minister intoned, "these are the words of Jesus."

I am the good shepherd: the good shepherd giveth his life for the sheep.

Sarah's mind veered to her own thoughts. Yes, Jesus was the good shepherd. One of her favorite stories as a child was of Jesus, the good shepherd, who went after that one lost sheep. She pictured Him going out in the dark and wild land, leaving the ninety-and-nine and risking his life to rescue the one.

Just as John had risked himself for her.

Her mind went again to the time in the mountains. She remembered John saying he was like a shepherd, an *under shepherd* he called himself. Did this mean a shepherd under Jesus?

John had risked his life, first to save her, then later, disappeared over that fearful precipice, to save Hob. Had that grubby, sinful man appreciated what John had done for him? John—respected and loved in the community—risking his life for that poor, dirty man who was probably drunk half the time. And just minutes before, Hob had tried to kill him.

Through selfless action to them both, John had shown what it meant to be a good shepherd. The inner strength of the minister amazed Sarah: that he should put himself out so. Remembering brought tears to her eyes.

And there, down the incline, John had told Hob about God, prayed with him. Hob had confessed his sin.

Sarah remembered praying a similar prayer in Sunday School when young. Her heart had been tender toward the Lord those early years. Why had she thought so little of this recently?

For a few moments she looked around the sanctuary. There were those who whispered with a neighbor or looked off distractedly, paying little attention to what was going on. Was she like those people, more concerned with herself and her own affairs than with God?

The minister continued to read. *"I am the good shepherd, and know my sheep, and am known of mine. As the Father knoweth me, even so know I the Father: and I lay down my life for the sheep..."*

Arresting words! Jesus, the Good Shepherd laying down His life. He had done so for her. And what had she given Him in return?

All these years, she'd never thought of herself as much of a sinner. She'd always been kind and thoughtful—a bright spot in people's lives. She tried to be good. But what did one call her taking for granted such sacrifice on her behalf?

Somehow this had all translated into thinking that extraordinary service was her due. She'd shown such little appreciation for the shepherding John had done for her—and now, a greater sin dawned on her. She'd had the same attitude toward Jesus, the Good Shepherd.

What had she been thinking?

The congregation began singing the familiar words, "Alas, and did my Savior bleed, and did my Sovereign die...for sinners such as I?"

Sarah sat very still now, no longer seeing the sanctuary or the people in it. She saw only her ingratitude. Ingratitude for what John had done for her. And gross ingratitude toward the Lord.

Had she even loved God these last years?

Life had become busy—she'd gotten caught up with society. God, such as John knew Him, had been absent from her life.

She bowed her head and leaned over, grasping the back of the pew in front.

God forgive her!

CHAPTER 22

John quickly put down his fork and held out his hand for the letter. His heart had jumped when Hannah announced a letter from Philadelphia. Was it from home or—some time ago Sarah had written him.

But as he glanced at the envelope, it looked official. His eyes darted to the return address: the church board. "Mind if I open this at the table, Hannah?"

"Go ahead, why should I?"

John smiled up at her. "You usually fuss about your food getting cold."

"Well, this looks important."

"Hannah! Have you packed my dress shirts, the ones you starch and iron so carefully?"

"I sure 'nough did. Packed them all."

"Good. I wouldn't want to...run out."

Hannah held out his pressed handkerchiefs. "In fact, when you get to Philly, why don't you put aside one or two, save them for something special that might come up." She turned to get something else from the dresser, then added, "Isn't that where Miss Whittington comes from?"

"I...I believe so." John could almost see Hannah smiling with her question, but even to her he couldn't admit this feeling of tenterhooks about traveling to Philadelphia. Sarah had invited him to dinner, or, in reality, her mother had. But he'd also heard that lawyer friend of Sarah's had staked his claim, even sealing it with a ring, and John felt uncertain how to handle the situation. Usually, he was pretty forthright, but this— Sarah was surely making wedding plans. He flung down the handkerchiefs on the clothes in his suitcase. He didn't know what he was going to do—or say. His mind jumped from one possibility to another.

He rubbed his hands over his face. Certainly, he'd need to play this by ear. And well, did he trust God or not?

A sudden thought occurred to him. When he went to the Whittingtons' for dinner, he would give Sarah something that reminded her of the West, something that represented their time together—for they *were* friends, weren't they? He couldn't give her jewelry—although he'd like to, but that was not now his place. However, he would stop in Denver and look up the art gallery he'd noticed on his last visit. The bank was conveniently down a few blocks if he needed extra funds. Yes, he'd get off the train in Denver.

<hr />

John exited the building on Philadelphia's Cherry Street. The Church Board had given him a choice that he would need to think through. Much of his decision would depend on Sarah. Sarah!

The first leg of the train trip East, when he'd gazed over the prairie, he thought of that day months ago when he'd escaped onto the plains east of the Springs. How he'd given both a final mourning for his wife and also recognized how much he wanted Sarah. Then, later, realizing the improbability of this last, had put Sarah away. Whenever she entered his thinking, he'd made himself think about something else. Seeing the stretch of plains, its many miles, reinforced how far apart they lived. And, spiritually, he wondered if they lived far apart as well. They'd spent little time together talking about such things. She had left so suddenly.

So, he had let the prairie settle him down. He'd come East to attend this board meeting, not sure if he'd even have a real talk with Sarah. He had let her know he was coming to Philadelphia for a church board meeting, but was unsure of his exact schedule. And he would be visiting his parents. His plan was to attend the Whittington dinner, make small talk, and maybe let things rest as they were.

Yet, now standing on Cherry Street with the Art Institute so near, their discussions about art, nature and God came back in a rush. He felt something rise up, something strong and searching, something difficult to put down.

Suddenly, he knew he could not leave Philadelphia without talking with her. Really talking. The feeling in him was so strong he wanted to go immediately to her house and make his presence known. What would he say? He wasn't sure. But he wanted to see how she was doing, really doing. Was she happy in her decision to marry this lawyer fellow? Yes, he wanted to make sure she was happy. That's what he would do, approach her as a minister, make sure of her wellbeing.

It was just after the noon hour. He would get a quick bite to eat then find her address. His hand clenched—he would *do* this.

John knocked on the door of the large Whittington house, a mansion really. He was somewhat taken aback. Mr. Whittington had done mighty well for himself. John was surprised Sarah was as sweet-tempered and amiable as she was, living in a place, a neighborhood like this. As he waited for someone to answer the door, his heart now squeezed in doubt. What was he doing here? Why had the thought crossed his mind she might leave this for the West? And besides, she was engaged.

A man in proper black apparel opened the door. "Yes, sir? What can I do for you?"

Ah, they had a butler.

"I'm John Harding from Colorado Springs. I would like to speak with Miss Sarah Whittington." For a moment, he didn't know if he should first ask for Mrs. Whittington, the mother, or seek Sarah straight away. Living out west, manners were more informal, more direct; he hoped he wasn't committing a social faux-pas. If he was going to do this, he wanted to do it right. He didn't want to present a boorish impression of western men.

He was ushered into what looked to be a parlor—or maybe salon would better describe the place. Deeply-hued blue and green velvet chairs and sofas occupied a room on whose walls hung ornate gold-framed paintings. Standing there, he felt the lavish apartment widen the gap between Sarah and himself. He crossed the room to better inspect a landscape hanging over the black marble fireplace. Was it from the Hudson River School? He wasn't knowledgeable like Sarah about individual artists—the signature in the corner left him in doubt—but he was sure she would know who'd painted the quiet river with its lush foliage.

"Ah, Mr. Harding, I believe." Turning from the painting, he saw a beautifully dressed matron enter the salon. But she had hesitated a moment, her eyes widening. Was he something unexpected?

The woman held out her hand, looking him up and down. "I understand you helped my daughter out West." He was glad he had worn one of Hannah's whitest, starchiest shirts with his dark suit.

"Sarah has, of course, spoken of you. My husband and I are most grateful for all you did—saving her life, really. I wish she were here."

"She is out?" John felt rather stupid in asking a question that had already been answered, but he couldn't for the life of him think of anything else to say.

"Yes, if she had known you were coming, she would have made a point of being here. And knowing her, she might come home just in time to rush upstairs to dress for dinner." She hesitated. "You wouldn't be able to stay? For our evening meal?"

All of a sudden he felt underdressed...and wondered if this mother really wanted him to be here. "As you see I'm not in dinner clothes. Hardly formal enough. Maybe I should return another day?"

"What you're wearing will do. We all know you're from the West." The way she said that made it seem like the last outpost of civilization. "We understand. And then, we'd like to hear about your work before you leave. And with Sarah's fiancé dining with us, I'm sure he'll be interested in what you have to say as well." Mrs. Whittington stepped to the bell rope. "Would you like some tea?"

"I've just eaten. I had a late lunch. Thank you."

"Being a cleric, I know you must be a great reader. Maybe you would like to spend time in our library before dinner? "

"Yes, I would like that. And since the day's so pleasant, I might take a walk around the neighborhood—to pass the time." He smiled with what he hoped was his most engaging smile. He could tell this mother was arranging everything to suit herself. Well, he'd fit in as best he could. Still, some part of him rose up in rebellion. He wanted to see Sarah—alone. Not with a lot of other people present at a dinner.

Sarah's mother smiled. "That seems a workable plan. Because I *do* have a meeting this afternoon, I'll send our butler to attend to any needs you have."

As John waited, he walked up to the painting over the mantle once again. He felt the need of a peaceful scene.

He'd noticed this mother had been sure to mention Sarah's *intended*. Something about the way she said it gave him a ray of hope. Did she find him a bit threatening to her aspirations for her daughter? Suddenly, he sincerely hoped so.

Could he put before Sarah what was really on his heart? She was engaged to be married to another man. Plans had already been set in place. Social decorum dictated, especially here in Philadelphia society, that he not disturb the roost.

But, most important, was Sarah happy? What did she want? He really had no clear idea. Back in the mountains, they'd seemed so much in harmony with each other. But she hadn't *said* anything. And he hadn't either. Of course, escorting her back to the trading post, particularly as a minster, he had felt the delicacy of the situation, especially with his feelings intensifying. He hadn't wanted her to feel threatened with any impropriety. When questioned, he wanted her to be able to say with perfect candor that nothing had happened.

Now, however, events were moving forward. She was engaged to be married, and he needed to make a decision about future ministry. He was here in Philadelphia, able to speak with her. If he was frank about his feelings, her answer would determine, to a large extent, what his future ministry would be.

Would it be among the residents of Colorado Springs or would he move farther out west—to those bands of Utes in southwest Colorado? Or to those in the northwest, that arid territory beyond Colorado where the White River Utes would undoubtedly be sent after the Meeker affair?

He sighed, uncertain about the whole situation. He discovered he needed more than a painting. He needed the open air.

⋄∘⋙∘⋄

Returning from his walk, John felt very much better, more like himself. Something about walking—any kind of exercise, for that matter—stabilized and energized a person. The Whittington butler once again opened the door, greeted him and led him directly to the library at the back of the house. "Mrs. Whittington said to give you tea. Dinner won't be until seven."

After a tray was brought, John was left to browse. He wandered around the room, noting the library's organization. There was a section of books on art. As he looked them over, he noticed a paper sticking slightly out from the top of one. He took the volume from the shelf, and opening it, lifted out a sketch of a woodland scene with a pool at its center. In the corner was a childish signature: Sarah W. His heart warmed. She had done this when young and forgotten about it. Even then, she'd an appreciation for beauty in nature. Suddenly, he wanted, desperately, to be part of her continued discovery of God and how He had created such beauty. And he wanted to show her that by worshiping God for the beauty, praise would be sent back to Him, making a full circle, delighting His heart.

John gazed at the sketch some moments longer then on impulse put it next to the small package, the painting he had brought for Sarah. He smiled. Maybe he'd ask to exchange one bit of art for the other.

He continued around the shelves. A goodly number of books interested him. Here were far more volumes than in his parents' farmhouse. He chose a couple and sat in one of the leather easy chairs and poured himself a cup of tea. The luxury of this chair was a far cry from that of his parents' home as well.

Though his childhood surroundings were far more simple, he had been taught to value orderliness and beauty from a young age. He'd learned to appreciate the finely furrowed field his father insisted on, scything weeds at the field's edge to give their farm a trim look. His mother's finely-tuned aesthetic had inculcated beauty in him from the way she arranged the food on a serving platter to the style of her well-made dresses, and the watercolors she'd painted, framed and hung on the walls of their modest farmhouse. These last—their freshness, simplicity, and delicate coloring—had fed something deep in his soul. In their own way, they were as lovely as the oil paintings in this grand home's salon.

Looking around the lavishly appointed library, he knew that with Jake's money, he could afford to live in a larger home. Yet he would not do so unless his wife required it. Or better yet, unless the scope of ministry for the Lord necessitated it.

He wondered particularly about the White River Utes. He feared they would have to make an inevitable move—to territory northwest of Colorado.

He'd been in that part of the country once, a barren landscape where the soul of the Ute would be weary for many a year until the younger generation grew up to view it as home.

Would he go out there to live and minister? That's the choice the Board had given him. That, or remain in his present church in Colorado Springs. Who would be there? A growing population of easterners, as well of British. Upper class in nature. Would he be suited to be their minister? Not if he didn't have a wife.

Sarah....

But that was a stretch—she was engaged to be married to another man. And the stretch felt even broader now that he had seen this stately home.

Yet if his wife required something larger, more elegant— where members of his congregation would feel more comfortable—he could see himself....

He felt the familiar clenching of his hand and made it relax. *That* was getting ahead of things, wasn't it?

CHAPTER 23

Sarah scrutinized herself in the long mirror. When Mother told her about their unexpected guest, she hastily donned this bright rose silk. Its vivid color set off her golden hair, and its wide, rounded neck framed her face. Why had Mother apprised her of the minister's presence just minutes ago? Was it because Sarah had been so late arriving home that she was sent directly upstairs to change for dinner? Sarah would like to have seen Mr. Harding— John—alone before dinner. But her mother's management had precluded that.

What would Sarah have said to him anyway? Couldn't it be said in front of others? She would certainly thank him in a more appropriate manner for all he'd done for her. Then introduce her fiancé?

Sarah had just seated herself in the salon when John entered. A little thrill of pride shot through her. Surely, no man looked more distinguished. His white starched shirt stood out sharply against his black broadcloth suit. A sudden memory crossed her mind of the day she'd first seen him at the western wedding. Someday he would undoubtedly be attending his own. Who would be his bride? That thought ignited a little flame in her breast.

John had just enough time to greet her and bow over her hand when dinner was announced. He was assigned to escort her mother. Sarah, of course, was accompanied by her fiancé. Prescott would sit next to her at table.

Before they were seated, her father proposed a toast to their guest and thanked him for what he had done for his daughter. All joined in heartily.

John had been placed across from Sarah, ostensibly so they would be able to better converse. He favored her with a few, bright words, then kept up a cheerful conversation with those around him. She could see in him the successful pastor, ministering to everyone's needs and interests. Every inch the informed Westerner, he gave insights on the country in general, then on the West in particular. He was doing himself proud, and while he gave her more attention than the others because of their previous acquaintance, he was careful not to single her out too much. He judiciously asked Prescott about his profession and sensitively handled them as a couple, yet he never alluded to or asked about a possible wedding.

Later, while Prescott was busy talking to Aunt Martha, Sarah glanced up from her dessert plate to see John gazing at her, his look sharp and intense. When had a man ever looked at her like that? Certainly, not Prescott.

During dinner, she had been sensitive to John's every word and gesture, yet now she felt something different stirring between them. At that moment, she knew something needed to be settled. He had something to say and it was to her alone. And she must give him an audience, for soon he would be gone.

With dinner finished, her mother rose. "Shall we ladies adjourn to the salon while the men talk over their concerns?" She looked at Sarah's father. "Then you can join us later for coffee." Her mother was keeping the evening on the pre-scribed social agenda.

"Mrs. Whittington, Mr. Whittington," John stood, taking in both her parents, "I appreciate your hospitality, but I won't be able to stay much longer. Before I leave, I would appreciate being able to speak with your daughter—in private. Could that be arranged?"

Her mother looked at her father, and Sarah could see the challenge in her gaze. But her father spoke up, more forcefully than was his wont. "Since you are leaving, Mr. Harding, I think a few minutes would certainly be in order. We're most grateful for all you've done for our daughter." Sarah saw resignation in her mother's eyes, but felt her own heart leap in anticipation.

"Sarah, why don't you conduct Mr. Harding to my study," her father offered.

Prescott rose and grasped the back of her chair, assisting her to rise.

John walked purposefully around the table and held out his arm in escort.

Feeling his strong arm beneath her hand, Sarah trembled slightly. Being this close, touching him, alerted her—to what, she wasn't quite sure. Was she apprehensive, or overawed by this man who was stronger, so much deeper than any other man of her acquaintance? She knew that what he had to say to her would be important. And necessary. And, in truth, she wanted to hear it very much.

When they approached the study, he said, "Wait a moment. I left something in the library." She looked around at the dark, rich paneling of the familiar room, the painting of dogs above her father's massive desk. On John's return, he held a flat package and a drawing on a piece of paper. He closed the study door, and Sarah momentarily wondered at the degree of privacy this suggested. He then led her to one of the chairs near the fireplace, its shiny brass surround and irons reflecting the firelight. Stirring up the fire a bit, he repositioned a log, then took the chair opposite.

"This is for you." He handed her the package. "Something to remind you of the West..." He didn't finish his sentence; instead, nodded for her to open it.

She took off the wrapping to reveal a small painting reminiscent of a Bierstadt, a grand mountain range with a lake and forest in the foreground.

She looked up. "Thank you! This means a great deal to me."

"I bought it in case you were unable to return...in the near future."

The thought of her not returning for a long time gave her pause. Surely, she would be able to visit her aunt and uncle, and Jean. Was he referring to after her marriage, when she'd be dependent on her husband's wishes? Inwardly, she sighed. Of course.

"Miss Whittington...Sarah." He smiled. "May I continue to call you by your given name? We've come to that place in our friendship, haven't we—back in the mountains?" Without her answering, he took her acquiescence for granted. And she let him. Her normal take-charge, sparkling self had quieted to a whisper inside her. She wanted to listen, catch every nuance of his voice, every expression of his face as he spoke. For it was not just words she sought. She wanted to drink in the whole man, every part of him.

"Sarah, your parents gave me permission just now to speak with you. For a few minutes only. So I will try to not overstep the boundaries of their hospitality. I came to Philadelphia, as you know, to attend a church board meeting. That's all anyone might know of my visit. But now, between you and me, I've decided to say what's on my heart."

He bent over, his hands clasped between his outspread knees. "I want to go back briefly to our time in the mountains. It was both exhilarating and painful for me. This last, because I felt I could not, should not cross the line between pastor and parishioner, especially as we were alone in the wilderness. Also, because you were all but engaged to another man. Under the circumstances, to be other than a shepherd caring for a sheep would have been wrong. So, I determined to wait to talk with you until a more appropriate time. I hoped that opportunity would come later in Colorado Springs.

"But then you left. Without a good-bye. It affected me more deeply than I could have thought possible. Because what had been happening, almost without my consciously knowing it, was that I was developing a deeper and deeper interest in you. When I learned, on coming back from General Palmer's mission, that you had been taken by Indians, there was no question that I would go after you. And use everything in my experience, my strength—even cunning—to rescue you. Everything! That should have told me right there how much you meant to me. But I was caught up in the moment, in the challenge of tracking your kidnappers and getting you back.

"When I fought that renegade I discovered an extra strength, extra quickness and shrewdness to do what needed to be done. Thankfully, my Indian friend arrived on the scene to stop us. Otherwise...."

He wiped his hand over his face, composing himself. Sarah, too, remembered those terrible minutes, the uncertainty of the fight's outcome.

John straightened up, looking at her directly. "Then the journey back to the post, the remainder of that day and the next, I delighted in being with you, in having you to myself. But I kept reminding myself that I was a shepherd guiding you back to the fold—in this case, the trading post to your aunt and friends. I wanted to be able to face them with a clear conscience as to my conduct. And that you would not betray by a word or a glance that I had been anything other than a pastor and a gentleman.

"But all that time, discussing beauty and talking about God—and His part in beauty—was like food for my soul. I will always remember that trip, the hours together as one of the highlights of—"

He paused, looking down at his hands. Sarah could feel his tension, his earnestness.

213

"And then you left without a warning. I reacted—well, the scales were ripped off. No longer was I thinking you were singularly attractive, a person with whom I felt a special affinity. You had become of paramount importance to me. I started wondering if this Prescott fellow was necessary to your happiness. If you were, in fact, meant for *me*.

"For I love you, Sarah. Love you dearly. And deeply." His eyes now had that look she'd seen as he bent over her in the hostelry, laying her on the bed. She felt her breath catch. Now she knew what that look had meant. Love and desire had shone from his eyes. Tenderness, too. But he had kept his want for her under lock and key—except for his eyes.

Something stilled within her...and wonder stole in.

He rose from his chair. "I came here today, uncertain of what I would say to you. I didn't know if I should break family and society's strictures by saying what was really in my heart. And, most of all, I didn't know how you felt in your present commitment to...your fiancé." She saw his difficulty in saying that word. However, he continued. "But then in the library this afternoon, as I thought about a drawing I discovered of yours—" he stooped to retrieve it, "something you did when young—I was reminded again of our mutual love of art. And how I wanted this to be one of the ways we'd discover the wonders of God together.

"So by the end of the time in the library, I decided I must speak to you. Show you my heart before returning West."

He smiled broadly. "And I faced the fact that if I didn't, I would be like a caged lion, pacing back and forth in a self-imposed prison, ignorant as to your feelings.

"I have to know, Sarah. I *have* to know." He made no move to touch her, but his eyes drew her to him. "Sarah, is there any hope that you might return my love?"

Sarah was gazing at him, putting together the pieces of their time in the wilderness. True, he had been the perfect gentleman, had treated her as a pastor. Yet, there had been

214

something she'd been unable to put her finger on. Something she'd begun to respond to. She remembered the time when she had felt so terribly tired before reaching the trading post, how she'd wanted rest, but more than that—had wanted him to hold her.

However, under Aunt Martha's urging to leave Colorado, she had put that all behind her. Not immediately. On the train with Aunt Martha looking forward so to Philadelphia and their life back home, she'd finally concluded she'd been weak and fanciful about the minister, that any woman would have reacted that way, being alone with such a man. And, of course, there was Prescott. She had an assured future with him.

Yet now, would her approaching, prescribed life be enough after hearing such a declaration of this man's love? Her hands twisted in her lap.

How did she really feel? Her fiancé was...she was confident he'd give her a good, solid life...a good home, well-run with lovely dinner parties and such. Was that what she wanted? Could she know for certain?

She stood abruptly. She *must* know.

"John, would you...embrace me, hold me?" She felt herself blushing. But she had to *know*. "And then would you kiss me?"

He took a step toward her. "Sarah, does this mean—?"

"No. Just that I must make certain of something."

He came near, slipping his arms around her, drawing her close. She waited for him to lift her face for the kiss. But no, he lowered his head and pressed his lips to her hair.

She felt his longing and held herself still, motionless.

Then John lifted her chin, and placed a gentle kiss on her lips.

Ah...this was like Prescott's kiss, sweet and chaste. It felt right and good. And proper.

John drew back and his eyes searched hers. Then he lowered his head again and this time his kiss was long. It searched her, sharing something of himself and of his yearning. It was a kiss different from any other she'd experienced.

She leaned into him, so close she felt almost a part of him. Was this what intimacy meant?

"Oh, Sarah...!" He crushed her to himself.

She had all she could do not to respond, *not* to let her arms go round his neck.

Where was Prescott in all this?

Hastily she drew away. She had felt herself about to give in to John—she could hardly think. "I think you should go now."

He looked at her. A look she could hardly bear. How could she assess this situation, know her true feelings when he looked that way? He loved her...too much. She was not accustomed to this need, this passion in a man. It confused her.

He grasped her hands, holding them gently, but firmly. "Are you *sure*? Do you really want me to leave?"

She hesitated. "I think you *must*."

He sighed and looked at her a long moment. "Then will you see me to the door?"

"Yes. Certainly."

He leaned forward as if he would give her one last kiss. But she stepped back.

He dropped her hands then, and stooped for her drawing. "May I keep this?"

At her nod, he placed it in his case.

When she led him out the study door, he asked, "Will you make my excuses to your parents? I appreciate very much their hospitality, especially your mother's inviting me to dinner."

As they entered the foyer, the butler appeared. He must have been on the lookout, because he had John's coat and hat in hand.

"I'll see Mr. Harding out, Yates."

"Yes, miss." He nodded respectfully and handed John his coat and hat, then turned and left.

As Sarah put her hand on the vestibule doorknob, John asked, "No proper good-bye? You know, I did without one once. I don't think I could again..." When she stood, struggling

216

silently, he caught her hand. Pressed it and raised it to his lips, holding it there a long moment.

He then picked up his case, and she gazed as his tall figure exited through the glass door into the vestibule.

Taking a deep breath, she turned to cross the foyer. She would join family and friends in the salon. Could she make small talk with this confusion and inner tumult inside her? Maybe it would be advisable to go upstairs, to be alone in her room for a while.

Suddenly, a thought pressed down on her—he was leaving *for good*. A pain struck so sharp, her breath caught.

"No!" Her whisper was sudden and vehement. She turned and rushed back to the vestibule. Had John gone far? She yanked the door open.

He stood quietly, back in the shadow.

"John! Forgive me!"

His arms opened, and she willingly went into them. "I couldn't leave," he said. "I had to see the last of you."

She now welcomed his kiss, indeed, sought it. And responded with an intensity that surprised her.

Lifting his head, his eyes alight, he observed, "This vestibule is cold," and drew away a moment to unbutton his top coat. Then wrapped it around her and drew her inside.

CHAPTER 24

Sarah stood at the rear of the Church of the Holy Trinity, waiting to march down the long aisle. The train of her wedding dress swept back gloriously. Mother had insisted on a dress that did honor to this magnificent church and the grandness of the occasion. It was what Sarah herself had envisioned long ago for her wedding. However, she would have done anything to please her mother after the broken engagement.

She would always remember the shock, then the good-breeding Prescott displayed once he realized he had lost her irrevocably to another man. For Prescott's sake, she had vacated the city—to ease what he called his humiliation. Then, too, by living those months with Aunt Amelia in Colorado Springs, she had fulfilled a fond desire of John's: to court her properly.

Sarah glanced at the back pew where she'd surrendered herself to God. How good He'd been to her. Then she looked to the distant dome where her husband-to-be awaited her. She felt the wonder, again, of how all this had come about.

A movement caught her eye. Hildie had put down her basket of rose petals and now pranced up to her. Sarah looked down at her flower girl, more than a year older since that last wedding, but still diminutive enough to fulfill the coveted role.

Hildie reached up to give Sarah a hug. The young arms clung to her neck and Sarah quickly planted a kiss on the soft cheek.

"Isn't this fun?" Hildie said, giggling. "And after your wedding, it'll be only a couple of months till Jean and Sid get married. I just *love* weddings."

Jean turned. "Hildie! Get back in line. The music's signaling the first bridesmaid to start down the aisle." Jean gave Sarah a sudden smirk. "It's time we get this show on the road. I know *John* is ready."

One after the other, the five bridesmaids stepped down the aisle in their filmy, pastel gowns, keeping careful time to the music. Hildie followed in their wake, carefully scattering roses as Sarah took her place at her father's side.

When she squeezed his arm, he said quietly, "You remember I realized John was the one only minutes after I met him. As much as I will miss you, I know I can trust you into his keeping."

Sarah remembered the time after that momentous dinner when John had confessed his love to her. The very next day, he had honorably approached her father and told him about their attachment. Later, her father told her when he had seen John and Prescott at dinner, he wondered how she could continue to be engaged to the one when the other had so obviously captured her heart. And as the dinner progressed, he sensed John's sterling worth. So he had readily assented to his being alone with her—despite her mother's chagrin. Sarah squeezed her father's arm affectionately again. He had been on her side from the beginning.

The organ music now swelled and Sarah, with her father supporting her, took her first sweeping step down the aisle. Such a glorious church and music! Her heart swelled with gratitude. Yes, God had been good to her. How she reveled in this moment with so many happy faces greeting her as she passed. The story had gotten around about the man she was to marry, his war record and his rescue of her in the mountains. She was glad, now, their love had been handled discreetly. Time had been allowed to pass before her relationship with John had been made public. Those months out West had helped heal the situation. In her heart she blessed her aunt and uncle who had understood and aided her wherever possible.

Up ahead, Sarah saw Hannah's eager face, saw her wiping away a tear. The gesture started a tear of her own. Dear Hannah...who'd been so fearful she'd lose her place in John's household. But Hannah had never had anything to fear. From the first, Sarah had wanted her to remain. But the issue was decided once and for all when Sarah's mother visited and had seen the larger house John was preparing for his bride. She'd immediately said, "Why! My daughter can't run that all by herself. I insist she have help." So, Hannah's place was assured.

Mother had come around to accepting what would be Sarah's new place in life when she attended the party the Bells had given them. It was a party to end all parties. No one in the East could have done it with more aplomb or pleasure. Mother had been suitably impressed, and it had helped reconcile her to the coming separation. She also realized her daughter would live just a few miles from her sister Amelia. "Well," she said, "I will just have to make time in my busy social calendar to visit the Springs. It wouldn't hurt me to take the waters as well. Martha and I will travel together."

John's parents, too, had made a welcome place in their hearts for her. How she'd enjoyed visiting their home that John's mother had so delightfully depicted in her watercolors.

Progressing down the aisle, Sarah's mind touched on all this as she recognized one person after another. Then, seeing the dome's reflected light shining down on the bridal party, her heart soared with happiness. Her husband-to-be, waited for her, so straight and tall.

The majestic sound of the organ swelled as she approached him. Their wedding ceremony would be more beautiful even than she had envisioned. She sensed the glory of God in this large, vaulted sanctuary.

John must have had the same thought, because when she caught his eye, it flicked upward with that certain look of his. He was feeling the same glory. Just the night before, he had spoken words from Scripture: "Thy kingdom come. Thy will be done in earth, as it is in heaven." Yes, a little bit of heaven was present in this place.

She and her father took their final steps to join the wedding party, and the music intensified into a last crescendo to its grand ending.

Then, with the music still echoing in the vaulted chamber, the minister began intoning the familiar words, "Who giveth this woman to this man?" Her father gently placed her hand on John's strong arm, then John, covering it firmly with his own, led her forward. A ray of sunshine touched them just then, a benediction on the coming wedding of their two lives.

John guided her into their hotel room. Sarah's eyes rested on the luxurious, prominent bed in the center of the room. Yes. The bridal suite.

In the lobby, he had already directed the bellboy to deposit her bags in the dressing room. He had thought of every detail for her comfort. Her eyes wandered again to the bed.

John helped her remove her wrap then led her to the window that overlooked Philadelphia. He had given her this gift of time together in the city she loved, the gift of walking around it, sharing favorite sites.

After returning to the Springs, he said, they'd continue their honeymoon by traveling to a cabin he'd been gifted by an old friend. He and Hannah and a couple men from his church had outfitted it as a place his bride would enjoy. Some of the "fixings" as Hannah called them, had been presents from members of the congregation.

John's arms now encircled her and she felt his gentle kiss. Yet it was searching as well. Was it searching *her* love—testing its depth—she who had been so easily persuaded by Aunt Martha to return prematurely to Philadelphia?

John turned to look out the window. "My dear, this is the city you hoped to live in, giving happiness to others as only you can. Are you sure you won't miss all this?"

"Hold still," she said and reached up to grasp his chin. She gently turned his face to his right side, and went up on tip-toe to kiss his cheek. "I love this scar," she said softly, "because it reminds me of so much."

She turned his face and looked into his eyes. "For me, that scar represents the tough, terrible times you've been through—the war and its terrors, the fearful times with the Indians and the whiskey brothers, and the deeper hurt of losing your wife.

"Yet it represents more. Your scar healed over the physical wound inflicted upon you, yet you've been healed of these other inner hurts as well. You've allowed God to do it, and I honor and love you for that. It gives me confidence for the future, so that no matter what happens, you will weather the storm. And if I falter, you will help me. To answer your question—it gives me confidence to go west with you, to leave this well-loved city where I thought I would spend my days in comfort."

She smiled. "I have glimpsed what it will mean to live life at your side, discovering together, weeping and joying together, ministering to the people who live in the Springs and surrounding area. As well as those who travel and decide to settle there.

"You see, I want to bring beauty to our home. The kind of beauty that my friends here in the East gravitate toward and understand. The kind of ordered beauty our friends from Great Britain are accustomed to." She paused and her lips curved upward. "I want them to feel at home in the *wild* West. And

222

the best part is that I see God in the beauty, in fact, realize He's the foundation of it all."

John drew her closer and whispered, "The *Alpha and Omega, the beginning and the end, the first and the last.* All comes from Him."

Sarah looked up into his dark eyes, enjoying what she saw there—his masculinity and his sensitivity. Especially, his spirituality. "I treasure your view of God. It's a big view, like the bigness of the West."

She reached up to touch his cheek. "Without really knowing it, I think that's why I was drawn to Bierstadt's paintings. They showed the bigness and glory of the West."

She pressed her hands lovingly to his chest. "He was the artist that brought us together—on a mental and emotional level. I will always be grateful to him and his art for that." She smiled mischievously. "And I'll never forget how determined I was, that first party at the Bells', to talk with you about Bierstadt. Seldom have I crossed a room with more resolve— and you almost slipped away from me, making that beeline for our hostess."

John laughed appreciatively. "At the time I didn't know you wanted to talk with me. *Wanted* me," he teased. "And now, my dear, I *want* you to make a similar beeline to your dressing room and get ready...for bed."

———— ⋙⋘ ————

Sarah stood poised on the other side of dressing room door. She had carefully, yet loosely tied the silken robe that covered her nightgown. The white bridal gown and robe had been a present from Jean. When Sarah had first tried it on, she blushed, seeing how it clung to her figure, but Jean had crowed, "John will love it!"

Sarah was a little unsure how she would respond on her wedding night, yet she felt happy in the knowledge of the pleasure the gown would give her husband. In a minute, she would enter their hotel bedroom where he patiently waited. She instinctively knew John's patience was a strong outer shell, holding back a desire he'd controlled these last months of courtship, a desire he assured her had begun in their time in the wilderness. How he must have loved her—and God—to govern himself and seek her higher good.

With that thought warm in her heart, she turned the doorknob and stepped into the bedroom. John turned from the window and Sarah saw in his eyes both the eager boy and the man deeply in love. He held out his hand and she crossed the room with what some might think was unmaidenly speed.

She wanted tenderness from John, but now discovered she wanted fire, too. She was a little surprised at this last and said quietly, "I don't quite know how to say this...but I've come to love the fire I've seen in you...when you fought that Indian and those whiskey brothers...the fire in your love for God...and the fire in your love for me. I wonder if a little of that same fire has seeped into my soul and become a part of me."

John looked at her for a long moment then lowered his head to kiss the top of hers. "I love your thoughts."

He lifted her face and kissed her eyes. "I love what you see."

Then he pressed her to himself. "And in the words of the marriage vows, with my body, I thee worship." She reached up to put her arms around his neck, and he quoted, "This is now bone of my bones, and flesh of my flesh," and his mouth met hers.

After a long minute, he drew slightly away. "Did I ever tell you I kissed you that night I brought you back to the trading post?"

"No," she said breathlessly.

"When I felt your soft lips, as I did just now, I felt fire rise up in me."

He bent down and lifted her, and carried her to the bed and gently placed her on it. Then he knelt. "You kissed my scar earlier"—his voice was tender— "now, roll over." After she acquiesced, he gently lifted the gown from her ankle and ran his hand caressingly over her calf. Then he kissed her scar, pressing his lips gently up its serpentine length.

He held her ankle firmly in his hands. "You shared with me that because of this scar, you felt imperfect. But don't you see that I love it? Just as God loves us with all our imperfections?

"Mrs. Harding, I've wanted to kiss that scar ever since I saw it in the mountains." He smiled, but then a hard, bright light shown from his eyes. "No other man is allowed near it. It is *mine*. Do you understand?"

"Yes," she said, her voice small with wonder.

He laughed. "That scar, curving around your lovely calf, has been on my mind, more or less, since the first time I saw it. If you had known how seeing it affected me, you might not have entrusted yourself to me for the rest of the trip."

Warmth rose up Sarah's face.

John grinned. "At that time I wanted to—well, I'll *show* you now that we're married."

"Show me?" Her own voice was now playful, because no longer was she unsure of how she'd respond on her wedding night. She would be bone of his bone, flesh of his flesh.

"Yes, *show* you," he emphasized. He got up from his knee and sat on the bed, inviting her into his arms.

He gave her a quick kiss. "There now, enough talk."

DISCUSSION QUESTIONS

1. Describe how the two weddings are bookends to both the beginning and end of this story. How does Hildie reinforce this?

2. How does Jean's attraction to John begin "a comedy of errors?" Discuss Sid, Sarah and Prescott as they take part in this "comedy." Also, tell how Aunt Martha and Sarah's mother aid and abet this comedy of errors.

3. Which characters guess what is actually happening between John and Sarah?

4. John shows strong emotion after he learns about Sarah's unexpected departure. Describe his reaction. Do you identify with his feelings?

5. The central theme of this novel revolves around Art and Beauty. How would you state the theme? How does God fit into it?

6. A sub-theme has to do with a shepherd. Explain how the following incidents illumine this: The cliff scene with the two whiskey brothers. Sarah's rescue in the mountains. Sarah's favorite shepherd story in the Bible.

7. What significance does the scar bring to the story? What does it tell us about Sarah? John? God? How does the scar also bookend the novel?

8. How does Sarah grow spiritually in this book? How
do John's faith, personality, and relationship with God
influence her? Does John change in the story? How?

9. This novel contrasts the West with the East. What are
some differences between the two?

10. In what ways did Colorado Springs differ from other
western towns? Include General William Palmer's
vision for this city.

11. What picture of the Indians does the author depict
in this story? And what famous General is quoted in
Chapter 11? Cite the quotations.

12. What character is associated with western railroads?
In 1879, the year this story begins, what railroads were
mentioned?

13. Which prominent artist of the time is discussed in the
story? How did his art affect the central characters as
well as the main theme?

14. What was a favorite scene in this novel?

Be sure to visit Ruth online!
www.RuthTrippy.com

Camping at 9,000 ft.
Pikes Peak backcountry

I would be delighted if you'd write a review
of A WESTERN BEAUTY for Amazon or Goodreads.
They tell me this is important to get a book noticed.
I do love this story so hope
many people discover it!

CPSIA information can be obtained
at www.ICGtesting.com
Printed in the USA
FFOW03n0709111017
40965FF